Coyote Trap

A Fargo Blue
Mystery Series

Coyote Trap

By:

Don McKenzie and Ron McKenzie

Published by
D.E.M. Publishing,
A Division of COMPASS Consultants Corporation

For information please contact:
COMPASS Consultants Corporation
ramckenzie.compass@gmail.com

ISBN: 978-0-578-08010-9
Printed in the United States of America
10 9 8 7 6 5 4 3 2 1
Published March 2011
First Edition

Dedication

To my twin brother, Donald E. McKenzie (1946 – 2008) the best identical twin anyone could ever have. I miss him with all my heart but he is still with me every second of every day. Together we have assembled hundreds of pages of notes, so Fargo Blue's adventures will continue in many books yet to be published.

To our Dad, Alonzo Max McKenzie (1919 - 1961), a proud member of the U.S. Coast Guard during World War II, who loved a good detective story. We wrote these stories for him, and for our Mom, Janis Grace McKenzie (1928-2003) who bought us all the comic books we ever wanted. Ever since then we have been filled with stories we had to write.

Acknowledgements

The authors developed the Fargo Blue character for a television pilot named Courier during their writing weekends on the campus of UCLA in the early 1980s. They turned the Fargo Blue character into a mystery series in 1995 while sitting at the off-track-betting lounge at the Excalibur Hotel in Las Vegas, Nevada.

*   *   *

We thank Pamela McKenzie of My Advertising Partner, Inc. who designed the cover, book layout and text style for Coyote Trap, and Marge O'Connor of TMC Resources, Inc., who edited the final manuscript.

Don McKenzie

Ron McKenzie

Introduction

From the Las Vegas Times

Blue Not Blue About Final Wrap

(Las Vegas, Nevada) Fargo Blue, known as Fargo, long-time homicide inspector for Las Vegas Metro Police ends a distinguished career after solving the latest in a series of puzzling homicides.

"I feel good about moving to the private sector," Fargo said as he checked in for his last day on the job with the Las Vegas Metro Police.

Fargo's career started over ten years ago when he made Homicide Inspector at the ripe old age of twenty-five. "First day out I found myself at the Sands Hotel where I was put in charge of a double murder. I was scared to death," he said.

One would never know it. Fargo, who believes in a basic "follow the clue" crime-solving approach, was able to trace the killings to a robbery gone bad on Fremont Street. The search ended with the arrest of one man who eventually confessed to the murders and is now serving a life sentence at the Nevada State Prison.

The Las Vegas hotels have been Fargo's best friends over the years. He developed a reputation within the department that when a casino had a problem, they requested Fargo Blue. Now that Fargo is in the private sector, he will be working for many of those same hotels as a private investigator on a case-by-case basis.

"I've busted down a few doors in my time," Fargo said. "Even went through a couple of locks, but I did what I had to do, to give the bad guys a new address in the county jail." Fargo Blue was all smiles on his last day. "The fun has just begun," he said.

Chapter One

I REACHED FOR MY GLOCK, chambered a round, and listened. With bullets tearing up the room, I felt more comfortable armed. A scream pierced the hallway. I belly crawled toward the closet and threw on some clothing as I heard footsteps outside my room at the Treasure Island in Las Vegas. I glanced at the bedside clock and it was a little before five a.m. I slipped into my shoes, and tucked the Glock in the back of my trousers letting my pants do the job of a holster. I cracked the door open and peeked into the hallway. I could see people sticking their heads out from their hotel rooms. I was amazed at the new turn of events, and thought about the meeting I was to have with my new client, Rapture. A lot had happened over the last twenty-four hours. I could still hear Sheri's voice as we ended an afternoon of sailing.

* * *

"Drop the anchor and secure the lines," Sheri yelled.

We were near Fisherman's Reef, off St. Thomas, in the U.S. Virgin Islands. *Noble One* came to rest and bobbed gracefully in the water. Sheri had the ticket and Abby and I didn't. She was a former member of the U.S. Coast Guard and knew more about sea-going operations than most captains. Sheri had pushed us all day to make port before an approaching storm. But Sheri worked hard at everything, particularly in my office, Fargo Blue Investigations, where she has a private detective agency of her own and works with me on special assignments.

Abby, the third member of the crew, is a line dancer at the Tropicana Follies Bergere Show on the famous Las Vegas Strip. We shared the forward cabin together. She wore more then her share of sun block to prevent getting a sunburn, which would get her kicked off the line. Abby's first love was dancing. I came in a distant second. Something we discussed quite a bit, but I always lost. We all lived in Las Vegas. My name is Fargo Blue. I'm a P.I.

It was the middle of May and we were enjoying a leisurely cruise -- five ports in twelve days. This was just to pick up supplies, a quick lunch in one of the many fine island restaurants, and then back out to sea. The rest of the time we cruised, seeking safe harbors only on rough nights.

No serious treasure hunting on this trip. We were scouting known shipwrecks by doing some light scuba diving. We found one interesting wreck that had eluded us for years, and we were doing preliminary dives trying to figure out the best approach to explore this shipwreck on later outings. Before we returned, we would do a full profile on this site, and find the origin and history of the vessel. We would then know its contents, and whether it was worth a return trip. It looked promising, and I expected we would be back here soon for some serious exploring.

The three of us had been in the islands around St. Thomas for almost two weeks. Two women and a man always got everyone's attention when we slipped into port. I have to say I enjoyed these moments, but when you're Fargo Blue, you get used to the idea of being noticed.

We were sailing a Shannon 38, a custom-built thirty-eight foot offshore cruising yacht designed to traverse the globe in comfort, safety and style. We had rented it before and enjoyed its amenities. The owner, Brad Gibson, had made two transatlantic crossings, and now rented Noble One out for touring the islands. It slept seven. The inboard three hundred horsepower diesel kept us out of trouble.

"We're in for a bit of a blow tonight," Sheri said, as she observed the winds starting to come up. "No use riding out a storm unprotected if we don't have to."

"How about dinner on deck?" I asked.

Sheri flashed her brilliant smile as she brushed her red hair out of her eyes. "Sure. We still have time for dinner and a movie, but we'll have to move down below early to get the cabin secured."

Dinner to us was a special time onboard, and we ate an extravagant feast lavishly prepared by all of us. We took direction from Abby, who had planned every night's meal and agenda for the entire trip. Fresh fruit and other necessities were picked up when we went into port. The evening fare was equal to any offered on the neighboring islands. Tonight it was a Caesar salad, followed by a small portion of Bombay Shrimp Balls, with Lobster Thermidor as the main course, all served with a special bottle of wine called Barn Blend from the Nelson Family Vineyards located in Mendocino, California. Brie cheese and fresh fruit followed with a blend of Guatemalan coffee. It was presented on a white linen tablecloth with full table setting. Elegant and gracious. We had all the time in the world.

After dinner, when everything was stowed away, we settled down to a movie via DVD. Other evenings we dug into Noble One's library of fine books, and settled into an evening of reading everything from classic and modern literature to sea faring stories with Captain Horatio Hornblower at the helm, which was another touch that set us apart from the normal yachting crowd. Tonight it was the 1960 movie "The World of Suzie Wong" with William Holden and Nancy Kwan. The romantic setting of early Hong Kong served as a backdrop for Holden, who falls for a "working girl of innocence". The location was not unlike our own, as Noble One bobbed gracefully in the bay, the sky above provided a rich palette of scarlet and burnt orange against the jagged peaks of St. Thomas. This was the ultimate drive-in movie.

Just before the evening entertainment started, I used my cell phone to pick up messages. A necessary evil. We had worked out a system. Uncle Leo, a former Las Vegas prosecutor turned private defense attorney, whom Sheri and I shared offices with, left any important messages on my office phone. Uncle Leo had got his name from the people he had helped over the years. Everybody called him "Uncle." I dialed in. Only one message had come in according to Uncle Leo. A woman by the name of Rapture had called. No last name. This aroused my interest. Rapture had left an urgent message for me to return the call. Uncle Leo had called back, but according to Rapture's secretary, she only wanted to talk to me, day or night. I dialed the number as Abby and Sheri set up the DVD. "This is Fargo Blue calling for a Ms. Rapture. Is she there?"

"Yes, please hold." There was a pause as the call was put through.

"Fargo, is that you?"

"Ms. Rapture. Hello, this is Fargo Blue."

"Fargo, you don't know me. I'm sorry to interrupt your tropical holiday," said a voice that was dark and arousing. Sort of like a velvet whisper on a foggy night.

"It's okay. I always keep in touch with my office. What can I do for you?"

"Listen, I need your help. I'm on my way to Las Vegas. Actually, to get right to the point, I was threatened."

"How so?" I asked. She had my attention now.

"I received an e-mail yesterday that if I showed up at a meeting, I

16

would meet my father."

"How is that a problem?"

"My father passed away about three months ago. Heart failure."

"Oh my...I am sorry."

"Thank you. It's hard to get used to. But I'm meeting my partner in Las Vegas about our mutual business interests. He was my father's long time associate before he died. Because of the e-mail, I wanted to have someone there that knew Las Vegas."

"Where did you hear about me?"

"You were the detective that broke open the Vegas Strip scandal, which ended up in that terrible murder. I followed the papers as you developed the case and applied the pressure. Nice work by the way."

"That was over three years ago."

"That's about right. When I got the e-mail message I called Vegas Metro and asked for you by name. They told me you free-lance and gave me...let's see...your Uncle's name. I dropped a message to him, and here we are."

"How can I help you?"

"I want to hire you to show up in the hotel, unknown to anyone."

"What hotel?"

"T.I."

"Treasure Island?"

"Yes."

"I want you to appear at my meeting at the hotel on Friday morning as my associate."

"It sounds like you need a bodyguard. I'm not in the protection end of the business."

"No, not really. Well, maybe just a bit, but you're there to investigate anything out of place. Just to keep a watchful eye while I'm there."

"Have you advised the authorities of the possible threat?"

"You know as well as I do that they won't take an e-mail message seriously."

"Well, I'm on vacation here with my two associates...and I...."

"I thought you worked alone?"

"Oh, I do. It's a lady friend and an associate, Sheri."

"Oh, I see. Two ladies and you on a yacht?"

"Believe me, it's not what it appears to be."

"Appearance is everything."

"True," I said smiling to myself. Rapture was very perceptive.

"Okay. So can I count on you?" Rapture asked, in a way that suggested the promise of gold at the end of the rainbow.

"I'd have to cut my trip short. Book reservations. I don't know." There were a lot of things happening at once. If I were to do the assignment I would want complete control.

"Listen, I have a suggestion. I don't want anyone local to know you're coming into town. You're on vacation in the islands so you're the last person anyone would ever suspect. I want to fly you in on my private jet with your two lady friends as decoys. You will be picked up at the airport by a jet helicopter, and flown directly to the T.I. hotel where you will make a big obnoxious entrance. No one would ever guess that it's Fargo Blue. Can you do that?"

"Why such an obvious entrance? Isn't that going to attract

A Fargo Blue Mystery
1
Las Vegas, Nevada

Be sure to discover the first thrilling adventure of The Fargo Blue Mystery Detective Series:

Don and Ron
MCKENZIE
POOLSIDE STING

Texas Hold 'Em!

A Fargo Blue Mystery

Book One

POOLSIDE STING

Fargo Blue: former homicide inspector and Las Vegas cop, turned private detective, is hired by a Las Vegas Casino to solve the mystery of who murdered a beautiful and glamorous hotel guest at poolside. Fargo moves into the hotel and goes to work. Following a twisting tale, culminating in a tense, thrill-packed game of Texas Hold 'Em Poker with a lady named Pleasure, Fargo works the case one clue at a time. Las Vegas is hot...and Fargo Blue is cool...

Book Three in the Fargo Blue Mystery Series: MIDNIGHT SAND - Coming Soon!

attention?"

"That's the point. You usually get into town undercover. It's not like you to make this kind of entrance."

"Okay. I can buy that. Deception is always a key strategy."

"Then it's agreed. You'll make the trip?" Rapture asked.

"I haven't shaved for a while, and I have a pretty good sunburn going. Add the right clothes, some sunglasses, and no one would ever know who I am."

"Good, good. Great idea. How about your friends? Could they pose as two trashy broads for your entrance?"

I looked up at Sheri and Abby. "Just a minute." I cradled the phone in the palm of my hand. "Hey, I have an interesting assignment shaping up and I need some help. I need to make an entrance into Las Vegas so I'm not recognized. Can you two ladies play the role of two trashy broads?"

Abby and Sheri looked at each other and giggled. Abby spoke first. "Honey, we could be the two most trashy broads you ever laid your hands on." Both Abby and Sheri laughed at the remark.

"Well, Ms. Rapture..."

"...Please call me Rapture."

"Well, Rapture, thank you." Abby and Sheri stared at me as I spoke Rapture's name. I just shrugged my shoulders. "It appears that I just happen to be with two of the most trashy broads in the islands. One redhead, and one blonde."

"Tell them they each get a thousand dollars for their entrance..."

I covered the phone again. "You're each in for a thousand." They gave me a thumbs-up.

19

"I'll make it worth your while Fargo. I'll pay two thousand for the entrance, and then a thousand a day after that. Of course I'll cover all expenses."

"That sounds fair enough to me. But I'd really like to know more about you, your specific problem, and do some checking before I take the case."

"I can understand that," Rapture said. "Here's what we can do. My meeting is set for nine in the morning. There will be a reservation for a Samuel L. Miller out of Miami for you. Your room is private of course, but there is an adjoining door. My partner, J.T., who is my father's former partner, will be staying in this adjoining room. I will drop by J.T.'s room at six-thirty a.m. for a breakfast meeting, to which you're invited. I will let J.T. know you will be knocking on the connecting door. If everything is to your satisfaction after our breakfast meeting, then you can accompany J.T. and me to our nine o'clock as Fargo Blue."

"Who are you meeting with?"

"J.T and I are going to meet with a potential...let's say, an investor. I can't explain right now all of the particulars. We'll do that over breakfast with J.T."

"What about the girls?" I asked.

"The girls will be long gone. That's just a cover to get you into Treasure Island undiscovered."

"Yes, that's true. But why don't I just come in as Fargo Blue?" I kept thinking this was a lot of work when I was going to be Fargo Blue when I get there anyhow.

"Because I don't want to tip anyone off before the meeting. The best defense is a good offense."

20

"You think your adversaries are local and might recognize me?"

"I don't think so, but I'm concerned they might hire local help. What do you say?"

"One more question. Is it J.T. who is in danger, or is it you?"

"Why do you ask?"

"I can't protect you if you're sleeping in another part of the hotel."

"Yes, I know. That's true. But I believe that J.T. would also be a target, since he had such a long relationship with my father."

"But the e-mail was to you."

"True. I understand your concern. But I'll be okay."

"Okay, it's your call," I said. "When would you pick us up? It's Wednesday evening now."

"My Lear Jet will be in the air within the hour. It will be at St. Thomas airport waiting for you Thursday morning. Everything will be taken care of for you and your shipmates."

"Okay, but just one more thing. We're cutting our trip short by a day. How about making that Lear round trip? When we're finished with the assignment, we'll catch a ride back here to refresh ourselves."

"Done."

"Great."

"Just ask for Rapture's Lear Jet. James, my pilot, will take care of you."

"Okay. One last detail. I want you to wire my bank account five grand as an advance. Do it through Uncle Leo. Three for me, and one each for the ladies. I won't leave until I get confirmation."

"I'll take care of it."

"I'll see you in Las Vegas on Friday morning. I'll knock on the connecting door to J.T.'s room promptly at six-thirty a.m."

"Good, good. Thanks for the help, Fargo. I'll get started on the money transfer. By the way, what type of weapon do you carry?"

"Why?" I asked wondering why she would care. Carrying while traveling was more difficult with the stricter regulations, but I had worked out the problems to get me through the airports without attracting too much attention. In most cases, the airlines and local authorities were cooperative if you followed their procedures. On this trip, the private jet made it easier.

"Just wanted to make sure you were carrying. I don't know where the threats are coming from."

"Do you expect trouble?"

"Wouldn't you?" Rapture said, throwing the question back to me.

"Yes, you're right. I travel with a Glock 17."

"Good choice."

"It's my 'away from home' handgun, if you know what I mean?" I glanced at Abby who was already planning a shopping attack at Caesar's Forum with her new wealth.

"Yes, I do. Good. I'll see you tomorrow. Looks like we're set."

"Okay. And tell your pilot to be careful. There's a storm brewing down here."

"Right. I will."

I hung up the phone and settled in next to Abby. "Well it looks like we're out of here tomorrow. We have to cut our trip short by one day, but you'll each get a thousand, and we can use her Lear for a return trip if we want to spend a few more days back here."

"Sounds good to me," Abby said. She lived day-to-day and never thought about money.

"Me. I'm going to invest," taunted Sheri. Sheri was the practical one who had an investment portfolio the size of Fort Knox. Her game plan was to retire before any of us, and I had fifteen years on her. Sheri kept telling everyone she was going to become independently wealthy, so she could become my full time partner. Sheri had probably started her retirement account at about the age of one. I was afraid to ask her for fear I was right. I was still thinking about starting.

"Sheri, I'll make some notes. Could you start a case file on this assignment when you get back?"

"First thing, Boss."

"Also, I need to run a background check on our new client. The usual stuff. But I also want to know what's she's being doing over the last ten years or so."

"Give me your notes in the morning. I'll tap in to a line when we hit port, and we should have something waiting for us when we get back."

"Thanks."

Abby clicked on the DVD. In the background a thunderstorm flashed inside a black cloud relentlessly drawing nearer. The sky turned instantly into a mirage of ghostly colors, as Noble One slipped gently back and forth. The secret to life is not to dwell on the past, or worry about the future. We all knew these were special moments to enjoy.

Chapter Two

SHERI AND I DID one last check of Noble One before heading down below. The movie ended just as the seas were getting restless. We could smell the rain that was headed our way. We spent the rest of the time packing for a promised early departure. Our arrival time was scheduled for Thursday afternoon in Las Vegas. The rain started and proceeded to pound Noble One harder and harder as the night progressed. In the morning we were greeted by a brilliant rainbow and sunrise of spectacular colors and clouds.

The money came through just as Rapture had promised. Uncle Leo confirmed the transfer just before sunrise. We moored Noble One, and took a limousine that magically appeared for us directly to the airport where we found a whining Lear waiting on the tarmac. We were airborne within twenty minutes. Three p.m. sharp to be exact.

"Beats waiting in line," Abby said.

"No kidding," I commented, watching Sheri open her carry-on and dump her clothes in a big heap on the cabin floor.

"What in the world are you doing?" asked Abby.

"Well, Fargo over there said we had to appear as trashy broads, so I'm checking my wardrobe."

"Trashy broads don't have a wardrobe," I commented.

Sheri laughed. "Yes they do, but they leave it at home. That's what makes them trashy."

Abby smiled and started to dig into her luggage.

Our ETA was in five hours. We had plenty of time to sort everything out.

We arrived in Las Vegas at dusk, the magic hour when fading light is replaced by the neon glow of the Strip. And true to Rapture's word, we were met by another limousine that escorted us to a Jet Bell Ranger helicopter. We lifted off the pad and headed toward Treasure Island. I wore dark sunglasses and had not shaved in several days. My complexion was red. I wore a white linen coat commonly found in the islands, with sleeves pushed up, and matching pants.

Abby was trashy. Sheri was really trashy. We decided Sheri won the award. She wore a loose tropical shirt tied at the waist with no bra. She bounced as she moved, and she moved a lot. Abby, the topless Tropicana line dancer was all modesty. She wore a black bra and a see through net shirt. They both wore short shorts that showed off their legs, dark sunglasses, and carried drinks.

We had left a tropical paradise and landed in a den of pirates. There is gold to be found on the tables, or at least that's what they want you to think. Any hotel guest arriving by private helicopter, which is highly unusual, gets a lot of attention. We played the role to the hilt. Our entrance was obnoxious, loud and demanding. Anthony, our new limousine driver, took care of the check-in and luggage as the girls swooned over me. Abby and Sheri never left my side. They kept kissing me suggestively, while whispering sweet nothings in my ear.

As we passed the roulette table I locked eyes with the most attractive woman I had ever seen. She was dressed in a long flowing silk gown that barely clung to her body. Dark sparkling eyes danced with diamonds of fire and had such magnetic pull that my heart actually skipped a beat. She blinked, and the trance was broken as she turned away, her thick red hair swinging in seemingly slow motion, as she faced a pile of chips she had just won. I was stunned.

We continued to dance through the casino toward the elevator that led to the penthouse. The tourists loved it. They knew this sort of thing happened all the time, but never actually experienced it first hand. It was a memorable Las Vegas entrance. Made their day. No one saw me. The tourists only saw Abby and Sheri and imagined them to be Las Vegas showgirls, who were partying with what they presumed was a high roller. I was enjoying myself, but my mind was filled with a vision I had just seen at the roulette table. Only in Las Vegas.

We checked out the suite on the sixth floor, and it was one of the nicest I've been in since my short stay at the MGM Grand. This Treasure Island suite overlooked the Strip and was complete with sunken tub, wet bar, and fireplace. The view was a carnival of neon lights dancing in the night. Champagne was already iced with glasses waiting. Abby poured and we sat back and enjoyed the view. Dinner was served about an hour later and we enjoyed a movie on the wide screen projection system.

Abby and Sheri left the hotel around one a.m. We were all tired, but Sheri wanted to stay on to assist as back up. I told her if she didn't hear from me by eight a.m., to beep me. If I didn't answer come and find me. I cleaned up and caught up on the local news. I even ordered coffee to save time in the morning. My mental alarm was set for six, and with the hotel computer working as backup, I drifted off to sleep.

It was around four-thirty a.m. when I was awakened by a large 'bump' in the night. The first thing I thought of was Halloween when I was a kid. Any noise that awoke me would find me gripping the covers in fear of the unknown. I heard a metallic sound of a slide being pulled back on what sounded like a high-powered assault rifle. My gut reaction took over and I dove for the floor just as bullets started to rip through the wall. I grabbed my Glock and cell phone and rolled toward the closet door for protection.

I speed dialed Sheri as I rolled myself into a ball.

"Boss!" was her one word answer when she read her caller I.D. I could hear the concern in her voice

"Roll. Lock and load!" I clicked off.

I heard a scream, and then short bursts of rapid fire lasting for over twenty seconds. I heard another magazine being slammed home, then silence. I listened for any clues and heard footsteps moving past my doorway. I peeked around the corner and could see shafts of light shining through the bullet holes in the wall. Pirates!

* * *

I peeked out the hallway door. "Hey buddy, what happened?" said a pajama-clad man that was also peeking out of a door down the hall from me. I glanced at the hotel guest as he looked up and down the hotel corridor. He was tired and bleary eyed. He would not make a good witness. He must have been in a deep sleep as his hair was as awful mess.

"There was some gun fire," I said, also glancing up and down the hotel corridor. "How about you? Did you see anything?" As I talked, I thought of J.T. who Rapture said was in the room next to mine. I need to find out if J.T. had been hit and then locate Rapture as fast as I could.

"Not a thing," he said, as he stifled a big yawn and ran his hand through his rumpled hair. His lumpy looking flower pajamas were almost hypnotizing. I would never have thought to wear them to bed. It would have kept me awake. Must have been a gift.

He looked around. "I heard what sounded like gun fire and then footsteps. They were moving fast. In a hurry. You all right?"

"Yeah," I said, as I stepped into the hallway and moved toward the hotel door that was next to mine. "Several rounds were fired from inside this room. You'd better get back inside."

As I turned he spotted my handgun sticking out of the back of my shirt.

"Hey, you got a gun!" he said, now fully awake.

I pulled out my I.D. wallet and flashed my gold detective badge. "I'm a private investigator."

"I'm from Kansas. We never have this much excitement."

I couldn't resist. I looked back over my shoulder. "You're not in Kansas anymore."

He smiled just as a security officer rounded the corner. The hotel guest stepped back into his room, and shut the door not wanting to get involved. Probably watched too many episodes of Cops.

Chapter Three

"**HEY, YOU DOWN THERE.** Stay right where you are," yelled a guard who was obviously wearing a brand new uniform. He was about ten years old – or least it seemed that way. The ultimate rookie. His uniform was a display of perfect creases. Another guard followed him and was working hard at keeping up. This guy did not care about his uniform. He was a beefy guy who shook the whole floor as he huffed and puffed his way down the hallway losing a little ground with each step. The buttons on his shirt were ready to pop at any second and I made a mental note not to stand in front of him. I held up my room card as if it were a badge. "Room 6370. Right next door to this one. Gunfire came right through the adjoining wall and door into my room."

"No kidding," the kid said as he stopped directly in front of me.

"No kidding," I replied.

The young one pulled his radio. "Name's Tony. This is Toby here. We're working security. We got a call that there is a problem on this floor."

I gave a nod in reply and checked to make sure my shirt was covering my Glock. I was legal for concealed carry, but didn't want the hassle right now, because their attitude would change if they knew I was armed. Statistics show that concealed carry lowers the crime rate, but the mainstream press rarely reports it.

Tony was all business. "Hotel guest says bullets were fired on the sixth floor," he reported to security. "I'll investigate and advise." That would kick hotel security into high gear, I thought to myself. Tony knocked on the door, waited, and then looked up and down the hall. People were sticking their heads out looking at us. "Okay everybody, back inside. Everything is okay down here."

I wasn't convinced of this, and neither were the other guests. They had heard the bullets and running footsteps, but like most curious people, they just had to sneak a peek.

I looked back at Tony. "I think we're not going to be too happy with what we find inside."

Tony pounded on the door "What do you mean?"

The beefy guy named Toby leaned up against the wall and was feeling his shirt pocket for a smoke. That's exactly what he needed was another smoke.

"Well, I bet they weren't shooting at the wall for target practice," I said.

"I suppose you're right." Tony tried opening the door but it was locked. Curious I thought. He pulled out a set of key cards, found the right one, and inserted it in the slot. The door opened about three inches, as it was secured from the inside with an interior privacy latch. He squirmed down to try and peak and the only thing he saw was a close up of the wall. He pulled out the card key and backed up, frustrated.

"Let me have a look." I pulled out my badge wallet and retrieved a very thin stainless steel mirror the size of a credit card. I stuck it through the door opening and angled it so I could get the best reflection. I could see a body sprawled on the floor, and was pretty sure it was a man. I knew it was probably J.T., and not Rapture, who wasn't scheduled to show up until 6:30 a.m.

"Hey, that's a pretty neat trick," Tony said, as he bent down right next to me and peered through the crack in the door. "Looks like we got a body." We both stood up.

I tucked my wallet back into my pocket. "Let's check the connecting doorway." Tony never asked me for an I.D. and I wasn't going to offer any information. Not yet anyway. I made a mental note to talk to Gilbert "Gil" Sanford, head of security at Treasure Island about security procedures. I had ongoing assignments with Gil, and this fit right into one of them.

"They're supposed to be dead bolted on both sides," said Tony. "This here's a suite, and it has another set of connecting doors on the other side."

"Let's check it out anyway."

"Okay. Toby here will watch this door." Toby raised one hand signaling that's what he would do. I didn't think he was going to live that long.

We entered my room and I pointed out the bullet holes in the wall and door by shutting off the lights. Small lights appeared in the wall where the bullets had slammed through the walls. I snapped them on again and Tony had pulled his radio out. He was quick on the draw.

"Ah...this is Tony again on the sixth. We've got bullet holes in room 6370. I can see where the carpet and walls are torn up in here, so they came from next door. The guest in this room said they came from there. Okay...okay...right...Metro's on their way," he said to no one in particular. He opened my side of the connecting door, and we were faced with the second one. He tried it and it was dead bolted. "Looks like we're stuck."

"I hope no one's alive in there. They might need our help."

It was obvious that the guard hated dilemmas. It meant a decision.

"Why don't we force open the front door? We can shoulder it and it will probably pop open. A lot easier than trying to go through this steel frame and deadbolt.".

"I don't think so," he said as he rubbed his shoulder. "We should wait for a locksmith."

Memories of all those times I spent with my dad in his locksmith business in San Francisco flashed through my head. I could go through this door in a matter of seconds, but I didn't think that would be a good idea.

"Your first responsibility is to clear the scene and help the injured, isn't it?" I asked.

"I...ah...I suppose you're right. How do you know someone is alive?"

"We don't, but we can hope there is. Someone locked the door from the inside."

Tony grunted a response at the obvious. "Oh, yeah. You're right."

We moved back into the hall and Toby gave us his famous one hand wave.

Tony and I lined ourselves up, and on the count of three we hit the door. I don't think Tony gave it his best shot, but nevertheless, the interior latch popped open and we were in. I immediately smelled gunpowder.

"Man are you going to get into trouble," Toby said, who was still holding up the wall. He had refused to help smash open the door because of a bad shoulder.

Tony flashed Toby a mean look, then turned to me and pulled out his revolver. "Better stay back while I check it out." His Smith and Wesson six-shot revolver seemed bigger then he was.

It was killing me that I could not enter first. All those years in Vegas Metro built habits that were hard to break. "Okay," I responded, having no intention of being left behind. Tony entered and I followed right behind. Tony walked right past the partially closed powder room door and headed directly for the body. I pulled my Glock, entered and cleared the powder room and returned without Tony ever seeing me. I stuffed the Glock in my belt and made sure it was covered by my shirt.

I followed Tony into a spacious living room with a sunken seating area and two sofas facing each other. The room lights were on but the neon lights from the Strip spilled into the room from floor to ceiling windows, casting an ominous glow that gave the room a pulsating effect, rich with color and style. The room was large and well appointed, with paintings that could have been in a museum. But it had been tossed. It was a mess with everything thrown about. It was going to be a forensics nightmare. A dead body lay on the floor. Boxer shorts, nothing else. I assumed it was J.T. He lay next to the end of one of the sofas that was covered in a rich textured fabric. In front of the sofa was a glass table with several crystal pieces that had been spared during the bullet parade. I could tell from the spray of gunfire that they'd nailed the guy while he was just starting to stand up, and the shooters followed him down to the floor where they really tore him apart. Tony was right; it was a suite. Another set of interior connecting doors was on the far side unopened. Another room to clear.

I moved to the far side of the room, which led to the sleeping areas of the suite. I spun around facing Tony while at the same time I reached for my Glock. "Just going to take a look, Tony." Before he could say anything I spun around so he never saw my weapon and entered the room. I was faced with lavish sleeping quarters with a connecting master bath and dressing room. Why can't I get rooms like this? I quickly cleared the room just as Tony entered and I tucked my Glock safely away. This room had also been tossed. I walked over to the nightstand and the billfold was open. A name was clearly visible. Jonathon Taylor. It must be J.T.

My whole concern now focused on Rapture. The dead body was J.T. and I had to find Rapture and get her out of the hotel.

"Hey, I told you to stay in the hall." Tony moved back into the adjoining space and stood over the body. "We're going to want to ask you some questions."

"I need some information. I need to have you call security and I need to get the room number of a guest, and I need to have you do it now!"

"Sorry, confidential information. I need to have you move back into the hallway."

"I want you to call security and patch me to Gil Sanford."

"How do you know Gil?"

"First, why don't you put your revolver away?"

Tony looked at his revolver with surprise; like it was the first time he saw it. He tucked the chrome beauty back into his holster and latched it. I breathed a sigh of relief. I didn't like how Tony had waved his revolver all over the place. "Okay. Now get out of the room."

As Tony was talking, I was sweeping the room for information. 7.62 mm cartridges were strewn all over the place. It most likely meant an AK-47. An SKS uses the same cartridge, but I knew I was listening to thirty round magazines. Since there was a magazine change, I knew it wasn't an SKS. A professional assault team would have opted for the current agency-preferred assault weapons such as Heckler & Koch MP5s that uses a variety of cartridges including 9x9 mm, .40 S&W or 10mm. Or they might go for an AR-15, which is readily available. And if you want something that wasn't traceable, you can pretty much build your own AR-15. But it looks like this team went for throwaway AK's. It's a big desert out there. Tony then bent over and started to pick up one of the empty shells that had bounced and landed on top of the coffee table.

"I wouldn't touch that if I were you," I said, with a great deal of urgency in my voice.

"What?"

"It's a crime scene. I wouldn't touch anything until the boys have been here and cleared the scene."

"The boys?"

"Forensics," I said. "They'll want to gather prints and DNA samples!"

"Oh," Tony stammered. "Hey, how do you know about that?"

"Call Gil."

"No. I thought I told you to go out into the hall and wait for Metro."

"Well, you've got a dead body. I think you better wake up Gil. And I need that room number." I pulled out my badge and held it out for him to see. "Fargo Blue of Fargo Blue Investigations. I'm a private investigator."

The stunned Tony stood there with his mouth open looking at my gold badge.

There was a lot of debate in the profession as to whether a private investigator should carry a badge. There were good arguments on both sides. Some felt that in a bad situation when law enforcement arrives on the scene with guns drawn they will think twice if they see a gold badge flashing at them. That badge could save your life. On the other hand, someone who is being interviewed by a detective may think they are being interviewed by law enforcement, and P.I.s can get themselves into situations where it appears they are misrepresenting themselves to get people to talk. Looks bad in court. I took the proactive side. In a bad situation I would rather have the badge helping the officer I.D. me as a good guy. So, whenever I pulled my gun, I pulled the badge. In normal situations, I just showed my credentials and told them verbally I was a private investigator and not with any law enforcement agency. It lets me sleep at night. This wasn't a normal situation.

My cell phone rang. I spoke into the phone as I put the badge away. "Fargo here."

"It's me, Sheri."

"I'm on the sixth floor, come on up."

I snapped the phone shut. It was now about five a.m.

"You should have told me," stammered Tony.

I locked eye contact. "You should have asked." I knew I would have to address this issue. I was on retainer with Treasure Island on two assignments, one was to report on security procedure in order to improve the department, and the other was an undercover assignment where I had hired an independent operative to assist me. Old Tony here didn't know that.

Tony looked frustrated. He knew he should have asked. "This is my area of responsibility," he stammered. "I would appreciate it if you would move into the hallway, and keep Toby company," Tony said, empowered with his authoritative direction.

"Okay. No problem." I returned to the hallway, and Toby was still holding up the wall. He gave me another half wave as I approached him.

"We got one down in there. You'd better call for an M.E. right away," I said. Toby started to make the radio call while I wandered down the hallway away from the murder scene. I half expected him to challenge me on what I was doing, but I reached the end of the hallway without getting any hassles. More security procedure problems to deal with later. I could have been the killer they were looking for. I stopped and studied the end of the corridor. I had heard the footsteps running in this direction, so I was curious as to what I would find. They had not chosen the elevators as part of their escape plan, which was in the opposite direction about midway down the corridor. I found an emergency exit stairs, but there was no way to view the stairs without opening the door. I didn't want to contaminate any possible evidence until forensics had cleared the scene, so I moved on making a mental note to find out where the stairs ended.

I then saw what looked like a window that was completely busted out. The window allowed light into the end of the corridor, and also gave visitors a spectacular view of the Strip. I poked my head out and saw three ropes tied off to what looked like brass fittings that window washers used to secure themselves and their equipment.

There was no doubt about it. This was a professional hit. Amateurs would have made the attack, and then escaped by way of the elevators. In the process, every camera in the casino would photograph them. There are usually cameras on the roofs of casinos, but I'm betting that most of them would have been knocked out. Obviously these guys were in good physical shape and adept at their job. Nobody else could have thrown themselves out the window and scaled down a wall to the roof below on a whim. I was glad that I wasn't following them. I would have made an easy target.

Just then the elevator door opened and Gil Sanford, John Morton of Metro, Homicide Division, and Sheri walked out of the elevator. I waved and we met halfway down the hall just outside the crime scene. Sheri was wearing a shoulder holster that was exposed with an I.D. hanging from her belt. She looked good despite being rolled out of bed so early. Morton was on shift and Gil had been called in by security. I could see the elevator door was still open, so Gil must have hit the 'hold' button.

Gil, Morton, and I shook hands. Morton gave me his usual strong grip that matched is physique. I placed my hand on Sheri's shoulder as I spoke and nodded toward her. My way of saying good morning.

"So Morton, you got the short straw huh? How's Johnston doing these days?"

"He's still at it."

"Fargo, give us the quick rundown." Gil said.

Just then Tony walked out of the room and started to say something and was immediately cut off.

"Okay, but please all of you join me in my room. I need to get a couple of things while we talk. You can also see the damage." They all followed me into my room.

"You can see the bullet holes on this side of the wall." They all moved over to examine it as I pulled on a different shirt, put on a shoulder holster and secured my Glock. As they examined the wall and I dressed, I talked.

"It went down like this. I was rolled out of bed at a little before 5:45 a.m. with gunshots coming in through the door and the wall of this room. Security showed up," I nodded in the direction of Tony, "and I finally got Tony here to agree to knock down the door to see if anyone was alive. We have one dead unidentified male, which is presumably Jonathon Taylor, according to the I.D. laying on the nightstand. All rooms have been tossed, and have been shot up by what appears to be an AK-47. Someone was looking for something specific." At this point I didn't mention the lack of procedure by Tony and Toby. Time and place for everything. I continued, "the deceased has a partner located someplace in this hotel. I need to find her and find her fast."

"How do you know that?"

"I was to meet with the deceased and my client early this morning.

"You can't find her?" Gil said, as he examined the wall.

"I don't know the hotel room number, and Tony was reluctant to call you."

Everyone stood there and looked at Tony who had a helpless look on his face. His day was getting worse by the minute.

"Fargo," Sheri interjected. "I stopped off at the office last night and followed up on the background check you requested. Rapture is clean, no record of arrests or warrants. Single, no kids and been living in San

Francisco where her family is located. She's been in her father's employ and apparently took over his real estate development business after his death. Graduate of Stanford. Well-to-do family. Her story checks out."

"Thanks Sheri,"

Gil hit his two-way radio. "Front desk. Yes...this is Gil Sanford, head of security...please hold." Gil looked at me, "What's the name?"

"Rapture."

Gil's eyebrow went up, and Morton, who had been quiet during this exchange, looked at Sheri and mouthed the name "Rapture"?

"Rapture," Gil said. He waited, then announced, "there is no listing for Rapture."

"Check under Jonathon Taylor at room 6368." I was hoping for a connection.

"Gil relayed the information. Seconds later the radio came to life. We have another listing for a Ms. Alice Woodward in room 1845."

"That must be it," I said anxiously.

We all moved to the hallway and headed toward the elevator.

"Morton, it's your crime scene," Gil said. "Tony and Toby, do whatever Morton says to do." Tony nodded and Toby waved. "I'm going with Fargo and Sheri."

"Morton, I plan on removing my client from Treasure Island into a protected controlled environment. When we land we'll let you know as you'll want to talk to her."

"When you get her secured could you come back to the crime scene so you can walk us through it?"

"Sure, no problem."

"Just keep me posted." Morton waved his approval as we all

stepped in the elevator and Gil released the 'hold' button and hit floor eighteen. The door closed as Morton and Tony started to head toward the crime scene.

As we began to move up, I had one overwhelming thought. There was a very good chance that Rapture had unwittingly saved her own life by staying in a different room. By using an alias it made it difficult for anyone to find her. The unexpected should always be expected. If she had shared a suite with J.T. she would have been dead.

Chapter Four

ONCE WE ARRIVED AT THE EIGHTEENTH FLOOR we broke into a run toward Rapture's room. Quite a picture if anyone had seen us. We came to a stop outside 1845 and noted that there had been no obvious attempt to break in the door. Gil rapped loudly.

"Security...this is security, please open up." There wasn't a response so he rapped again.

This time I yelled. "Rapture, this is Fargo. There has been an incident. Please open up."

Faintly from the inside we heard someone say something, and then the voice got louder and we could hear Rapture. "Just a second, just a second."

"Who is it?" came from behind the door.

We stood back from the door just slightly so she could see us through the security peephole. "Rapture, it's me, Fargo. I'm here with security."

There was a slight pause and Rapture stuck her head tentatively out the door.

"Ma'am I'm with security. Gil flashed his badge and Sheri and I displayed our own badges. After all, we had never met in person. "And you know Fargo here. May we come in?"

Rapture swung the door open and we all entered her suite.

I suddenly became very aware that I had seen Rapture before. She was the knockout that was playing roulette the evening before when I made my entrance. "Rapture, I'm Fargo Blue." We shook hands. She was beautiful even at this hour of the morning. "This is...." "Sheri," Rapture said, completing my sentence. They shook hands in a warm greeting.

"Rapture, I have some bad news for you and you may want to sit down. J.T.'s been shot and killed." I didn't know any other way to say it.

Rapture immediately sat down and put her hands over her face. She clutched the robe to her chest in a protective, defensive manner and sort of rocked back and forth. Sheri sat down next to her and put her arms around her to comfort her.

Gil had walked around the suite to check everything out. "Did anyone tried to get in here during the night?"

A big tear rolled down Rapture's cheek. "No one."

"Was there any commotion outside your door? Anything unusual?"

"No."

"We need to get her out of here," I said.

"Everything is ruined," Rapture moaned.

"Everything is a mess, but we're here to help you pick up the pieces," I said.

Rapture looked up at me and her face brightened a bit as she rocked back and forth. Another tear rolled down her cheek and I innocently brushed it aside with my hand. I looked at Sheri and she nodded toward me. We were all here to help, and something as innocent as tears can bring people together.

Gil Sanford pulled out his two-way radio. "Security. I want two men on floor eighteen outside of room 1845. Also, get a security car on the side entrance. We're going to move someone out of here for protection."

"Rapture," I said, as I knelt in front of her. "We need to move you.

If you could get dressed as fast as possible, Sheri will help you pack."

"I don't want to leave. I need to have the meeting at nine. It's important."

"I know it's important, but I will help you set another meeting."

"You...you don't understand."

"Rapture, you hired me to protect you. Right now, I'm going to make the decisions based on your safety. Right now, I want you to go with Sheri and me. We're going to take you to another hotel where you can rest, and where we know that you'll be safe. Sheri is going to be staying with you for a while until you are comfortable. Okay?"

"Okay." Rapture got up and she and Sheri moved into the bedroom and the door swung closed.

I turned to Gil. "I wonder what this is all about?"

"The one thing I have learned on this job is that people's lives are sometimes extraordinarily complicated."

"I'll say."

"You get her moved, and I'll let Morgan know what's going on. Sooner or later he'll want to talk to Rapture."

"Yeah, I know."

"How did you land this client?"

"I think she was the one that landed me."

Gil and I talked for a bit and we exchanged information. I told him I would be back in touch and would file a report about his security team. He knew he had some weaknesses and I admired him for addressing it.

When Sheri and Rapture emerged they were ready to go.

Rapture had slipped into casual clothes and we each pulled one of her bags. She looked good and was calm despite the awful news she had received.

"Sheri, we'll run a standard armed escort. I have security downstairs waiting. I want you to leave before us and get your car in position in front. Also, call Uncle Leo and let him know we'll both be in to brief him. I think we need to get a couple of legal opinions on this one."

"Right Boss." She gave Rapture a hug and was gone.

We all stood there sort of lost in thought for a few seconds, and then picked up Rapture's luggage and moved into the hallway. The two security guards were there and accompanied us to the elevator.

Gil's two-way radio broke the silence. "Security One, do you copy?"

"This is Security One, over, " Gil said.

"Security Two."

Gil gestured his head to me asking if I needed anything else. I held out my hand to request that I speak. Gil gave me the two-way.

"Hi, this is Fargo. A Miss Sheri Austin, a detective in my employ will be emerging from the elevator shortly. She will be working the front end of an armed escort. We will be following with the subject. Could you have security there to assist when we get off the elevator?"

"Yes, no problem."

"Good. Could you arrange for a follow car for Gil?"

"Yes, no problem."

"Good, see you downstairs."

"Security Two, out."

Just them the elevator arrived and we all stepped in including the security guards.

Rapture brushed her hair off her face. "All of this for me?"

"A little extra protection right now is just what we need," I said.

We arrived at the main casino floor and the doors slide open and were converged upon by two additional security guards. They surrounded us, two in front and two in back, and we walked straight through the casino past the roulette and crap tables and exited a side door. Rapture and I climbed into a black Cadillac. I could see Sheri's Lexus up front and as soon as the door shut, the driver moved out. Gil moved into a car behind us and was joined by a plain clothed security man. We were off.

"My, said Rapture, "that was fast."

"It's the best way, sometimes."

The Cadillac turned to the right and I could see him talking to Sheri who had briefed him on our route. I glanced in back and could see the third security car following. I relaxed a bit.

"Thank you for your help, Fargo. Thank you." She put her hand on my arm in a gesture of thanks. It was the kind of first touch that you sometimes remember. It sent a charge though my body. It was not Rapture; it was, but it wasn't. It was the realization as to why I was in this business. I had helped someone, and that feeling of helping is worth more than any amount of money. I loved my job as a detective. I loved it.

"I don't know how I can ever thank you enough," Rapture said.

"You hired me to have someone local to assist you, and your hunch paid off. And staying in a separate room also saved you. Right now, you're lucky to be alive."

"Yes, I know."

"Tell me something. J.T.'s room was tossed as if someone was looking for something. Does that surprise you?"

"No, not at all."

"What was so valuable that cost J.T. his life?"

"It had to do with the meeting we were going to have."

"Tell me, give me an idea of what we are up against?"

"It's complicated. We were going to discuss a business transaction that would terminate in an exchange of a document for money."

The car turned another corner and I could see Sheri out front, and I again glanced in back and saw security behind us. "Who were you going to meet with?"

"A woman."

"What is her name?"

Rapture turned her head to the side. "Her name is, Coyote."

Chapter Five

COYOTE "SLEEPING" HOLLOW glided into the waiting stretch limousine outside the Venetian Hotel early Friday morning. She sat back as the driver whisked her out of the driveway. She glanced over and saw a small girl with long, tangled strawberry blonde hair. Her thoughts traveled back to when she was twelve years old.

* * *

Coyote watched Priscilla Joyce open her locker. Priscilla carefully removed a sweater from her school locker and draped it over her shoulders just like a grownup. Priscilla was eleven years old. Her mother gave the sweater to her. She was especially protective of it, and very proud of the first sweater she had ever owned. It was green to match her eyes; together it was a dramatic combination. She was short, and rather diminutive in build, so she had to stand on her toes to reach the top shelf of the metal locker to get her notebooks for the next class. As she pulled the books down, a common garden snake fell on her face and immediately became tangled in her thick hair. He baby face turned pink as she hysterically dropped everything and went screaming out of the aging school building. In the process her very special sweater slipped off and she tripped on it, causing her to take a vicious fall. She gathered herself and grew more hysterical as the garter snake weaved even deeper into her hair.

Coyote watched the scene play out with quiet intensity. She moved behind her locker further down the hallway and watched with great interest as the incident unfolded. When Priscilla had run uncontrollably out of the building, a freckled chubby kid moved out behind a door with a few of his pals, and raised a clench fist as a salute of victory. Red, as his friends had named him because of the constant sunburn on his light complexion, continued with slaps on the back to celebrate his latest prank. As they left, Red slammed his own locker shut, which unlike all the other lockers, Coyote observed, had no padlock. No one would ever dare to touch Red's locker.

Coyote thought about how Red had taken advantage of Priscilla. Having no friends of her own, and a product of a broken home, Coyote had no one to talk to, so she began to formulate her own plan. She stayed up late that night working in her room. The following morning she left for school early, and began to watch the movements of Red. She spent the rest of the week observing and noting all of his habits and exactly what routes he took. She then placed a sign on several bulletin boards indicating a reward for a lost package by the school administration. Because she now knew Red's habits, it was easy to place them where she knew he was going to read it. Each night she spent more time plotting in her room.

The next day Coyote hid from view, and watched as Red walked through the open courtyard surrounded by school buildings. Unseen by anyone, Coyote had left a package right in Red's path. Red saw the package as he rounded the corner. It was partially hidden and covered with dirt. It obviously had been there for some time. Red noticed printing on the package right away: "If this package is found, please return it to the school administration office, and you will receive a cash reward. Important. Do not open." Red was infatuated with his good luck. He had put two-and-two together and knew this was legit. He gathered up the package and proudly headed off toward the administration building.

Not only was he going to get some money, he was going to make some points with school officials. He did have somewhat of a bad reputation, and had done more then his share of time in the principal's office. Red would level the playing field.

Dorothy, who headed up school administration, looked puzzled about the package when Red proudly delivered it to her. She opened it and found approximately fifty sheets of paper with the words, "If you need a snake in your hair, call Red on a dare." in very large bold letters. Red had been conned, and had delivered his own undoing.

Red left the office in a hurry only to discover everyone pointing at bulletin boards and picking up handouts. Everyone was laughing and pointing. Someone had left small stacks of flyers where kids could pick them up. Eventually, everyone, all four hundred-fifty six kids, and the faculty, had a copy or had seen it.

There was so much talk that the school had to do something. Soon, the inevitable happened. Red was summoned to the school principal's office where he was chastised. Red denied everything, and with each growing moment turned a deeper shade of red – out of guilt and anger. Soon a procession started that lead to the front of Red's locker. Since it was between classes, quite a large crowd joined the walk. When they got to Red's locker, he was asked to open it. Red's eyes were as big as the old school clock on the wall, as there was now a combination lock on his locker. The click, click, click of the old school clock on the wall matched the pounding of Red's heart.

Of course, Red couldn't open his own locker, which looked like refusal from the principal's point of view. So he sent for Henry, the school janitor, who brought bolt cutters. With little ceremony, they busted open the locker, found more sheets of the same notes, and a dozen snakes. They crawled out and started to squirm their way through the crowd, which created a huge commotion in the hallway. Kids were running into each other trying to escape. Several kids went down, and the snakes slithered under them, creating more panic. Red had never seen these snakes, and was as mesmerized as the principal, who suddenly became quite vocal and slammed the locker shut, catching Red's hand. Red screamed in pain. It just was not his day.

The result was Red's immediate suspension from school for the rest of the school year. He now realized that he had been had. But who had done this to him? The girl he had terrorized had not even returned to school and was out on sick leave. Red knew his buds would never do this to him. He would never learn that Coyote "Sleeping" Hollow, age ten, orchestrated the revenge, nor would Priscilla, the victim of Red's stunts, ever know.

Coyote, sweet as she was, was also cunning. The Priscilla incident forever gave Coyote the driving incentive to help other people. Unequal justice was her model. Not just getting even, but getting a bit more. She also developed a stealth-like approach to targeted events, working behind the scenes, unnoticed by others, but helping to right the wrongs of the world.

Coyote's real name was Catherine, and she was part Cherokee Indian. Coyote was a nickname from her school friends, created as a symbolic gesture to her Indian heritage, and her quiet movements. Legend has it that we all have three names: the name given by your parents, the name given by your friends, and the name you answer to. Coyote Sleeping Hollow was a version of her real Indian name.

But the beautiful light skinned girl was as tough as nails. She became stoic in manner, internalizing everything while letting nothing escape her sight. Some teachers always felt she under-performed; worse yet, others though she just wasn't capable of meeting the school's standards. In reality, Coyote was far ahead of her classmates and spent a great deal of time deeply observing her surroundings. She sat quietly watching the other kids play. She wondered who she would help next.

* * *

Coyote's thoughts were broken as a car attendant jolted her back to the present. She had arrived at Treasure Island. It was eight forty-five Friday morning and she was just in time for her meeting. With strawberry blond hair accented with red lipstick, and good figure, she always got attention. She was wearing a long sarong that was slit up the slide revealing tanned legs that had all the car attendants watching intently. She handed the attendant a five-dollar tip for opening the limo door. He received broad smiles from his co-workers, and secretly hoped Coyote would return before he ended his shift.

Coyote had checked into a high roller suite at the Venetian Hotel. She was a comped player and spent a good deal of time playing roulette. Her play was seemingly random with no distinguishable pattern. She was an astute money manager moving her bets between one-hundred and five-hundred dollars depending on whether she won or lost. She also usually attracted a crowd.

Always interested in their guests, the Venetian tracked her every move, and referred to her as Miss C. But little was known about her. She seemed to present a range of complex behavior patterns that had the

Venetian higher ups guessing. On one outing she had taken a limo over to Caesar's, and wandered around the Forum shopping mall. After a bit of haggling she purchased a painting by an artist whose work was known as a contemporary of the early Flemish masters. The painting reflected the bridges and canals of early Venice not unlike where she was staying. She paid fifty thousand dollars and had it delivered to her hotel suite. It was hung the very next day. As far as management at the Venetian could figure out, she was tired of hotel art.

Coyote smiled as she watched the tourists in Treasure Island as they accustomed themselves to the low ceilings, like one might find on a pirate ship. But the glitter of pirate gold was too much for most people, and they would try their hand at finding treasure in the tables and slot machines that the hotel so conveniently provided. Most of them would lose the money they came with and some would lose hundreds, if not thousands, of dollars. Others, who could afford it, or not afford it, would lose hundreds of thousands of dollars. Millions were lost every year in Vegas, but everyone always came back to try again. It was a gold mine for casinos that spun the wheels of fortune day and night taking only a small percent of every dollar bet. Someone had to lose.

But they all go home feeling like a winner. That's the magic of Las Vegas for all those who make it part of their vacation. The tourists are happy and so are the casinos – nothing like a happy tourist with twenty dollars in their pocket walking across the casino. But the twenty dollars would never see the light of day. The percentages were always in favor of the casino.

As Coyote moved through Pirate's Cove there was a tremendous amount of security about. She approached an elevator where a security guard was standing.

"What floor, Miss?"

"Sixth floor. I'm going there for a meeting."

"Sorry, that floor is now secured."

"What happened?"

"There was a problem on the floor, Miss. That's all I can say."

"Thank you." Coyote moved away from the elevator and turned to see the security guard talking into his two-way radio. Coyote moved into the casino and blended into the crowd. She then went to a house phone and dialed Rapture's hotel room.

There was a pause, then an answer. "Hello, who is this?" said Morton.

"Who is this?" Coyote responded very agitated. The hairs on her neck went up. Something was not right.

"Who is calling?"

Coyote waited and listened. She could hear movement and other voices. She remained quiet.

Morton finally spoke breaking the silence. "This is Morton, Las Vegas Metro Police. I need to know who's calling this room."

Coyote hung up immediately and started for the entrance. The limousine she had arrived in spotted her when she walked out. It pulled up, a bellhop opened the door and Coyote slide in. The door closed and the limo slipped into traffic. She knew now there was a problem and she would have to wait before trying to make further contact with Rapture.

Chapter Six

TREASURY AGENT DAVID HOLDEN turned onto Las Vegas Boulevard, three cars in back of Coyote's white stretch limousine. Holden, wearing black sunglasses, was dressed in a neon-Hawaiian shirt, shorts, and driving a dark green Mustang. He would never be taken for a U.S. Treasury agent on the prowl for tax invaders, but that was his current assignment. Holden had played the role many times before, pretending he was a tax accountant from Montana, while he dug into the affairs of other people. As a CPA, he knew the routine, and was documenting the spending habits of his targets.

For two weeks now he had been tracking "Willie," his nickname for Coyote. His field controller believed she was involved in a large scam, and Holden had been assigned to gather any kind if incriminating evidence linking her to a crime. Any crime would do, according to his controller.

Dogging her day and night, he had not been able to find any criminal activity. His field controller felt it was imperative that they follow her closely in Las Vegas. The money she used for betting was being transferred out of a Louisiana bank, and records revealed the money had been duly recorded, with taxes paid in full. If she wanted to lose her money, that was none of the Treasury's business. But hiding unreported assets was.

Coyote had only one pattern. She traveled daily to a casino and played roulette. She played for about two hours and then left and returned to the Venetian where she ate light meals with wine, and did some shopping in the hotel malls before returning to her room in the early evening. In the evening she had the full attention of the Venetian where she played for about three hours betting heavily. Right now, she was up about one-hundred thousand dollars. Casinos like to have the high rollers on their own playing field. Keep them happy, and they keep betting.

Holden watched as Coyote's limousine moved down the strip as it left Treasure Island, which was situated right next to the Fashion Show Mall. To the left was the Mirage Hotel and Casino. One cab was in front of Holden's Mustang, which didn't make the light. Coyote's limo continued down Las Vegas Blvd and Holden was stuck behind the cab. The cabby got out, looked at the front of his cab, and then waved at Holden. Holden just waved back and watched as the cabby got down on all fours and examined the front of the car. Holden imagined that the steam and heat from the pavement was unbearable. He hoped he was not going to have to help the cabby because it was nice and cool in his Mustang. The cabby got up, brushed off his pants, and then approached Holden's car on the driver's side. Holden rolled down the window and the cabby leaned down to be at eye-level with him.

"Looks like I got a problem with my engine," the cabby said.

"I can push you across the street so traffic isn't blocked."

"Yeah," the cabby said. "You think the bumpers will match?" Holden glanced at the cab to judge whether or not their bumpers would be okay and noticed there was no license plate on the cab. Thinking that was strange, he turned his head to look at the cabby again. In a split second he knew he had made a mistake. The cabby was wearing rubber gloves and held a small 9-millimeter semi-automatic equipped with a silencer. It looked like a Berretta. Without hesitation, the cabby put two bullet holes into Holden's temple. "Don't even worry about it," the cabby said. "Things will work out."

Holden had finally developed a clue, but it was too late. He was dead.

The cabby walked back to his taxi and drove away making a U-turn on Las Vegas Boulevard. Twenty thousand dollars had tempted Carl Collins to make the hit. He usually didn't work the U.S. market, but he was in need of cash and had opted to "cowboy" Holden at his first opportunity. The Las Vegas police would find his cab dropped in an airport parking lot several weeks later. But they would find nothing of value. The cab had been lifted two days earlier from the overnight yard of the Vegas Cab Company. Collins had worn gloves when he picked up the cab and left the cab "dirty" in the back. There were hundreds of fingerprints to keep the detectives busy when they found the vehicle. But he had switched out the license plates with one he had stolen from another cab. The plates would be traced back to the Vegas Cab Company, but they wouldn't match the car. A little something to slow down the investigation process. He didn't want to be picked up by an over zealous patrolman, who wanted to score a few points with his captain.

Trying to guess what plane he had taken out of McCarran was another matter, and close to impossible. He had picked up his own generic Buick and headed for Salt Lake City and then to Canada.

Carl had learned his trade in the military as a long-range sniper where he was trained by the best. He had natural talents, and was coached in the secret world of thousand-yard hits. The problem was, he was good, too good, and continued to ply his trade after his tour of duty. It started with a simple hit on a skimming drug dealer caught by the supplier. Now, he moved from country to country after every assignment, leaving no trail behind.

Chapter Seven

MORTON FROM LAS VEGAS METRO had asked me to return to Treasure Island Friday morning after I had Rapture safely tucked away. Sheri would stay with Rapture until she was settled in and then head back to the office after giving her implicit instructions. We had her stashed at the Orleans Hotel where we had special arrangements when we needed a safe house. We had used it before to protect a witness and it was the perfect answer to our current problem. It was off the Strip, it had good access to freeways and back streets. One of the best kept Las Vegas secrets.

The murder room had been sealed off as forensics went to work. My room was included in the crime scene, as they needed to trace the angle and trajectory of each bullet that smashed through the common walls of the two hotel suites. Fortunately for me, none of the bullets had struck the closet where I had put all my belongings, so after everything was inspected, they were released to me.

Morton was gone when I arrived, but he left a message for me to give a statement to the homicide inspector who was on site with the forensics team. Since I was a former Metro cop and detective, John Morton gave me some slack. I knew the drill. I provided the statement recounting how I was rolled of bed and the subsequent investigation of the primary crime scene. It was made with the stipulation that this was to be reviewed by my attorney, Uncle Leo. I had received Uncle Leo's lecture more than once. Even so, it took some time before I left the crime scene.

Having been released by Metro, I headed downstairs to take care of some unfinished business with the hotel day manager. Treasure Island apologized profusely for the inconvenience, and quickly comped me a suite on the tenth floor. They even gave me a credit for the room service I had ordered, but never received.

"Say, do you have a list of all the people staying on the sixth floor?" I asked the manager. You don't get what you don't ask for. I flashed my badge and told him to check with Gil.

"Yes, certainly. I will have it printed off and sent to your office."

I gave him my business card with the fax number. "Thanks, that will help."

I did have an ace in the hole, however. Only top management and Gil from security knew I had Bobby Lawrence working undercover for me in the casino. I contacted Bobby by cell and arranged a meet at Mandalay Bay. Bobby Lawrence was a freelance P.I. working undercover as a tourist trying to track a slot team, which moved in on progressive slots that were getting ready to pay out. It was a science, and also a war between teams who hit the hotels as innocent tourists, and the slots manager who wanted the hotel guests to win for their long hours of spinning the Wheels Of Fortune.

My client was Treasure Island security. Casinos often supplemented their own security forces with shills who worked the floor in a security role. Treasure Island hired me to investigate, and I hired Bobby to go undercover. Actually, that was Bobby's cover assignment. We were also investigating security for Treasure Island because of several thefts from the service area that supplies uniforms for the employees.

Bobby kept a careful watch of what they did, and we would assemble his case notes into a report with a list of recommendations. Now with my first-hand experience I had a pretty good idea of what they needed in the way of changes.

I was on my way across Las Vegas choosing to use the Strip instead of one of the many short cuts that all the locals knew. I left Treasure Island around a quarter after ten and drove down to Mandalay Bay. As I pulled into the hotel entrance, Bobby Lawrence popped out of the hotel and stuck his head in the open car window. He was wearing a plaid sport jacket that even Steve Martin might have passed on. I had to smile at how Bobby fit in, by not fitting in. Only a tourist would wear such an outfit.

"Hey Fargo, glad you called. I heard you were involved in some action at Treasure Island this morning. I didn't see you, but from what I heard, there was a lot going on."_

"Word travels fast," I replied, wondering how much Lawrence knew. Las Vegas was really like a small town. Gossip travels fast in small towns.

"Anything you want me to keep an eye on down there?"

"Yeah. Keep an eye on Metro and who they are meeting and interviewing. Metro doesn't know you exist. Who knows what this will turn into when we sift through the details.

"Okay, will do. I'll report in as usual. I like the work. Keep it coming."

"How is the slot operation going?"

"Right now it's a bust. The team is moving around from hotel to hotel. There are two spotters. They locate a progressive-island that is due, call the crew in, and then take over all the seats and play till they hit a jackpot. The whole operation is bankrolled by an investor who pays off the crew and pockets the rest. We'll find out sooner or later. I thought they were going to hit the five-dollar slots for a bundle, but it didn't happen. Almost got em.'"

"Anything else happening?"

"I caught a cup stealer this morning."

I grinned when I heard this. It happened to every hotel that had rows of slot machines. An innocent looking tourist would create a distraction and then grab a cup full of coins. They usually headed for the exit playing a couple of slots along the way to blend into the crowd. Sometimes the thief would team up with a "distracter" who would drop some coins on the floor near where their target sat. The target would turn his head for just a second, providing the cup stealer with just enough time to make the grab. The problem is, it's always on video. Every hotel is hit by them. "You're a regular one-man crime stopper," aren't you?"

"Yeah, the security team was grateful when I caught this guy. But they had a good laugh over it. Here I am watching for a team to hit the progressives, and this idiot tries to get a cup of coins, and I'm sitting there watching him. He must have been totally blind."

Fargo laughed. "I would have thought that your sport coat would have scared him away."

"Thanks."

We both laughed. I said my good-byes and was out of there. Treasure Island was a hotspot of activity. I left Mandalay Bay and marveled at this wonderful casino. The Hacienda Hotel and Casino was blown up years ago to make room for this fabulous hotel. Lance Burton had made the Hacienda come alive in its last years. His magic act at the Fiesta Theater in the Hacienda was sold out every night. But Lance made a deal with the Monte Carlo, and it was one of the greatest packages ever put together in Las Vegas. In included a custom theater for Lance. This was a first rate hotel, with a magician's magician.

I was now backtracking toward my office, since I needed to review the case and talk to Sheri as soon as she left Rapture. I had a client that could have been killed and I needed to figure out what was going on.

I looked around and examined the Strip as I drove. It was a changing monolith of pleasures, sin, and romance all dressed up to attract tourists. I remember the lyrics from an old Meat Loaf song. "Good girls go to heaven, bad girls go everywhere." Sort of sums up Las Vegas.

Over the years I have learned to love this city with a passion. Driving down the Strip that connects all the hotels together is like being on vacation. I glanced over to the left lane and there was a couple with their new video camera focusing on the hotels. The casinos loved to see that. Those videos would get shown to neighbors and friends and everybody would tell stories about their trips to Las Vegas. The legend grows with each tourist who leaves with hours of Las Vegas on videotape.

I was passing the Bellagio and watched the ballet of water jets accompanied by the voice of Andrea Bocelli that echoed along the Strip. People lined up every fifteen minutes to watch the modern-day ballet of water and music. An ingenious idea and one the Bellagio was proud to have. Hotel guests made sure they dined on one of the patios overlooking the water, or they lined up around it on the outside where small viewing balconies had been created. The manpower support team for this feature attraction was extensive and consisted of the maintenance crews to repair the miles of pipes, and the computer techno geeks who made the water show work. But visitors only see the European Spa and lake complete with a Chris-Craft handcrafted mahogany powerboat gracefully bobbing on the water.

Traffic slowed at Treasure Island, as everybody stopped to gawk at the flashing red and blue lights of several police vehicles. I slowed also, and could see yellow tapes around a car, which I took to be a rental. I spotted Henry Brill, a long time friend and patrolman.

I rolled down my window. "Hey Henry!" Henry turned around and waved. He walked over to me even though I was slowing down traffic. Henry had that police swagger that came from being loaded down with his duty belt of defensive hardware that goes with working the streets and the job.

"How goes it, Fargo? I thought you never drove the Strip?"

"Nah...that's when I was assigned to the North side. I love the Strip...love the lights...what happened here?"

Henry took out another wad of gum and tossed the mint-flavored habit into his mouth. "Business card says he's a tax accountant. Took two bullets in the head. "Pro-job. We don't see this around here very much anymore."

"Really?"

"Yeah."

"Somebody must have been really unhappy with their taxes."

"Either that, or this accountant was a corporate tax attorney working one of the big guys skimming his client. Happens all the time. Brother's an accountant. You wouldn't believe the stories of accountants skimming. After all, they've been trained in the art of making numbers add up differently. Hide the expenses and make the company profitable. Just a matter of time before they balance somebody's account into their own. Even the big guys do it."

"Everybody's got an angle."

"This guy doesn't anymore," Henry said nodding his head in the direction of the stiff.

I nodded my head in agreement, and then glanced in my rearview mirror and saw the line of cars. "I'd better get going."

"Right, Fargo. "I'll see ya around," and Henry walked away back toward the flashing police lights.

I pulled back into traffic. Boy, that was really something. A 'hit' on Las Vegas Boulevard This just doesn't happen in Las Vegas. There are murders but they're usually isolated to streets off of Fremont Street, and areas off of West Las Vegas. Las Vegas was tumbleweed tough. I wanted to stop and investigate the scene myself. Old habits die hard. It was something to think about anyway.

I knew that Uncle Leo was going to be waiting for my arrival. We would discuss what had happened last night in the casino. I looked in my rearview mirror and saw the flashing red lights of a black and white. I pulled over to let them by and wondered why the officer never used his siren to alert the cars in front of him of his approach. Needless to say, I was stunned when he hit the siren and pulled in right behind me. Smiling faces from other drivers beamed from cars driving by knowing that another reckless driver was going to be pulled off the streets. I looked into the rearview mirror again and saw an officer with mirrored sunglasses approaching me. Great, I thought. I've got a patrolman with an attitude.

I continued to watch him from the mirror as he approached my car door as I placed both hands on the steering wheel. "Afternoon officer, what can I do for you?"

"Like to see your driver's license."

"Sure, no problem," I said, as I pulled out my wallet from my left inside jacket pocket. "I'd like to know what I was stopped for?"

"Changing lanes without signaling," said the officer, as I flipped open my gold badge showing that I was a licensed P.I. I flipped it again and it showed I had a concealed carry permit plus my driver's license.

"You're a P.I. huh?" Could you remove your license?"

I handed it to him, which he studied.

"Are you carrying?"

"Yes Sir," I responded. I still had both hands on the wheel. "I have nothing illegal in this vehicle. I was also a homicide detective with Metro a few years back." The officer grunted. He probably didn't like to hear that.

"Just sit tight and let me run this. Keep your hands where I can see them."

"Of course," I said as he walked back to his car. Just to amuse myself, I toyed with the idea about making a run for it. I had a good lawyer, but I would probably take too much grief from Uncle Leo for doing so. Besides, I never had any conflicts with Las Vegas Metro. A few officers, maybe, but not the general department. Better just to sit it out and be done with it.

The officer once again rose from the driver's side of the patrol car and walked toward my BMW. This time as he approached he looked into the back seat carefully.

"Sir, the computer shows you as a P.I. with a valid concealed carry permit."

"Yes Sir."

"Ahuh...right. You're now carrying, is that correct?"

"Yes Sir, I am," I said as I waved my hands as I talked.

"Would you please put both hands on the steering wheel, Sir."

"I don't think that is..."

"Please put both hands on the steering wheel, Sir."

I put both hands on the steering wheel. I was wracking my brain trying to find something in my first year at law school so I could nail this guy.

"Is your weapon loaded, Sir?"

"Yes, it is," I replied trying to keep my cool. "You have seen my permit and license?" I was a P.I. and allowed to carry. Nevada residents are also allowed to have a CCW once they have been cleared after a State and a Federal search of their background and with proper training. The local gun shops do a thriving business holding required classes, selling revolvers and semi-automatic handguns to casino employees who travel the streets in the late of night. My permit was an extension of my work as a private detective. Sort of feel naked without one.

"Yes, Sir. Do you have a round chambered, Sir?"

"Yes, I do?"

"You said you were a member of Metro homicide. I was able to confirm that when I ran your license."

"Thanks,"

"I'm not going to write you up. Just try and hit the blinkers once in awhile, at least when I'm behind you."

"Thank you officer...?"

"Bennett..."

"Officer Bennett...say, didn't your dad work vice for a couple of years?"

"That's right...vice...illegal gambling operations...he's seen everything."

"How's he doing? Haven't seen him in years?" I asked, relaxing into the conversation a bit. Now that I knew I was not going to be arrested and thrown in jail, I felt better. Everybody usually does at that point.

"He's retired. Lives out by the lake. Talks a lot of the old days. You know how it is?"

"Not yet, I don't."

"Officer Bennett smiled for the first time. "I've got to write some more tickets so I'd better saddle up. Drop by and see my dad whenever you get the chance."

"Will do. Say, what's the routine with asking if my gun is loaded and whether a round has been chambered?"

"My particular routine. Not police policy by any means. Officer's discretion. I just want to know if a round is loaded or not, and that might give me a jump if the "stop" goes bad. Knowing a round is chambered means I might shoot straighter the first time. Besides, the more we can get them to talk, the more chance there is to incriminate themselves. And if you want to get real technical, if the suspect says a round is not chambered, and we find out it is, there might be some legal grounds for, "endangerment-of-an-officer" by deception. Of course, to my knowledge, this has not been tested by the courts."

"Understandably so. Thanks, for the info," I said, as I shook Bennett's hand. He walked back to his car and I could see him on his microphone clearing off the stop so control would know what was happening.

I pulled back into traffic thinking about how many people now carried either semi-autos, or revolvers with them everywhere they went.

No question about it, there were problems in Vegas. Especially after dark. Being a patrolman on the beat for many years before I became a detective, I was trained to always think that the suspect was "armed" and ready to use deadly force to make their escape. We didn't go by the old adage, "shoot first and ask questions later," but we were ready to shoot back, that was for sure.

When I was out on the street as a cop and I walked into a situation, the right hand automatically moved over to feel the butt of the handgun. To this day, I do the same thing, and when it's not there I go to the shoulder where my Glock is safely nestled. Reassurances came in a variety of calibers.

Chapter Eight

MY BMW FIT PERFECTLY NEXT to Sheri's Lexus. The two-story stucco buildings with Spanish tile roofs blended into the desert architecture. Several fountains located between the buildings were joined together by a bubbling stream that worked its way through the complex. On a hot summer day everyone in the area hoped the stream would cool the air, but it mostly knocked out traffic noise from Sahara Avenue. The bronze colored buildings and the abundant plantings artfully placed around the water made it a great place to work.

I entered our offices on the second floor and could sense that something was different. Sheri immediately waved at me and put her finger to her lips in the universal gesture of silence. She came up to me and spoke quietly in my ear.

"Fargo, Uncle Leo has a gentleman in his office that looks like a government agent. His name is Dick Barnes and he is asking for you by name. Uncle Leo said not to mention the incident at Treasure Island. You just arrived back from vacation. I don't like him."

I whispered in her ear. "Okay. Start a background check on the guy from what you know. Did you brief Uncle Leo about what happened?"

Sheri nodded yes.

"Good." I headed for Uncle Leo's office, wondering what was waiting for me. I knocked once, and then opened the door and stuck my head in. Uncle Leo's gray head looked up from his desk and he motioned me into his office. I entered and looked to the right. A middle-aged man was standing a few feet from Uncle Leo's massive oak desk. This was strange, I thought. Why was he standing? Why was he not sitting? I glanced at his shoes first, and the story started to unfold. They were well traveled and a bit scuffed. The suit was in better shape, but it had that government look to it, like he was trying to fit in. Close cropped hair, narrow set gray eyes and a starched white shirt that fit him perfectly. He looked like a clone. A government clone.

"Fargo, this is Dick Barnes," said Uncle Leo. "He is with the U.S. Department of the Treasury and has requested your services in a matter that is of some importance to the federal government."

"Nice to meet you," I said, as I walked over and shook his hand. I could tell right away that Barnes worked out and I bet he had some type of martial arts training. I looked for signs of a weapon, but was not able to trace one under his jacket. But I was betting he was carrying. Uncle Leo had given me all the information I needed to make a fast assessment of the situation.

"I'm glad I was able to catch you," Barnes said. "Please have a seat."

"After you, Mr. Barnes." I stood my ground and Barnes smiled and seated himself with his back to the wall of library books. He shifted his chair just a bit so he could see the door leading to the lobby. I was guessing he had agency training, and knew the tricks of the trade.

"We need your assistance on a project," Barnes said, glancing at the door.

"I have an assignment right now, so I'm not really interested in taking on any extra work."

"I believe that you just returned from a vacation. You must be in high demand if you were able to locate work so quickly on your return,"

Barnes replied, smooth as silk.

"Ongoing case. What can I do for you?"

"We have this situation..."

"Does it involve me?" I asked point blank. I could see a bit of a smile on Uncle Leo's face.

"No."

"That's good. Could you please tell me what you're after, and why you picked my office?"

"You come highly recommended."

"By who?" I asked.

"By sources that I care not to discuss."

I had a feeling this guy knew more about me than I knew about him. He was polished and non-committal. I glanced at Uncle Leo, who continued to study Barnes.

"Let's try this again," I said. "How can I help you?"

"I like somebody who is aggressive."

I just sat there and stared at Barnes. I crossed my legs, and moved my right hand to adjust my shoulder holster to a more comfortable position. Barnes just stared back at me, but he caught the move. I had to start wondering if this guy had something on me. I mean it takes a lot of nerve to pull these types of stunts in somebody else's office.

"We have a situation at Treasure Island," Barnes finally said. "We know you're familiar with the hotel, know your way around Las Vegas, and in fact, know your way around most of the hotels."

"Do you need me to book you a room?" I asked. I was laughing hysterically inside, but Barnes never changed expressions.

"No, I don't need a room."

"Okay," I said. No sense of humor there, I thought. I glanced at Uncle Leo and could see the slight trace of a smile.

"This matter is of great concern to the Department of the Treasury. We need to have somebody in the hotel with eyes and ears. You will be paid well."

"And you've decided that I'm your man," I commented.

"Yes."

"I think I'll pass, if you don't mind. I have some pressing business to take care of and I think you have at your disposal a wide selection of men and women who can handle this 'situation' as you call it."

"But I do mind," Barnes said.

"Sorry. I generally work only in the private sector."

"I must insist that you look at this opportunity."

"No."

Barnes looked over at Uncle Leo. "I feel that I'm not getting through to Mr. Blue."

"You offered him an assignment, and he has refused your offer," said Uncle Leo. "I think he got the message."

"My, I'm surprised and sorry that the private sector is not willing to help out the U.S. Government with some of its problems. There must be a way."

"I don't think so," I said. "If you will excuse me, I have some work to do."

"The U.S. Government has an investigation running at this hotel. A criminal matter. You could be a great help to us. You know how the Department of the Treasury works. We could shut down your office."

"Is that a threat?"

"Look, I just want your help. I just want an agent working Treasure Island to keep an eye out for anything suspicious."

"Could you excuse us please," interjected Uncle Leo. "I'd like to have a few words with my associate."

"By all means," snickered Barnes.

Uncle Leo hit the intercom. "Sheri, could you come in here for a minute?"

"Yes sir," answered Sheri. The door swung open a few seconds later. I could tell that Sheri knew something was up. She never looked at Barnes. She only looked at Uncle Leo, watching for clues.

"Please come around to my desk and sit in my chair. Watch Mr. Barnes, and don't let him steal anything."

"My, my, my...aren't we trusting," Barnes said.

Uncle Leo smiled. "Watch him closely."

"Yes sir," said Sheri, as she sat down.

"Come on Fargo," leading the way out of the office.

I walked behind Uncle Leo and glanced over my shoulder at Sheri and Barnes. I felt sorry for Barnes if he tried anything with Sheri. Uncle Leo closed the door.

"What the hell is going on?" I asked. "Who is this guy?"

"We know who he says he is, but we really don't know for sure. What do you want to do?" asked Uncle Leo.

"I want to run a background check on him. I already got Sheri started on it. But we're going to have to go deep on this one. Then I want a forty-eight-hour surveillance on this guy and find out what he's all about," I replied.

"Not a bad idea actually. If he is government, he can make every

74

area of our lives miserable. I say that you agree to work for him for a couple of days. That will give us time to get a line on this guy and see what we are up against."

"Did Sheri brief you on what went down last night?"

"Yep. More reason to work with this guy for a couple of days. I agree with you, I don't like a gray suit coming in here and causing us problems. But we have to watch this closely. If this overlaps with your current case, I don't want you to have a problem with conflict of interest."

"It's only a conflict when it happens. But we'll watch carefully."

"We'll see about that. Right now you have no knowledge of any conflict of interest. It might be better to be on the inside than the outside."

I nodded my head in agreement. Uncle Leo opened the door and we entered the office.

Barnes and Sheri were just staring at each other, but I could see Barnes' eyes working her.

"Well, I believe I found some time to work for you," I said. "When do I get started?"

Barnes rose from his chair. "I knew you would find a way to help me out. Tomorrow morning let's meet for breakfast at the Mirage. They have a breakfast buffet, and I believe we'll be able to find a quiet table."

"Is nine a.m. okay with you?"

"Fine."

"What about compensation?"

"You'll be paid our normal rate."

"I only work for my normal rates, not someone else's."

"It will be cash," Barnes replied not answering my question.

"Cash? The U.S. Treasury is going to pay me in cash?" I looked at Uncle Leo.

"That's how we pay outside agents. Cash."

"Cash?" I again questioned. "Do I get a 1099?"

"Yes, if you want one. But I will be honest with you. In some cases we can't have a trail leading back to the Feds, if you know what I mean."

I knew that all the agencies had their covert operations and they paid in cash. Isn't it interesting I thought, that the IRS often pays money under the table in covert operations to catch the guy doing the same thing as they're doing. "Okay. My normal rate is two thousand a day plus expenses. Two-day advance, plus a thousand deposit for expenses," I said. "That's five thousand dollars, and it's not negotiable."

"I can add," Barnes said, flippantly. "But, sorry, it can't be done."

"Well, it looks like we don't have a deal after all." I just stood there and looked at him. I folded my arms and leaned against the wall. The office was completely silent. Uncle Leo didn't say anything. Sheri didn't say anything. And Barnes didn't say anything. We all just starred at Barnes. You could hear the fountain bubbling outside through the open window and an occasional squeal of tires from a car on Sahara trying to make the turn into the In-N-Out Burger.

"Okay, Okay. I will accommodate you this one time. I'll bring the money tomorrow morning. It has been nice meeting you all." We each shook hands with him but it wasn't sincere. It was a dance as we circled each other and positioned ourselves.

"Just one more thing," Uncle Leo said. "Fargo will bring a contract for you to sign. Standard, nothing fancy."

"Sorry, no way."

"Fine. But the cash payment and the delivered contract, even if it's not signed by you, won't look good in court. Particularly when this entire office is a witness to your offer to hire."

Barnes headed for the door ignoring Uncle Leo's comment. Sheri rose from behind Uncle Leo's desk. "Sir, your shoe's untied." Barnes looked down at his shoe. "Made you look," Sheri said, a smile spreading across her face.

Uncle Leo and I burst out laughing. Barnes looked at Sheri, then to Uncle Leo and I. He nodded to us and then walked out of the office. Sheri followed him to make sure he didn't steal anything. He let the screen door slam behind him. No sense of humor at all.

I grabbed my digital camera and made a dash for the back door, which opened onto a walkway balcony. Sheri grabbed another camera and headed down the stairs after Barnes. I moved over to a connecting bridge and caught Barnes getting into a non-descript four-door sedan. The car backed up and was gone. I snapped away and was able to get two good shots, plus the car plates. I then moved down the exterior stairs to snap another photo as he drove away. I met Sheri in front and we walked back upstairs together.

"Did you get his picture?" Uncle Leo said to both of us as we entered.

"Yep, no problem there," Sheri replied. She took my digital camera, and removed the disc and went to work on the computer.

"What about the car plates?"

"I got a good shot of those," I commented.

We all peered over Sheri's shoulder as the screen began to fill with images.

As she worked I had to ask a question. "Sheri, how is Rapture?"

"She's fine Boss. I gave her the lecture and we'll be in touch this afternoon."

"Good."

Up on the screen came crystal sharp images of Barnes both in profile and in full facial. Still photos taken in sequence have the ability to make the subject appear guilty. These were no exception. There was something strange and cunning about the images. There was also a shot of the car and of the plates. The wonders of digital photography.

"Good," Uncle Leo said. "Fargo, get a call off to one of your security friends and tell them we've got photos to run on their facial image identification systems. Sheri, you run the plates. Let's see what we're working with here."

"No problem. I'll take care of it."

"One more thing," Sheri said as she dug into her pocket. Sheri was the one who always saved the day. She handed Uncle Leo a scrap of paper. Uncle Leo looked at the numbers written on the paper.

"What's this?"

"When Barnes introduced himself he flipped his badge and I.D. and I memorized the numbers."

Uncle Leo shook his head and left the room.

Chapter Nine

I STOOD IN MY SUITE in the Treasure Island Hotel and marveled at the complexity of neon lights mixed with the energy of swarms of people on the Las Vegas strip. It was late Friday afternoon, and I had returned from upper Sahara where I had a small condo in a gated community. I had changed clothing and cleaned up. I grabbed some more clothes and returned to Treasure Island and the new suite the hotel had comped me. It would be easy to return to my home each evening, where I had all the creature comforts including an office library that Sherlock Holmes would envy. But when the opportunity presented itself, I liked to be close to the scene of the crime. Every time I had done this in the past, it had provided me with a better feel for the case. I pondered the problem at hand. I had three clients: Rapture who had originally retained me to attend a meeting with her; Dick Barnes, a U.S. Treasury agent; and my undercover security assignment with Treasure Island. I would see Rapture this evening and Barnes tomorrow morning. Those meetings should set the agenda for both cases.

Each neon sign below flashed a promise. The Strip was full of promises. My thoughts returned to how the Feds operated. All federal agencies hired freelancers as field agents when the situation called for a certain expertise. This would also remove the agency from being directly involved in any action in the field. If the surveillance went bad, the agency could officially claim they were not involved and had no agents present at that time.

These black bag jobs were not what I really liked to do. The first concern is you can never trust your employer. When they force you into a situation where you have to agree to gather information, which sometimes meant breaking the law, they always had you. It was difficult to break away. Once employed, always employed. That's why they liked to pay cash.

This potentially was the real problem in working for the government. One step at a time. How to accomplish what they wanted, and be able to walk away when I wanted to. I hoped the meeting tomorrow with Barnes would answer some questions. I was hoping that Uncle Leo and Sheri could come up with some background that would help. Uncle Leo was concerned, so I was concerned.

I left my suite and took the elevator from the eighth floor down to the sixth floor where everything started. Sure enough, the hotel door was taped with a yellow police ribbon making it clear this was a crime scene. I did not think the room would have been "released" at this point, but I had to check. I continued to walk down the hallway until I reached the window overlooking the roof. It too was taped off, but the broken glass was gone. I was able to move close enough to look down. I could see a few forensic investigators going over the roof in detail. In daylight, they might be able to locate and document some valuable clues. The ropes, which were tied there earlier, were gone. Metro had most likely secured them for forensic evidence.

I made a notation in my notebook about it. Once a cop, always a cop. I still preferred the small black notebooks used by most law enforcement agencies like the ones I used when I was in the field. But I also used a Palm Pilot for my database of names and contacts. It also had my calendar, which came in handy. Every night I would take the notes

the hotel, and followed a possible trail with our eyes.

"Why not use the service elevator? Plenty of exits to the street from there," commented Morton.

We started to walk toward the edge of this roofing complex. I noted several other police officers checking the edges of the building. Looking for signs of ropes I guessed. "Yeah, the service hallways provide an exit to the street, but there's too many employees wandering around there."

"How is your client? Rapture, isn't it?"

"We got her moved. I'm going to have a chance to talk with her tonight. I think she'll be a bit more rested and we can take some steps to figure this out."

"None of these crimes make any sense until we start to put together the details."

"That's for sure," I responded. "Any more info on the victim?"

"His name checks out with his I.D. We've got a background check going now, but it looks pretty straight forward. No record. How about you?" Morton asked, throwing the question back to me.

"Never met him. First time I saw him he was dead on the floor. Any ideas?"

"Don't know. We should know later today."

My eye caught something and I glanced down at it laying on the roof. "Look at this." We both bent down and examined a blue fiber, which could easily have come from a rope.

"You thinking what I'm thinking?" Morton said.

"Yep. They dragged the rope to this spot, slipped it around that air vent, threw both ends over the side, then repelled down the side and pulled the rope free."

"Possible. Very possible," Morton said, as he walked over to the edge of the building and peered down.

I followed him and we studied the side of the building and an alley. I could easily visualize a van sitting down there in the early morning darkness waiting for the killers to make their escape.

"What else your boys got?" I asked Morton.

"Nothing."

"That's why we have jobs," I commented.

Morton shrugged. "I'll keep forensics working the scene. We'll go over this area with a fine toothcomb. It will take a while, but we'll find pieces of the puzzle. Always do."

"What about down below," I asked, pointing to the area where a waiting van could have been hiding in the dark at the time of the murder.

"It's been cleared by our department. We came up empty. Puzzling."

"Why?"

"There's activity down there, but I cannot pinpoint any of it having to do with the murder. Nothing. Just normal everyday wear and tear."

"Always a trail, always," I said. I left Morton on top of the roof as more of his crew showed up. Forensic work never seemed to end on a case like this.

I exited the casino and worked myself around to the spot below that Morton and I had looked at just a short while ago. It looked like the crime scene had been cleared. I first examined the lighting situation. I expected to see a couple of the halogen lights knocked out. A professional hit team would have wanted a dark alley to limit visibility. The lights were bright and intact. I then examined the plants at the base of the wall looking for any kind of damage to the leaves. They appeared in great shape. Next I examined the grass and dirt surrounding the plants. I was looking for any kind of depression caused by men either climbing or repelling down from the wall. I could not find any. I scoured the wall in detail and found no marks whatsoever. As one final test, I jumped as high as I could and landed on the grass and then with a second jump landed on the dirt. My heels dug in and I made distinct depressions. I examined the soil, and about a half inch down it was moist. Unless the team landed on top of a vehicle, and then jumped to the pavement, they had not exited the building from this point. I didn't think they would plan that far ahead, so I figured they made their escape from another point in the casino. So, why the ropes?

Chapter Ten

THE PEPPERMILL FIRESIDE LOUNGE was legendary. Located on Las Vegas Boulevard next to the La Concha Motel across from where the Stardust used to be. It was a place where Vegasites, visitors, and stars met to hide and fathom the dancing flames. It was a chain restaurant that started in Reno and expanded to multiple locations across the country. It was sort of a dark Denny's with a lounge, complete with a cozy fire pit. The decorator must have liked orange and brown and thought it went well with faux flowering cherry trees. The hostesses at the Peppermill were famous for their long legs that were the eye appeal when their full-length cocktail dresses, slit up the side, swirled gracefully as they walked.

It was dark when I arrived, and since it was a Friday night, I was tired. Sheri had picked up Rapture and they were meeting me for a late night meal to discuss the case and the direction that Rapture wanted to take. I had to come to terms with what her problem was and whether I could help. I picked up my glass of Merlot, absentmindedly swirled the wine, and sat the long stemmed glass back down again. Habit.

I felt someone rub my right shoulder. I looked up and saw Sheri and then Rapture. I stood and gave Sheri a hug and a kiss on the cheek, and extended my hand to Rapture.

"Good to see you."

Rapture took my hand, and kissed me on the cheek. "I can't thank you enough. You have been so much help to me." She was as tall as I was. She settled herself into the wingback chair and snuggled close to the fire. Sheri took a seat next to Rapture.

"Well, your instincts were right," I said as I stared into her beautiful green eyes.

"I knew something was wrong when I got those e-mails."

"Do you still have them?"

"Yes, but what good are they?"

"We can do a search to see if we can pin down who owns the account, or what ISP they originated from. It's a start."

"Okay. My laptop is in my hotel room."

"At Treasure Island?" I asked.

"No, where I'm staying now."

"Good. Show Sheri the computer tonight and the selected e-mails. Do not try to copy them, or send them to anybody. Sheri's the computer expert. She'll look into it and see if she can come up with something right away."

Rapture turned to Sheri. "You're really something. What kind of girl ends up being a P.I.?"

"I spent a good deal of time in the Coast Guard, then traded the sea for the desert. My life ambition is to be Fargo's full time partner." Sheri said as she smiled that smile.

I countered. "We discuss it often."

Both Sheri and Rapture laughed.

"Now to the subject at hand. Rapture, I have quite a few questions for you. But, before we start, would either of you like a glass of wine?"

"Please, whatever you're having would be fine."

"Same for me," Sheri responded.

I waved at the hostess, poked three fingers in the air, and pointed to my glass. I was drinking a Sonoma County Merlot from Mietz Cellars in Healdsburg, California.

I seated myself across from Rapture. The Peppermill's fireside lounge was dark and the fire created most of the light. It provided an atmosphere that I had to assume helped many reflect on the good times, or maybe the problems, of the moment.

"If you would excuse me for a bit," said Rapture, as she rose from our table. "I'll be just a second."

I leaned over and put my hand on her arm, which stopped Rapture from rising, and I nodded at Sheri. Sheri left the table to do a walk through of the ladies restroom, while Rapture slowly sat back down, knowing the security precautions we were taking were for her protection. We both sat in silence. I swirled and sipped my wine. A peaceful moment, but one that I think made Rapture truly understand what kind of trouble she was in. Her eyes cast downward as she reflected on the situation.

Sheri appeared and nodded to me. I turned and smiled at Rapture. She got up and disappeared. Sheri did not miss a beat as I turned to her.

"Successful, very successful," said Sheri, as she turned in her chair and watched the ladies bathroom door, never taking her eyes off of it while we talked. "She was a distinguished corporate exec in Phoenix for a large real estate company. Worked her way up from an associate in sales, then to a broker, and was looking at a vice presidency before she left the firm to work with her dad."

"Real estate is good background for becoming a developer," I said, studying the flickering flames, and taking a sip of my Merlot.

"Probably part of the overall plan that the family had. A lot of owners ship their sons and daughters out to other firms to gain knowledge, insight, and make their mistakes before entering the family business."

"Makes sense. Relationships?"

"None to speak of. Off and on flings through the years. Nothing to get excited about. Knows when the time is right, it will happen. Very happy working."

"Any hits?"

"Confusion over how this situation got out of control. Not understanding what some people will do for money."

"Could it have been avoided?"

"J.T.'s death?"

"Yes."

Sheri pondered the question, and I watched as her eyes glance momentarily at the flames. She turned back to me. "I always like to think that situations like this can be avoided. But, when it's your time, it's your time."

Sheri and I had this discussion more then once, and she knew that I was not looking for this kind of answer.

"Possibly bringing in more security. Putting a guard in the room. But they were convinced that they were not in a life-threatening situation, that no real action was needed."

"What about the e-mails?"

"Yes, that was a concern, but she took action right away. They hired you...us...to protect her."

I smiled at bit when Sheri used the word 'us.'

"After all," said Sheri, "they thought they were safe in a Las Vegas hotel. Who would expect that a hit like this would be attempted at the Treasure Island?"

"Why would the killers tip off Rapture with e-mails? Why not make it a complete surprise?"

"Don't know. Doesn't make sense."

"Here's something, though," said Sheri, as she leaned close to me, "Rapture has not told me yet what the meeting here in Las Vegas was about. We don't know yet what was really going on."

"We only know she was meeting with Coyote," I said as I caught Sheri's eyes glancing behind me. I leaned back in my chair. So far all we had was a wild entrance into Las Vegas, a murder and an early morning meeting that was canceled. Something to think about.

I looked up and saw Rapture edging her way between our chairs until she reached hers. A bar hostess brought our Merlot. I put down two twenties, and gave the hostess a wave. That got a big smile.

Rapture picked up her Merlot and gave the wine a quick swirl, and I could tell she had a practiced hand when it came to wine. "I can see why you would want to come here," she commented, studying the flames. "It's solitude in the middle of a world of excitement and risk taking. Something to remember."

"Everybody who is anybody ends up here," I said. It makes every list in Las Vegas. There's something about a roaring fire that captives the imagination."

Rapture held up her wine in approval. "Thank you."

I took a sip and then set my wine glass down. "Let's start at the beginning. Why were bullets streaming into my room at four-thirty in the morning?"

"My partner was in that suite. I was going to meet the both of you there."

"Jonathon Taylor?"

90

"Yes," Rapture said, tears welling up in her eyes. "J.T. is what everyone called him. I've known him for years. He was my father's partner, then mine."

"So, you inherited your father's business interests?" I asked.

"Yes. They worked together for years and shared many adventures. After my father passed on, I became J.T.'s partner, and we agreed to work together to transition my father's business. J.T. wanted to retire, and I was going to exercise an option for his share of the stock."

"He had no family?"

"He had family, but they had made a decision as a family to sell the stock to me. The whole family would be very well off. No money worries."

"I see."

"I had been working in the business, learning it, finding out what makes it tick."

"I'm sorry about your father, and your partner."

"Thank you." A smile flashed, the kind of smile you see at funerals. Polite, filled with grief.

"What was your father's name?"

"Andrew Buck Hiller. They called him Buck for short. I called him, father."

"Your father passed away from natural causes?"

"Yes."

I finished the remainder of my first glass of wine while Rapture sipped on hers. Sheri was quiet, listening.

"How did you find my room?" Rapture asked.

"According to security, there were two rooms booked by Jonathon

Taylor.

"I see."

I pulled my notebook from my coat pocket and jotted down the date, time of our meeting, and the name of Andrew Buck Hiller. I already had J.T.'s name from our first phone conversation. No doubt the police already had this information, but I like to keep records just the same.

"Were you aware of this possible attack before you checked in?"

"I knew there was some threat, but I believed that I was safe being in a popular hotel on the strip."

"They were certainly ruthless. I have never heard of someone using an AK to take out a guest on the sixth floor of a hotel, then making their escape."

"Do you think there was more than one?"

"Yes. From what I heard, at least two."

"I see."

We all sipped our wine. It was a good point in our conversation to stop and order our meal. The Fireside Lounge's menu had a lot of variety and the portions were large and the food fresh. Rapture went for the Cobb salad, Sheri had the Peppermill Burger with fries and I went for the meatloaf with a dinner salad. We would not be disappointed. The food was always excellent.

"So where do we go from here, Rapture?"

Rapture took a very deep breath. "I need help," she said.

"Why do you need me?"

"Treasure."

"What kind of treasure?"

"Buried treasure." She took a sip of wine never taking her eyes off of me.

Magic words for my ears. She had my attention. The mention of treasure was frosting on the cake. I stared at the fire that dominated the Peppermill Lounge just like a campfire deep in the desert or high in the mountains would do. It threw off light as well as memories. It stirred up dreams of forgotten men that once combed cavernous mountains from here to Alaska in search of gold. Whether a treasure hunter or a pirate on a rampage, the search for the world's treasures were the fantasies of young boys who grew into men that never tired of searching and hoping.

Many years ago I ran into a rough and tumble kind of guy outside a courtroom in downtown Las Vegas. We were both sitting in the waiting area passing time before being called to testify.

"Nice way to spend an afternoon," I commented.

"Yeah," the man said, leaning forward and placing his elbows on his knees. "Time I was out of here."

"Fargo Blue," I said offering my hand.

"Gerry Heisig," he replied, and we shook hands. They were strong hands, callused and tough.

"Glad to meet you."

"Same to ya." Gerry wore a red and black checked flannel shirt that had seen better times, but it was buttoned neatly at the top. That was Gerry's concession for his "maybe" court appearance. I wore my usual shirt, slacks and sports coat. No tie. Never.

"Been here long?"

"Nah. Just waitin' for my sister. She's testifying against a couple of punks who broke into her car. They might call me as a backup witness."

"At least the cowboys caught them. Times are improving," I said.

"Nah...the cops didn't catch them. Mary, that's my sister, walked out of her house and made them crawl on the ground."

"How'd she do that?"

"9-millimeter Beretta."

"That would do it."

"A neighbor called the police and they were there quick-as-you-please. They confessed to knocking in her car window and trying to get her stereo. They hauled them off and here we are."

"What do you do when you're not hanging out in court rooms?"

"I'm a treasure hunter."

As a young police officer on the beat I had toyed with the idea of treasure hunting. Everybody in Las Vegas thinks of it at least once when you hear about the lost mines in the region waiting to be claimed. Stone Cabin and the Silver Gate to name a few. Outfitters dot the landscape ready to rig you in the latest garb to tackle the desert's heat. My early forays into the desert were uneventful, and just plain hot.

"Professional?" I asked.

"Nope. Professionals have funding. Deep pockets. Me, I don't have anything. I've been poking around these mountains all my life. Looking here and looking there...and then going back to look again. My dad was treasure hunter. We used to spend evenings pouring over maps searching for lost mines and claims. We ransacked bookstores, libraries and old estates searching for evidence of lost treasures or Indian legends that might turn into gold. I continued in his footsteps. I find enough to keep me going. It's the hunt that's exciting."

Shared stories unraveled throughout the afternoon and before we left the courthouse we were like long-time best friends, and I was a bona fide, want-to-be treasure hunter.

"You interested?" Rapture asked, snapping me back to the present conversation.

"Sounds promising," I replied staying as calm as possible. "I have spent a considerable amount of time treasure hunting."

"Rapture looked up. "You?"

"Yep. I have been involved in it for years. Treasure hunting and detecting have a lot in common. Think about it. They both involve searching for something, asking questions, bumping around in the middle of the night, digging here, and digging there."

"I would never have figured you for it."

"Me neither," said Sheri. "But that's what Fargo is all about. Always full of surprises."

"What kind of treasure, and where is it buried?" I asked.

"Good questions, but I can't possibly answer those at this time."

"I'm your private investigator. Emphasis on the word private."

"Yes, yes you are."

"So, what's the next step? How can I help you?"

"I need to generate capital to purchase a map."

"A map?" Sheri said.

Rapture turned toward her and then back to me. "Yes, I need capital."

"Is this about Coyote?" I questioned. She had told me about Coyote in the limo when we were removing her from Treasure Island.

"Yes, I mentioned her before."

"So you need funds to buy a treasure map from Coyote?"

"Yes."

"You don't have money to buy the map?"

"No, I don't."

"How are you going to get it?"

"Roulette."

"Roulette?" I stammered.

Sheri sat back in her seat.

I also sat back and took a sip of wine as I glanced at Sheri. I bet she was thinking, "I'll let Fargo handle this one." I caught a twinkle in Sheri's eye, and knew I was right.

"You're going to win it playing roulette?" I said, as calmly as I could.

"That's the plan."

I remembered seeing Rapture as we made the obnoxious entrance to the hotel. So she was a player, I thought. "Seems to me that if you had the wherewithal to bring me to Las Vegas in a private Lear Jet, put me up in a better then average hotel room while you're also staying in a luxury suite, that the funds for buying a treasure map would be available."

"The map is expensive. Very expensive."

"Really?'

"Yep."

"Who owned the jet?"

"Leased."

"Why not a line of credit. I'm sure any financial institution would love to have your company as a client."

"We're tapped out and lenders would be leery of that use of the funds."

96

"Do you believe her to be connected to J.T.'s murder?"

"No. I believe it to be a third party. She would have nothing to gain."

"Why do you say that?"

"When you meet her, you'll understand."

"Okay, I'll believe you for now."

"I believe I'm right," Rapture said. "She wants to sell her half of the map. She has no interest in my half."

We sat in silence for a few minutes. I was going over the facts carefully and I believed Rapture to be telling the truth.

"Will you help me?" asked Rapture.

"To do what?" I asked.

"Find J.T.'s murderer and help me acquire the map."

"That's a rather tall order, and quite a switch in assignments."

"I need the help."

"I can help with the map, and look into the murder. Homicide wants to talk to you. This is really their investigation."

"I can't stop that." Rapture said. She leaned forward and looked me in the eyes. "I'll figure out a way," she repeated, and I believed her.

I sat back. "Let's do it this way. I'll stay on the case for a few days and see what happens. Let me snoop around and see what I can dig up. Treasure Island has comped me a suite. The hotel has been very co-operative. They know I'm a detective, and I told them I would inform them of any information that I find. I have a good working relationship with them. I'm a private detective and a treasure hunter. You couldn't find anybody with a better background to help you."

"I agree," said Rapture, leaning back and taking another sip of her wine.

I swirled my Merlot again. It was like panning for gold, and I remembered when I found my largest nugget ever. I had traveled to the Western slopes of Colorado and hiked up a trail where gold was discovered long ago. At least that's what I read in an old book about treasure hunting that I found in a junk store.

The Colorado Rocky Mountains were always beautiful, and on that crisp autumn day I had waded into the shallow banks of a small tributary creek that fed into the Elk River. The ice-cold water that flowed from the melting snow in the high country splashed relentlessly into the river forming a small but shallow pool. With rubber boots on, I bent down, scooped aside the first layer of gravel and mud, and loaded my pan with the small gravel, sand and silt that made up the river bottom. I started the swirling and dumping and it developed into a rhythm that could relax the soul of the devil himself. I picked up more water to wash the material, and the rhythm took over and melded with the sound of the river. Eventually the heavier material ended up in the crease in the pan, and there it was, a large gold nugget.

I looked down at my gold Hong Kong Jockey Club ring. I still had that nugget with me to this very day. I gave it up in Hong Kong, and it came back to me in a beautiful ring.

"First gold find?" Rapture asked.

"What?" I said, drawing myself back from Hong Kong.

"Your ring?"

"Yes, long story. I'll tell you someday."

Rapture composed herself. She absolutely defined the word beauty. "When I get the money for the map, you can help me make the buy. And when I find the treasure, and all is well, you can tell that story. Agreed?"

"Yes, it's a deal."

"How did your father and his partner find their half of the map?"

"Right here in Vegas. The story goes he bought some land, and when they were excavating, they unearthed a small mine shaft."

"Right, I remember that. About two years ago out on lower Sahara up against the foothills. They had parked a giant rig out there – a grader. And one of those huge tires sank down during the night."

"That's the one. They did some excavation and were able to recover some gold. Not much, but enough to make it interesting. Right when they were wrapping this up, they found a small box, some notes, and half a map. After that, J.T. had gold fever. He ended up chasing the world's treasures, and evidently was contacted by the party who has the other half of the map."

"You're in danger. I have to assume that the gunmen know about you."

"I would think so."

"So, the map explains the hit in the hotel room. Why fly me in so suspiciously?"

"We were set to make the map purchase here in Las Vegas. J.T. and I wanted someone who knew Las Vegas who could watch over the transaction. I was going to bring you up to date in our meeting that morning before we met with Coyote. I was trying to play it safe and have a card up my sleeve at the same time."

"Why the elaborate entrance?"

"Didn't think you would come."

"You're right. What else?"

"I believe Coyote is going to contact me soon."

"How much cash does she want?"

"Three million."

"So Coyote's got the map, or half of the map, and someone else is killing people for it, or at least we think so. This is very dangerous for all the players," I said, glancing around the lounge. I wondered if we were being watched. I also wondered if the killers knew about Coyote and if she was also a target.

Rapture sensed my uneasiness, and she too looked around the room. "Perhaps you're right."

"Okay. Here's what I would like to do. I would like Sheri to continue to keep an eye on you, and for you to continue to stay where you are, at least for a couple of days. As I sort things out, we will be in touch."

"Fair enough. The accommodations are very nice and I can use the rest. Besides, I have a lot of work to do since J.T. is...is no longer part of the corporation." Rapture looked away, and then composed herself.

"I understand."

"So...so I think the arrangement will work just fine. I have a lot of transition issues, and a board meeting to prepare for."

"Is the board meeting here or in San Francisco?" I asked.

"My call."

"Okay. I think it should be here. But we'll address that later. Sheri will take good care of you." Sheri nodded in agreement, and put her arm around Rapture's shoulder. Rapture's smiled said it all. It was a smile of thanks.

The food arrived. We were hungry, tired and somewhat content. My mind traveled to my morning meeting with Barnes. Perhaps some questions would be answered. Life as a detective is somewhat like being a philosopher. You think things through, project tangents, consider consequences, and do your best to help your client. It was honorable.

Chapter Eleven

PRETENDING TO READ A NEWSPAPER, I stood near the entrance to the Mirage buffet. It was Saturday morning and I had been thinking about the meeting with Rapture and her quest for treasure.

People could approach the buffet from two different directions, and I had them both covered. Sure enough, right on time, Dick Barnes walked in holding a newspaper. He looked cautiously over his shoulder as if he was trying not to be spotted. I laughed to myself. The sale of so many newspapers can be attributed to all of the people hiding behind them while spying on other people. It's like, if you have a newspaper, you're invisible.

Barnes flashed a badge, and a chubby buffet employee lifted up a rope barricade to let him through. Several people gave him a dirty look because he had obviously cut in front of them. About halfway through the restaurant he slid into a booth facing toward the front. Coffee immediately appeared, and he looked up and scanned the casino, which he could easily see from his table. Barnes nodded his head, and I followed the nod across the room to an overstuffed suit sitting at a slot machine, plugging quarters, and looking for cherries. Neither one of them had noticed me.

Barnes was double-teaming me. I moved cautiously back, and went around to a service entrance and took one last look. Barnes' partner hadn't picked up my movement. I disappeared behind the doors and found my way into the back of the restaurant. I went through the kitchen flashing my badge all of the way. I gave a waitress a twenty spot to buy my entry. I emerged from the server's entrance, stopped at the buffet, and loaded up a plate of scrambled eggs, bacon and threw in a couple of sausages for good luck. I also added some potato pancakes. I've always believed in a balanced fat intake. I added a pile of sour dough toast, and on top of that stacked several pats of butter. I walked as if I was on the high wire at Circus Circus. I stopped a couple of booths behind Barnes, but across the aisle. Talk about blending in, I thought. I was the ultimate tourist packing it in so I could fortify myself for a day of sitting in front of the slots.

Coffee immediately appeared. "Ma'am, could you ask the gentlemen over there to join me," I said keeping an eye on Barnes. I spread out the food, newspaper and coffee. How could Barnes expect me to move over there? It was all about strategy.

The good spirited waitress stopped at the table, said a few words, and they both turned around and looked at me. I waved for him to come over. Big smile on my face.

He was somewhat pissed and knew I had him. He reluctantly got up and walked the few steps to my booth, and had no choice but to sit down facing me. Covert-operation types hate sitting with their back to the entrance, as evidenced by our first meeting. Barnes threw down the newspaper as he slid into the booth. He was pissed.

"Morning," I said.

"Same to you." Barnes said aggressively with an edge in his voice.

"Say, would your buddy out there playing the slots like to join us?" I picked up my coffee mug and leaned over to the left, caught the guy's eye, and toasted him. His eyes got big, and then he turned and fed more quarters into the machine while trying to hide behind a newspaper.

The third invisible newspaper of the day.

"Okay, okay. So you nailed us. That's why I want you. You're good."

"You want your friend to join us?"

"No, the guy's an idiot."

The waitress appeared with Barnes' cup of coffee from his table, then topped off mine.

"Thanks," I said.

"Welcome," came the reply.

"Barnes, get some food, and we'll talk."

He got up, still somewhat disgusted for having his partner spotted, and not having his choice of seats. He ambled off toward the buffet. I watched him closely as he stepped into line. I could tell he was a picky eater by the selections he chose, and the amount he decided upon.

Every hotel has a buffet, but Mirage was one of the best. Tourists traveled from other casinos just to have breakfast in this delightful setting. The hotel felt like it was built around a rainforest, and it provided a pleasing sense of comfort. Many Saturday mornings Uncle Leo, Sheri and I would meet here for breakfast and a casual office meeting. First would be the fruit and coffee. Then about a half-hour later we would get a selection of sausage, bacon, country-fried steaks, eggs, and every type of bread under the sun, followed by more coffee. We were set for the day. Abby often joined us, but barely ate a thing. Keeping her figure was one of the major challenges in being a line dancer at the Trop, particularly the late night show when the dancers were topless. Abby watched her diet like a hawk.

Barnes returned with a moderate pile of food. Before he started, he spent several seconds straightening his plate, knives and forks. Typical accountant, I thought.

"Good bacon," he mumbled.

"The best. This town eats more bacon than the entire state of Texas. People starve themselves all year, and when they hit the neon lights they eat everything in sight." I reached into my inside coat pocket and unfolded several sheets of paper and turned it toward him. Barnes thumbed it open with his right hand while eating bacon with his left.

"I see you've done your homework," Barnes commented.

"We always do a background check." I had Sheri run a check on him with the Treasury Department. Many times Uncle Leo had said, "If you work with an agent, make sure they're an agent." Destroys my court case if they turn out to be a rogue. The Treasury Department responded quickly letting us know that Barnes was indeed a Treasury Agent and was on assignment in Las Vegas. They declined to comment on his specific activities.

"I was happy with the results."

"Picture's not too good," Barnes grimaced.

"Government photos are like that."

"Suppose so. Thanks for checking me out. I received a voice mail from the office that you had requested the check. I like working with people who know who I am, and trust what I'm doing." Barnes bit into a slice of wheat toast, and followed up with a sip of coffee. "Look, here's the deal. As you know, I work for the U.S. Treasury on special assignment for the IRS. We have a group of people here in town right now that we think...how should I put this...let's say they are suspicious, and we think that they're up to a potentially illegal activity."

"What kind of activity?"

"To start, I can say it always has something to do with taxes."

"So, how can I help?"

"Well, we know from information that we've uncovered that this activity will occur at Treasure Island. They know who I am, and that's where you come into play. We just need your eyes and ears on anything suspicious happening at Treasure Island."

"I do work for the hotel."

"You work for them? What do you mean?"

"Well, I'm reporting to the hotel on a number of issues. You, of course, know about the murder last night?"

"Yeah, I heard. Unfortunate."

"Really? How do you know what happened?"

"Word gets around. I heard you were part of it?"

"I was in the room next door. It was sort of a rude wake-up call. I worked with hotel security until Metro arrived."

"They any good, security?" Barnes asked, as he took another bite of his pancakes.

"The usual weaknesses."

"Anything else happen?"

"I poked around a bit. Went on the roof this morning. Didn't find too much."

"The roof?" Barnes asked.

"You know, just checking details." I needed to get Barnes back to the main topic, I thought. "Is this a pro team working the hotel?"

"Maybe. More than likely it's one person. We have several people we are looking at. Okay, let me give you more information. Here's the angle. We're obviously interested in potential tax evasion."

"Tax evasion?"

"Tax evasion is still the way to land the bad guys. People don't claim everything. We're here to make them honest."

"Mighty suspicious, aren't you?"

"It's my job to be suspicious. It pays the bills. But, in this case, we're suspicious of something – we don't know what yet. So we're taking the steps to keep us involved. A little investigation, a little poking here and there can sometimes reap big rewards for the department. Sort of like undercover surveillance, you never know what you're going to find."

"You going to audit me?"

"Nope, you're clean. We already checked."

Thank you Uncle Leo, I thought. Uncle Leo was a stickler for conservative, documented tax filings. Our office worked closely with an accounting firm and we all made ultra conservative tax filings. The strategy was if we were ever audited, we would be the ones asking for money back, not the IRS.

"Who are the targets?"

"Like I said, I can't say. But I will tell you that one is a female. A real looker who likes to gamble. We think she's going to hit the casino for a lot of money. She's waiting for something. Could be the right time. But we'll be there when she makes her move."

"What do you want me to do?" I asked as I dug into my potato pancakes. Only the Stage Deli at the Forum made better ones.

"Since you're already working for the hotel, it will be natural for you to get a feel for what's happening in the casino. Are they preparing for a run on the tables? Are the floor personnel nervous? Things like that.

Then just keep me posted."

"Why not just have hotel security look into this problem?"

"Too many barbeques..."

"Meaning?"

"People talk too much...eventually, every casino employee would know there is a take down coming at one of the tables. If this team has someone on the inside, they'll be tipped off and will try another casino. Sometimes, like this one, a private detective is the best solution."

"Sort of like treasure hunting," I commented.

"How do you mean?" asked Barnes, as he moved his plate to the side and centered his coffee right in front of him. He looked up with eyes that revealed nothing.

"The more people who know where the treasure is, the more problems you're going to have in getting it."

Barnes toasted me with his cup of coffee. "Gold holds many secrets."

I toasted him back with my coffee. "I agree, gold holds many secrets."

"Fargo, can I ask you a favor?"

"Sure," I said.

"The jerk they assigned to me is pretty tied up in his game. I would like to sneak out the back if you don't mind."

"Why is he a jerk?"

"Trainee. They assigned him to me from the local office and the guy is a complete loser. So I figure, if I'm to train him, then I'll do it. So I figure, if we disappear out the back, he's going to be sitting there wondering what the hell happened. And then when we meet up, I can give him a lecture about covert surveillance and what to do and what not to do. Hopefully, he will learn from his mistakes and I can give him a positive write up."

I smiled, agreeing. "Don't see any sense in disturbing an avid gambler."

Barnes laughed and I joined in. We both thought of what the agent would do when he saw we had disappeared.

"Before we leave, are you forgetting something?" I said.

"Not that I'm aware of."

"Payment."

"For services to be rendered?"

"Something like that."

"Don't you trust me?"

"It's business." I took out an envelope and dropped it on the table. "Here's my end of the deal. Just read it, sign it, and drop it in the mail. Copy for you is in there. If I don't get it back in a day or so, signed, I'll stop all work."

"Fair enough." Barnes pulled out an open envelope from his jacket pocket and pushed it toward me. I could see stacks of hundred dollar bills inside. I gave them a quick riffle and estimated the amount.

"It looks good. But why the cash? Are you baiting me? I will still have to declare. Wouldn't want the IRS to get upset."

"Thought it would be easier."

"Just creates more paperwork."

Barnes slapped a business card down on the table. Picking it up I noted that it was a formal IRS card with the official address and contact numbers. I looked up at Barnes.

"Unlisted number."

"Where you staying?" I asked.

"Like I said, unlisted."

I nodded my head understanding, and then glanced over Barnes' shoulder and glanced at his partner. I made a mental note to check out his partner in more detail.

I waited to make sure that the agent was hooked on his game, and gave the signal to Barnes. He dropped a twenty on the table and ducked into the kitchen area. As soon as we entered, we both pulled out our I.D.s and held them up for a hatchet carrying Chinese cook who was startled to see both of us come through the door.

"Back door?" Barnes questioned.

The Chinese cook responded in his singsong voice. "You want back door...you go that way...you go that way..." chopping with his hatchet to his left. "Garbage...garbage go that way."

I broke into laughter, and Barnes joined in. Honoring the cook's territory, we headed down the hallway next to the cold storage rooms, and out the side door to where dumpsters of garbage were waiting to be picked up.

Chapter Twelve

I SWUNG OPEN THE SCREEN DOOR and entered our offices.

"Hi, Boss," Sheri said as she handed me a stack of phone memos and my mail. I glanced at the memos and there was nothing urgent.

A bang sounded behind me. I turned and looked at the screen door. "Just can't get used to that door banging behind me every time I came in. Makes me feel like I'm back at our summer house by the lake."

"Or the pop from a .38," Sheri said.

"Yeah, that too," I smiled.

"Uncle Leo wants the office to have this warm and cozy feeling, and it reminds our clients of their summer vacations when they were kids. Besides, it saves on the electric bill for cooling down the office in the early morning hours."

"Makes sense," I said, somewhat amused. "After I talk to Uncle Leo let's get together to talk about our new client."

"Okay, Boss."

"Where is the great legal mind of Las Vegas?"

"He just hit his office. Wasn't in too good of a mood. Something about speed ratings not being correct."

I smiled and winked at Sheri as I rounded the corner, and went into my office to drop the mail in my inbox that was now about a foot high. We had a system, or Sheri had a system. We were afraid to say no. Everything was routed to everyone, and we had to sign off on it before it was file by part-time help. It kept all of us informed about the law and investigation issues. I passed Sheri's office, which was as neat as a pin, and knocked on Uncle Leo's door.

"If you're the horse that won the third race at Belmont, I don't want to see you. Anybody else can come in," replied a humorless voice from inside.

I entered Uncle Leo's office that any seasoned lawyer would be grateful to have. Surrounded by bookshelves on all four sides, he had two computers beside his desk, and a small laptop sitting on a stack of files in front of him. An arched window gave him a nice view of the courtyard and fountain outside our office. Uncle Leo was ready for battle. After his wife's untimely death a few years ago, he began to slow down. His main concerns were long shots, overlays, trifectas and any number of betting options the track provided the bettor.

I sat down and studied Uncle Leo, who continued on with his activity. Probably speed ratings, but I wasn't about to ask.

Uncle Leo leaned back in his chair and stretched. "What happened?"

"A lot."

"Brief it for me."

"First, Sheri and I met Rapture last night for dinner."

"Where?"

"Peppermill."

"Good choice. Why didn't you invite me?"

"Ahaaa...."

"Just kidding. I like the Peppermill."

"Next time. Anyway, we talked. When her father died, Rapture inherited the business and became partners with Jonathon Taylor, also known as J.T. He was the one killed at Treasure Island."

"Go on."

"It turns out that J.T. and Rapture were negotiating for a treasure map."

"A treasure map?"

"Yep."

"Right up your alley," Sheri answered, as she came through the door with her morning tea. Clutching her cup, she curled up in her normal chair right next to mine like a baby tiger. I never could figure out how she did that. She was a private detective in her own right, and we were lucky to have her. We should give her a raise for all of the extra stuff she does for us. Sheri shot me a look. She was also a mind reader.

"Keep going," said Uncle Leo.

"It even gets more interesting." I continued. "Rapture is going to play high stakes roulette in order to win the money to purchase the map from someone named Coyote."

"That's not the best business decision given the odds at roulette."

"True. I'm going to try to talk her out of it. But she seems determined.

"What else did you advise your client?"

"I told her she was at risk. We have her at our usual safe house and she is going to take it easy for the next couple of days. Sheri is going to look in on her from time to time plus regular telephone checks by both of us."

"Good. What else?"

"I'm looking into the killing at the hotel."

"We'll get to that. What about Barnes?"

"We met for breakfast at the Mirage. He's cagey."

"Doesn't surprise me."

"Yeah, but wait until you hear this. He ditched his backup man."

"You're kidding!" said Uncle Leo.

"Have you ever heard of an agent dumping their backup partner?"

"Never," said Uncle Leo, as he got up out of his chair and moved toward the window. "Do you think it was part of his plan -- sort of teaming up with you and dropping his partner routine was just to throw you off?"

"Possibly, but I wouldn't bet on it. My instinct tells me that Barnes does not like partners. Either way you look at it, it's something to be studied. It's manipulation of one form or anther."

"And he's supposed to be following somebody who the agency suspects of tax evasion?" asked Uncle Leo.

"Yes, but he wasn't too specific. Said it was a women."

"I ran a background check on Barnes," said Sheri. But he came up clean. Agency through and through. Dedicated and even brave. Took a bullet a few years back."

"What do you think, Fargo?"

"My gut says we don't know the half of it. I smell something big. I don't know what."

"You, Sheri?"

"My feeling is Rapture is clean. She is doing her best to take her father's position, and now she even has a greater burden on her with J.T. gone. I think her quest of this treasure map is emotional. Sort of the way she can wrap up her father's death. Not revenge, but something she has to do."

"Fair enough."

Sheri uncoiled herself from the chair. "I also think it's too much of a coincidence that Barnes is interested in Treasure Island right after the killing."

Uncle Leo turned and then sat down. "How do you find these cases, Fargo?"

"Just lucky."

"What about Treasure Island?"

"They just want current information. They expect the police will solve this one, or at least announce that it is under investigation, which means they won't be able to solve it."

Sheri took a sip of her tea. "Is it true what they say about AK's? Press is making a big deal out of it."

"Yep. AK's are the hot topic on the street. Never expected I would see an AK used inside a hotel. Pretty unbelievable," I said.

"The AK certainly brought some attention to this story," commented Uncle Leo, as he studied the screen on his computer.

"There was one magazine change that I heard clearly. It was an AK all right," I said, sitting closer to the desk.

Uncle Leo pulled down his reading glasses and looked at me. "I think whoever committed this crime wants to distract the investigators with the fact the target was murdered with a high powered semi-automatic. An assault weapon inside a hotel? Pretty spectacular!"

I sat back in my chair and thought to myself. Uncle Leo was right of course. I had been mulling over the use of an AK since last night. I'm sure homicide is doing the same thing, and it would probably lead them down a dark, dead end road. But there are a lot of bodies buried at dead ends when you live in the desert. Everything must be followed up relentlessly, to the last detail.

"There's something I'd like to know," Sheri announced.

Uncle Leo nodded his head at Sheri. "Shoot," he said. He had a knack for selecting just the right word.

Sheri turned toward me. "You found the hotel door locked, which security opened."

"Right, but it was still latched on the inside," I said.

"And with your mirror you were able to see a dead body on the inside?"

"Right."

"How did the killers get out of the room, if the door was locked and latched on the inside with a privacy lock? Dead men don't usually get up and lock the door."

Uncle Leo looked at me. "I'll let you answer this one."

Of course I knew this all along, but I hadn't addressed it head on. How could the killer escape, if the door was locked? True, it wasn't dead bolted, but the privacy lock counts for something.

In all my detective work I had only encountered one "locked door" mystery. This involved a dead man in a room with the front apartment door bolted and chain locked from the inside. Neighbors heard the POP from a handgun, and the victim crashing to the floor. When the police busted down the door, they found one dead body, and a bullet casing on the floor. Eventually the gun was found tucked away in the bottom of the bureau in the living room. The telephone was off the hook, and all the windows were closed. There was no back door, and being on the eleventh floor, you would have had to been Spiderman to make a clean escape scrambling up the outside wall to the top of the complex.

The telephone was the clue that solved the case. There was no pushing *98 to find out who the last caller was, but the phone off the hook led me in the right direction. From the apartment complex next door the killer had called the victim, got him to open the window, and used a Smith & Wesson Model 17 K-22 to put one bullet into the victim's chest. When the victim was hit, he let go of the window, which crashed down closing itself. Lodged in the window was the shell of a previously fired .22. The crashing of the window dislodged the casing. The victim then swung around and collapsed on his living room floor. The neighbors heard the window crash and the coffee table splintering from the dead man falling on top of it. Since it was a .22 long hollow point, the bullet exploded on impact, and did not exit. There were no blood splatters for forensics to use to establish where the bullet had come from. They did establish that the casing came from the gun in the bureau, but how did the .22 get back in the bureau?

It looked like an apparent suicide. The only problem was the gun in the drawer. Was the victim so neat that he shot himself, then put the gun in the drawer and died? It became obvious that the bullet was not one in the same. The .22 used at a close range, would do far more damage than one shot from a distance. I lifted the window, and noticed it would not stay up; this led me to study the other apartment complex directly across from the victim's. I thought of the movie, "Rear Window" and was able to put it together.

I looked up at Uncle Leo and Sheri. "Yes, it's been in the back of my mind. I haven't addressed it yet. Once I saw that there was somebody down in the hotel room, I convinced security to bust down the door. He could have been still breathing."

"Let me ask a couple of questions," Uncle Leo said. "First, good job Sheri. We might have Fargo getting the coffee for us soon while we solve the problems of the world."

"Thanks, but I've tasted his coffee."

"Good point. Now Fargo, did the officers or detectives figure this out while you were there?"

"Nope. Never questioned me about it at all."

"From what you got to see, were the bullets fired from inside the hotel room, with some of them straying into your room?"

"Not all the bullets strayed, but a fair number."

"Could you tell if they had been fired from the adjoining room to the victim's room?"

"No, they were fired from inside J.T.'s hotel room. There were empty shells all over the place."

"Did you get any info from the scene in terms of the shell casings? Anything that can point us in a direction?"

"I observed brass casings. I know the original design was of Russian origin, and the official nomenclature is Cartridge, 7.62mm, M1943. Since they are shorter than full-size cartridges, the weapons made for them can be shorter and lighter than those made for full-sized cartridges. An AK-47 uses this type of cartridge in 30-round magazines. The magazines can be changed in about ten seconds. It's a short-range bullet and is perfect for assault rifles in close range. Ala AK-47. This type of bullet is almost never used for sniper work because the range is not good."

"How about an SKS?"

"Too many casings on the floor, and SKS's are usually loaded via a stripper clip. Ten to a clip. The clip is inserted on the top and the load is then pushed down into the SKS."

"Impressive, and right on the money," Uncle Leo said.

"Ever fire an AK?" Sheri asked me.

"Yes," I said.

"Where?" Uncle Leo asked.

"Hong Kong, a long time ago. This is not the time for details. How about you Uncle Leo?"

"Yes, in Nam. Like a million other guys. As an advisor we had a lot of opportunities and saw way too much. Way too much." Uncle Leo's voice drifted off.

"So Uncle," as Sheri fondly called him. "What does this all mean?"

"I think it means the AK should be treated as a very strong lead. It's a common weapon, but not that common. Unfortunately, it's been used in a number of mass killings in recent years. Homicide is going to have to tie the killers to an AK." Uncle Leo leaned back in his chair and looked at Fargo. "Sounds like you've got this case on the right track?'

"Yes. We've run a background check on Barnes, but I think we need to dig deeper. Same with Rapture. I also want a detailed history on J.T. Perhaps there's something going on that we ought to know. I am also going to visit Morton and see what is going on over at Metro and see how they are approaching this case. And of course, we need to track down the AK. Someone always knows something."

Uncle Leo thought more about it. He was always thinking about complications with the law. "Sounds good to me, Fargo. Also, on this assignment, I think we need very detailed case notes of every interview and every morsel of a clue. That's the only way I can help you if we end up in court. Three separate cases and cross-reference it to the three interests, Treasure Island, Rapture, and now Barnes. If there is any conflict, we stop."

"Agreed," I said nodding my head. "How about you Sheri?"

"I'd like to shoot one," Sheri said.

"What?" I asked.

"I want to shoot an AK."

"Good idea," said Uncle Leo.

"Interesting. I think Sheri and I will go undercover and get into the local AK scene."

Uncle Leo smiled. "That will work. In fact, that might be a nice diversion."

"Why the smile?" I asked.

Uncle Leo's eyes bobbed up from the paperwork he was always scanning on his desk. "One, it's a smart move. A step ahead of the police. And two, the AK world is not ready for Sheri." Uncle Leo looked over at Sheri. "No offense of course."

"I took it as a complement," Sheri said, smiling.

"You're going to love an AK, Sheri. You can shoot from a shoulder position like this." I stood up and pretended to shoulder a weapon against my right shoulder. "Or shoot from the hip, like this," I said as I dropped the invisible semi-automatic rifle to waist level and pretended to mow down the books. "An AK is a good jungle weapon, light to carry, doesn't have much kick, great for magazine changes in a firefight, and also makes a great all purpose kitchen utility."

"I want one," Sheri said. Uncle Leo and I laughed.

"No, I wasn't kidding," Sheri said with a sting in her voice. "I really want one." We stopped laughing.

Chapter Thirteen

I WAS ON MY WAY TO HOMICIDE to check in on the latest development. It was unusual to have a Sunday afternoon meeting, but Homicide was always working overtime. I glanced at my watch and it was just after noon. I swung into Starbucks just past Decatur on Sahara and entered the drive-thru with the rest of the coffee addicts. As we inched forward I watched the sparrows forage for food in the bushes that separated me from the mist-covered patio. This had been the setting for so many meetings between Sheri, Uncle Leo and me.

The sparrows were not unlike the people flocking to Las Vegas to live and earn their piece of the pie. The birds fight over scraps of bread they haul away from the tables, or receive as a gift from a customer who's leaving. Las Vegasites act the same way. A new hotel opens up, and hundreds of applicants appear all seeking full-time work. Every one of them is trying to scratch out a living. But with the hordes of people also come the misfits who prey on targets for their daily bread. The sparrows claw the earth to find and devour a worm. The dregs of life fire bullets to wipe out competitors for their share of the catch.

"Here ya go Fargo," said Wanda, a University of Nevada law student and part-time Starbucks employee that I'd come to know. I jumped at the sound of her voice and realized that I had been deep in thought. Wanda handed me my iced Café Americano.

"Thanks. How's the law?"

"Hawkins vs. McGee."

I smiled. "That will keep you busy."

"See ya tomorrow," Wanda said, as she brushed her blond hair behind her ear. Probably a habit she did all of her life. "And catch those bad guys so we're all safe on the streets. Then maybe I won't run into them in the courts."

I gave her a big smile and nodded, thinking of how law students need plenty of caffeine to keep going through long nights of reading forgotten law cases that only students read. I moved ahead, keeping the line going so those behind me could get their midday fix. Caffeine was addictive. Just ask Coca-Cola how they were able to build such a huge business.

Life in Las Vegas is good. I was glad the sparrows had found a home at Starbucks, but my mind wandered back to trying to determine how Rapture and Barnes figured into my new assignment.

Barnes was going to be an okay guy to work with, but I needed to watch him closely. He knew the tricks of the trade, and he had pretty well established who his target was. My assignment with Rapture had turned into two murders and a treasure hunt. Conflict of interest crept into my mind, but I moved it aside. I always went by the philosophy that the other side knows something that you don't. I knew Barnes was not telling all, but the Coyote connection was my secret. One step at a time.

I love staying in the hotel where I'm working a case. I can study the patterns of tourists as they check in and out of the hotel, move from the gambling floor to various eating establishments, and then to their rooms. Watching these flow patterns often helps solve puzzling problems when you study the options criminals have as they work the hotels.

At this point, I knew I was up against two major problems. The first was the murder of a hotel guest by an unknown. I was hoping that

Detective Morton would have some leads that might point to a possible suspect. It usually turns out that the victim knows the killer, so a random shooting in a hotel like Treasure Island is very unlikely. That means the police will be tracking everyone J.T. ever met looking for motive and opportunity. In this situation, I was hoping Homicide was going to solve the case right away, and I could keep Treasure Island informed of their progress.

The second problem was that of the locked room. It presented numerous challenges for the detectives trying to solve the mystery, and the prosecutor trying to bring charges against a possible suspect. How could you convict somebody of murder, if you could not show how they entered the room? It kicked my imagination into high gear. A locked room mystery. If you could prove motive, but not means, it would be a difficult problem for a jury. I could just hear the defense attorney argue the case.

"If you truly believe my client committed this hideous act of murder, the prosecutor is going to have to prove how my client, an upstanding citizen of this city, entered the hotel room, committed the murder, and exited the room, leaving the doors locked from the inside. My client is not a Las Vegas headliner with a magic act. I dare say our local prosecutor has an overactive imagination and is leading you down a garden path that he says is covered with the blood of the victim and the guilt of the defendant. The prosecutor is spending way too much time at the Garden Court of the Bellagio trying to develop his case."

I could hear the laughter in the courtroom. I was always told I have an overactive imagination, but that's probably why I am a good detective.

It only took me thirty minutes to cover the distance from our office to Las Vegas Metro. I entered the station and made my way to Morton's office waving at some familiar faces along the way. I tapped on the partially opened door and peered in at John Morton. Heavy set with a tanned face, he was one of Las Vegas' most distinguished investigators having solved more murders than all the five-year rookies combined. When his rotation came up for a crime scene investigation, you knew he was going to follow through till the case was solved. He was readily available with information for the rookies who became stumped and needed some input on their investigations. Holding court every evening at The Academy, a local cop bar, Morton discussed on-going cases and was easily the biggest influence on bringing justice to dead men and women in Las Vegas.

"How ya doing, Fargo?" Morton asked, as I entered his cubbyhole of an office. Morton pointed at a seat and I removed some file folders and sat down. Morton used the chair filing system.

"Employed, after that shooting last night at Treasure Island."

"So am I. So, tell me again, why were you staying next door?"

"I was meeting my client at six the next morning and she offered to put me up at the hotel."

"Rapture?"

"Yes."

Morton looked back down at his paperwork. I knew the routine with Morton and smiled to myself. Morton had probably checked her out. Besides the computers, Morton would roll the name through his memory, which was just as fast and accurate at producing rap sheets on people who Morton had dealt with years ago.

"Anything on the dead guy?" I was fishing, detective style. I was here to find out what the police had, and what they didn't have. I remembered my meeting with Rapture at the Peppermill, and it crossed my mind that maybe Rapture was involved with this murder. I had to believe she wasn't, and would believe her to be innocent until proven otherwise. They would be talking to Rapture soon enough.

Morton put on a pair of reading glasses and studied some notes on his desk. Not that he didn't remember, but wanted to get the facts exactly right. "Jonathon Benjamin Taylor. People called him, J.T. No warrants. No arrests. No contacts with Vegas Metro. Business interest here in Vegas with main offices in San Francisco. Looks like he had been coming here the last ten to fifteen years or so for business. We've contacted San Francisco Police and they're making notification of next of kin, and running a background check for us. You know, the usual. I would assume Rapture's is the same."

"That's all you have?" I commented, and thought about my hometown of San Francisco. Born and raised there, I had some contacts in the Bay area that might prove useful. Abby had been bugging me to take her to the wine country for the last year. I had promised to take her after our St. Thomas trip.

"Who wants to know?" Morton asked.

"Treasure Island. They're looking for an update." A little information never hurt anyone, I thought. It was true, I just left out some details. Like Barnes was also looking for the information.

Morton took off his glasses and rubbed his nose. "I'll let them know when I'm ready to release information. Not before." A knock at the door and a thin squeaky looking guy wearing a white short sleeve shirt popped his head in, then kind of slid through the opening and dropped a foot high stack of papers onto Morton's desk.

"Here ya go," Squeaky said.

Morton slapped his glasses back on and pushed them up onto his nose. "I don't have room for this crap in here," Morton said, waving his hands at his cramped office.

"I'm just the messenger. When we all get computers the world will be a better place." Squeaky backed out of the office and shut the door.

"Paperwork," Morton said.

"Yeah, I know what you mean. I know the routine."

"Computers are creating more paper. I'm surprised there are any forests left." He leaned back into his chair seemingly overwhelmed with the volume of work facing him. "You need anything else, Fargo? I know you're digging around."

"I'm on retainer with Treasure Island. You know, the usual, trying to make Treasure Island happy so they can spin a story to the press."

"Sorry, everything is internal here. We'll get back to the hotel eventually. You know the routine," said Morton. He picked up the top sheet of the stack and glanced at it.

"Yeah, I know," I said getting up. "I hear J.T. was into treasure hunting."

"What?"

"I heard J.T. was into treasure hunting."

"How did you know that?"

"Hey...just digging around."

"Tell me more."

"Want to trade?"

"Trade what?" asked Morton.

"Information. I tell you a few things...you tell me a few things... we'll solve this case together for old time's sake."

"Okay, I'll go a round with you," Morton said. "J.T. was supposed to be meeting with some pretty important people, according to the hotel desk."

I sat back down. "Old news. That's why I was there in the first place. You're going to have to better than that. What do you have on the murder itself?"

"Like what?"

"Weapon of choice was...?"

"Rounds on the floor indicate an assault rifle. Probably an AK-47. Lots of rounds in the entranceway. I'm sure you saw that," Morton said

"Pretty unusual weapon to use in a hotel."

"We're on it. There'll be talk on the streets. It will lead us somewhere. Not exactly a throwaway weapon, so it's going to be sitting somewhere. Somebody will give it up. We put some money out in the right places. Money talks."

"How did the killer, or killers, get into the hotel room?" I asked, wanting to move away from the AK-47 topic. I wanted to chase this lead myself as Uncle Leo had suggested.

"We assume they were let in."

"How did they get out?" I asked.

Morton looked at me and then at his reports. "I don't know. Door was locked."

"Exactly," I said. "Mystery of the day. Have your boys been

through the room a couple of times trying to figure it out?"

"Yeah, we went through that place all night long. All the doors were locked."

"What about the room next door?"

"The one of the other side, not yours?"

"Right."

"It was occupied for the evening, but the hotel guest was downstairs gambling. We've got video of the party playing poker for most of the evening. His door was locked on the hallway side, and also the connecting door."

"Connecting door?"

"Yeah, his side lead into the guest bedroom of the suite J.T. was occupying. The connecting door on J.T.'s side was locked, and the other side was locked solid."

"And the door leading out to the hallway was locked?"

"Bolted solid."

"And J.T.'s hallway door was locked?"

"Bolted from the inside. Nobody came out through there. They didn't come out through your room, and didn't come out of the connecting door on the other side."

"The security guard opened the door?"

"Right. It was latched from the inside, I used a mirror to see the body, and then we broke down the door."

"You checked the windows?"

"No way out." Morton nodded at the obvious and made some notes on this pad. "What about the ropes down at the end of the hallway?"

Morton raised an eyebrow. "How did you know about that?"

"Looked outside and saw them."

"Being awful interested in this case, aren't you?"

"Well, I was the one who had to tuck and roll out of my bed from the streaming AK rounds. Being attacked by stray gunfire always makes me curious."

"I'm sure it does," laughed Morton. "An AK-47 wake up call always works."

"Besides, I had to move my client out of the hotel for her protection."

"True. How's Rapture doing?"

"Fine, considering."

"Good. We'll want to talk to her eventually."

"Just let me know when and I'll arrange it."

"How about tomorrow morning?"

"That should work. I'll have Sheri bring her in. Say nine o'clock?"

Morton leaned over and checked his calendar. "Okay, that will work." Morton penciled it in.

"Great," I said. "I have one more question. From your perspective, where did the shots come from?"

"Fargo, with you it's never one more thing."

I smiled and continued without missing a beat. "From what I could tell, the bullets had to be fired from somewhere around the entranceway into J.T.'s room. This was followed by bursts, as they got further into the room. Those are the ones that served as my alarm clock."

"Exactly. The murderer fired from just on the other side of the door."

"Any blood markings on the floor in front of the door?"

"None. J.T. died instantly. Didn't have a chance."

"What was J.T. doing on the sofa at four-thirty in the morning?" I asked.

"We're checking," Morton covered.

"Was there any blood anyplace besides around the body?"

"None. Everything was clean as can be."

"Any results back from paraffin tests?" I asked. Besides doing the normal work up, they had taken some swabs of my hands, shirt and face that evening. Very straight forward. I told them I had not been shooting for at least five days.

"Hallway by the door. All over the walls. No where else. You turned up clean, but that was expected. A little bit on your hands, but you handled a firearm that evening. No fresh signs of gun powder."

"Thanks."

I sat back and thought about this crime scene. "It just doesn't make any sense. How can you have a murder and no visible signs of how the murderer got out?"

"We got one dead person, and all the doors locked from the inside. There is no way the victim could lock the doors after he died," Morton said.

"You brought in the experts?"

"They were there all night. Our on-call locksmith verified that all the doors were locked. The only way anybody got in was when you and Treasure Island Security broke down the door. We don't know how they got out."

"They had to come through the connecting doors."

"They were dead bolted from the other side. No way for that to happen. How did you know he was a treasure hunter?" Morton said changing directions and bringing me back to my comment.

"From his partner, Rapture."

"Can you get me details? Something to follow-up on."

"Why?"

"You know, everything's important in a murder case."

"You're right. But what have you given me?"

"Well..."

"Come on. We had an agreement."

"Okay. I'll give you this. Drop back in two days and I'll let you read the Murder Book."

I got up and headed for the door. "Deal. And I'll call you when I find something out."

"You do that," Morton said.

I got up to leave.

"I've got one more question for you," Morton said as he leaned back in his chair.

I stood by the door, waiting.

"Tell me, what was that entrance all about last night?"

"What do you know?" I sat back down.

"That you and two babes made a rather noticeable entrance into the casino after landing in a helicopter. What was that all about?"

"Understand, I don't have to tell you this as it is client sensitive."

"Understand that I can always subpoena you. Hell, I'll just pick you up on false charges and hold you for a while." Morton smiled.

"Why is it I don't have a tape recorder when I need one?"

"Planning."

"My client, Rapture, was having a business meeting, and she hired me to attend the meeting. But she didn't want anyone to know that I would be attending. So we cooked up this little charade to throw off any would-be onlookers interested in why Fargo Blue was at the hotel."

"Where were you coming from?"

"St. Thomas. We cruised the island for about a week."

"So, let me understand this. You, Abby and Sheri shared a boat together for a week or so, and they came back with you." Morton leaned back into this chair thoroughly enjoying the exchange.

"Yep. I'm one lucky guy," I said. I might as well propagate the rumors since he was so interested. I was curious why he was. It would have been easy enough to pick up this information from the hotel. "How do you know about our entrance?"

"Video and rumors."

"I see. Okay, I'm out of here. Good hunting."

"Same to you."

I left, and then stuck my head back in. "Hey, who is J.T.'s next of kin in San Francisco?"

"Nobody you know," Morton said.

"Just curious," I replied, as I disappeared from Morton's view knowing I wasn't going to get any more information out of him. I was still at square one, but I knew I was on the right track. Homicide was as confused as I was about the locked room, and they had no leads. Nobody likes getting locked out of a mystery. Nobody.

Chapter Fourteen

CURIOUS CASE, I thought. I was sitting outside of Metro looking out over the mountains. Red Rock loomed in the distance, and I thought of the pleasant times I had in the desert, and how different they were from my times spent on the water. I enjoyed them both because the desert and the water always gave me something back, perhaps an inner strength and a different perspective on life and on work. For some reason I had a sort of flashback that I was sitting on a houseboat on the Mississippi River. Now, there is something I had never done.

I was thinking about my conversation with Morton about Rapture. Then there was Barnes. He was clean, but I was suspicious. Too much of a coincidence. Morton doesn't know much more then we do at this point. But what really bothered me was that I just couldn't figure why Rapture, with her wealth and business experience, would resort to a roulette game as a means to go after a treasure. That didn't add up. Right now Rapture was safety tucked away, and in the process of setting the transition into place. It must be tough. I made a mental note to profile her business in San Francisco. My cell phone buzzed breaking my concentration.

"Fargo here."

"Fargo, it's Sheri. I'm in my car. I got some information I want you to see. Where can we meet?"

"I just left Morton's office and was going to swing by the Trop to see Abby. She should be there working out. If I don't catch her now, I won't be able to talk to her until after the second set."

"Good. Perfect. She needs to see this too."

"What are you talking about?" I asked.

"Nothing we can't handle."

"Okay. I'll be there in about thirty minutes."

"I'll be waiting."

Now that was interesting. What information could Sheri have that would have anything to do with Abby?

I dialed up Abby as I headed toward my car, and she answered a little out of breath. Always exercising and dancing.

"What's up Fargo? Are you going to catch me in the late show tonight?"

As a line dancer at the Tropicana, Abby knew that I hated that she went topless in the Adults Only show. The "show of shows" is how I referred to the late night review. The girls really didn't like it either, but it went with the territory. Las Vegas was moving away from a family playground back to what the columnist called, "sin city."

"No, but I was thinking of picking up a beautiful Tropicana dancer for my own late night show and tell."

"Oh, you're so romantic."

"Hey, I'll be pulling into the lot in about thirty minutes. Can I use the dancer's entrance?"

"Sure honey. I'll be waiting."

"Right. Look for Sheri. She should be showing up about the same time."

"Okay."

Eventually I turned off of Tropicana Boulevard and wound my way to the back of the hotel where the stage entrance was located. I spotted Sheri just as she was getting out of her Lexus.

About two months ago Sheri and I bought a basic '96 Dodge conversion van to use for stakeouts. I used to have an old black '91 Cadillac Deville for surveillance but sold it to Uncle Leo right after I bought my 635 SCI BMW. I also had a '96 Jeep Grand Cherokee that I used when I went into the desert. The van was in the shop being refitted for surveillance work, and it would be done shortly. We would keep it out of sight at Uncle Leo's place. Sheri and I had a lot of meetings to work out the details of what we wanted in the van. On the outside it was as plain-Jane looking van with dark windows all the way around. We'd use one of our many magnetic company signs, such as Desert Lawn Care, that fit on the van's front door panel so that we could blend into a neighborhood.

Inside the van was everybody's dream of dreams for stakeouts. We had two comfortable chairs in the back that swiveled, so that long stakeouts would be much easier. It also had a bench that could serve as a bed and had professionally installed drapes separating the front from the back. The front and the back also had completely separate electrical systems with separate batteries. With four DC outlets, we could have a computer running as well as radios for communication if our batteries failed. We had racks for equipment for both still photos and video.

There was also a full alarm system that looked like it was on even if we were in the van. No one expects someone inside if they see an alarm system engaged. We also had a manual telescope so we could check 360 degrees around us. No blind-sides for us. Extra heavy-duty shocks were put in so that moving around in the van would not attract attention. A special cooling system was installed that used dry ice so that we could sit for hours and not have to run the engine to cool the interior. A refrigerator filled with basics was always ready to go.

Sheri clutched a notebook and I knew this was what she had called about. She flashed a smile and greeted me as we entered through the dancer's entrance. I was a lucky guy.

Abby was waiting dressed in leotards, knee high warm up socks and a St. Thomas sweatshirt. She gave me a kiss, and Sheri a peck on the cheek with a big hug. They were the best of friends. Abby ran her fingers through Sheri's thick red hair with a sense of admiration.

"Are you sure you don't want to try out for the line? I keep telling you, with hair like that, you would be a knockout."

"Thanks, but I can't dance, and Fargo tells me they wouldn't be looking at my hair."

I grimaced, and had the urge to check out a plane flying overhead.

Abby shot me a look as she spoke to Sheri. "We can teach you to dance. What we can't teach are manners."

"Nah…people been trying to teach me to dance for years," Sheri said.

"I'll come to all the late shows," I commented.

"Yeah, I bet you would," Abby said.

"Just being supportive."

"Well, you would be sensational," Abby said, tousling Sheri's hair.

Curiosity got the best of me. "So, what's going on?"

Sheri, her usual bundle of energy, answered in quick penetrating flashes of information. "Something going on, that's for sure. Take a look at this." She handed me a letter from Las Vegas Metro along with the envelope. "It came Saturday afternoon."

"What's up?" asked Abby. She did a deep knee bend. Probably still cooling down from morning stretching exercises. She was in such great shape that Sheri and I hated her equally for it.

"I don't know yet," I responded as I read in disbelief. The message was quite clear. It was from Las Vegas Metro, and it stated that Sheri was to contact the department for questioning regarding her entrance into Treasure Island the night before. The questioning was connected to the death of one of Treasure Island's guests. She had 48 hours to contact the department and come in voluntarily, or there would be a warrant put out for her arrest. It was signed by Morton.

"Abby, did you get a letter that looked like this," I said holding up the envelope.

"Yep, but I didn't read it. You know I rarely open junk mail."

"If only we could all live like that, the world would be a better place. But in this case, it would have been a free ride to Las Vegas Metro."

"So, what do you think?" Sheri asked.

"Well, it looks like Metro thinks there is a connection between our entrance at Treasure Island, and the murder of one of the hotel guests. I just left Morton's office and we discussed our arrival. Why didn't he say something? I can straighten this out." I pulled out my cell phone and dialed Morton's direct number.

"Morton," was his quick one word greeting.

"It's Fargo. I've got a question for you. What's this about Sheri and Abby being pulled in for questioning?"

"Routine. We want to know more about their entrance last night."

"I thought we discussed that."

"Like I said, routine. Did you check your morning mail?"

"Office yes, home no."

"Well, you got the same letter, but we've already talked. If we need any more info we'll give you a call."

"So, why the girls," I insisted.

"We've got to cover all of the basics. There is no suspicion that you or your girlfriends are in any way connected with this…."

"They're not my girlfriends," I said, overriding him. I caught Abby's stern look. "Well, one of them is." I turned and looked at Abby. "At least most of the time anyway. But why the official notice?"

"Procedure."

"Why not ask me?"

"I already did. And when I have more to ask, I'll call you."

"Okay, here's what I would like to do. I'll arrange for Abby and Sheri to come down together and meet with you. But I would like to be present."

"No."

"What do you mean, no," I said. I glanced at both Sheri and Abby and they were watching me intently. Another dancer walked in. All legs, blond and peppy. I checked her out and glanced up to see Sheri and Abby looking at me. Sheri stuck her chest out mocking the dancer. Abby just frowned and looked away, arms crossed, foot tapping. I was busted.

Morton continued. "I mean no. You're not going to dictate

police procedure. We want to talk to them individually. And we don't want you there. Clear?"

"I thought we were working together on this?"

"No, we're sharing information, at least some information. I have my bosses. And again, I repeat, this in no way is an indication that you or your girlfriends are in any way under any investigation. We just want information, and some details. We want to put together a complete picture of what was happening at Treasure Island the night of the murder."

"I would like Uncle Leo to be present."

"That would be fine," Morton said. "They are allowed to have legal representation when being questioned, but I assure you that this is just routine procedure. They are not targets."

"Okay. They will contact you," I said.

"Fine," and the phone went dead.

I closed my cell phone.

"So Fargo, what does this all mean?" Sheri asked.

"It's nothing and it's everything. Old Morton wants to find out the details about our trip, and why we made the entrance that we did."

"So, what's the big deal?" Abby asked.

"It's not really. But it's a big inconvenience for you and Sheri."

"What's this about girlfriends?" Sheri asked.

"Oh, he was just making wisecracks about our vacation. When he gets the details of our little island hopping excursion, he really will give me a hard time."

"So let's run a little interference."

"How?"

"Since old Morton is so interested in our trip. Let me go in with some photos of us out at sea."

"You mean the ones with us in our skimpy suits," Abby said.

"Yeah. The guy will be beside himself. I bet I can get more information out of him than he can get out of me."

"I bet you're right. Would that bother you, Abby?"

"Me? Are you kidding? Buy a ticket for the late show and you can see as much skin as you want."

I ignored Abby's comment.

"So, you think the photos will be enough to distract Morton?"

"It's obvious they would distract you," Sheri said, nodding toward the direction the dancer went.

"Very distracting," I said. "But first we'll talk with Uncle Leo. I'm sure he will have some advice for you. Morton said you could bring him along if you wanted."

"Okay," Abby said. "Just keep me posted. I've got two shows today, everyday."

"I have a feeling you two are going to be the new pin-up queens of Las Vegas Metro," I said. I kept remembering what Rapture had said...two ladies and you on a yacht?

Boy, was Metro in for a surprise.

Chapter Fifteen

I WAS SITTING IN THE SPORTS BAR at Treasure Island. It was Monday evening and I had received a call from Rapture earlier that she had made contact with Coyote. They scheduled to meet here, and Rapture asked me if I would attend. It would be the first time that Rapture would be in Treasure Island since I had hustled her out of here. I also wanted to keep track of Barnes, and I dialed him up. He answered on the first ring as if he had been waiting for the call.

"Barnes."

"Fargo here."

"What's up?"

"Just checking in with you. Anything happening?"

"No. How about you? What's happening at Treasure Island?"

"Not a lot. I'm going to take care of a few details regarding last night, and see what I can find out," I said evasively. I really didn't want him to know that I was meeting my client and I was at Treasure Island right now. It wasn't his business to know, and I needed to keep as many options open as possible. I kept thinking I had three unrelated events: Rapture hiring me, the killing of J.T. and then Barnes showing up. I'm a detective that looks at seemingly unrelated events and asks the question: Are they related?

"You're kidding. Nothing new? I thought you were with the 'A' Team?" Barnes leaned back in his chair.

"I am the 'A' Team. What's up with you?"

"Just following the thread. Details. Anything else I should know about?"

A loaded question I couldn't answer. "Brief it for me one more time. What is it that I should be looking for down here?" I asked. "Explain it to me again." Sometimes the more you get someone to talk the more inconsistencies you find. Once a cop, always a cop.

"One more time for the record. We're after unpaid taxes. That's what we're all about. We have reason to believe that there are people gambling there that forget about us from time to time. That's it. Just look for something unusual."

"And you say it's a lady that I should be watching out for?"

"You'd watch her even if you didn't have to watch her, if you get my drift?"

"Right. A knockout. Okay, we'll talk tomorrow."

"Okay. When can we get together again to review the case?"

"How about tomorrow sometime. I'll give you a call when I know my schedule."

"Sounds good."

"Will you be bringing your sidekick along?"

"Nope."

"What happened to him?"

"Agency demoted him. He's up for reassignment, and he is on his way back to D.C."

"That fast?"

"Yeah...got to get going...see you tomorrow." Barnes hung up with a click.

I closed my cell phone and then flipped it back open to give Sheri a call.

"Sheri, where are you?"

"Driving in circles. Right now on Eastern."

"Any luck on Barnes?"

"Not a shot in the world. There is no way he is going to lead us to where he lives. He's pulled every trick in the book to lose any tails."

"Yeah, I suspected he was well trained."

"At least today he's good. Tomorrow is another day."

"Good girl," I said.

"I'm not that good."

Our little jabs added a sense of humor to the day. "Listen, I want you to stay right on top of him. I'm meeting Rapture here at Treasure Island, and I wouldn't want Barnes to show up. I want to know if he's in the area."

"Okay Boss, I'm on it."

"Keep in touch. It's important."

"You got it."

"And one more thing. I want you to follow-up on Barnes' partner."

"The one that was keeping an eye on you when you met Barnes?"

"That's the one. According to Barnes he was demoted. Let's see if we can get the Agency to loosen up a bit, give us a name, and let's run a background check. Cover our bases."

"Okay, Boss."

"I'll get back to you." I begin to think back over the conversation and wondered if I had any conflict of interest. So far, no crossover, but still...I was suspicious. Well, a conflict occurs depending upon where you draw the line. Rapture and Barnes don't know each other, and I'm in the middle. The hotel is paying me to keep an eye open regarding the murder in their hotel, as was Rapture. All I could think of right now was how glad I am that I share an office with Uncle Leo. Maybe it's the potential conflict of interest that is going to break this case wide open. Some defense. But if they are connected, how are they connected?

I spotted Rapture as she approached the Sports Bar area. She was strikingly beautiful.

"Mr. Blue, how are you?" asked Rapture, as she arrived, hand out, charming. She gave me a kiss on the cheek.

"Please, call me Fargo," I said, as I pulled out a chair for her to sit on. I took the chair opposite Rapture. "You would be easy to pick out of a crowd today," I said smiling. "All business today?"

"Today and everyday. She waved her hand to indicate the people around us just as a couple of gamblers in jogging suits ambled by. "More people should pay attention to their wardrobe in these places."

I nodded in agreement. They probably had a blood pressure monitor in their hotel room along with a cholesterol-testing machine. We both followed their march through the casino.

"Probably never exercised a day in their lives," I commented creating laughter between us. "How are you doing?"

"I've been very busy dealing with the details of the last several days."

The announcer started the call on the current race coming out of Belmont. "Playing the ponies?"

"Not really, just a nice place to relax. How about you?"

"I'm here to play roulette."

"To practice."

"Yes, I love the game."

"I bet you won a lot of money a long time ago playing roulette?"

"Yes, how did you know?"

"Just the power of Las Vegas. Most people play games they have won at before, and are trying to win again. Just a guess on my part."

Rapture laughed, a deep throaty kind of laugh that answered my question. Her awesome beauty hid the real Rapture. I was guessing she was a warm loving creature. Warm and loving creatures were always a weakness.

"So, how was your meeting with Morton this morning?"

"Uneventful. Told him the story and answered his questions."

"Did he read you your rights?"

"No. He said I wasn't a suspect."

Just then there was a scream from the crowd as a slot machine lit up. Someone had hit it big and went into the slot dance, jumping up and down. A crowd formed as security and the slot manager moved in to congratulate.

"Another instantly wealthy person. If they ever understood the odds, they wouldn't be there," Rapture said.

"Why do you really gamble?"

Rapture brought her gaze back to me. "I like the action."

"And what about Coyote? Is she a part of the action?"

"Yes, without a doubt."

"She called?"

"About three hours ago. Said she wanted to have a terms-of-agreement meeting."

"Where?"

"Right here."

"Convenient," I said, looking around at the Sports Bar. One general entrance on each side of the lounge area with the giant screens and tote boards on the opposite end. It was the end of the race day with only a few night tracks open in California, which made for an ideal location for negotiations.

"Are you friends with Coyote?"

"No."

"Have you had other meetings with her?"

"No. J.T. had. His only comment was that she was all business."

"He said that, did he," a voice with a slight southern drawl spoke.

I turned around to my left and there stood Coyote, I presumed. Smiling with sparkling eyes, she was dressed in a white suit that somehow exuded wealth and taste. The Southern accent confused me for a second as she looked like she was raised on the beach in Malibu. Tan, with a rosy complexion, she was a vision of youth and beauty. Everything about Coyote was a contrast of expectations.

"Hi, my name is Coyote. I do believe your name is Fargo Blue." Her hand was outstretched, offering and promising.

"Yes," I said, knowing I was meeting a truly unusual woman. I stood to greet her, "My, you are well informed, aren't you."

"One has to be in my line of work," she said, in an alluring, sexual kind of way.

Rapture stood up and there was an awkward sort of polite hug with lips brushing cheeks. I offered Coyote a chair and she sat down, or rather nestled herself into place.

147

Coyote addressed Rapture directly. "I am so sorry for your terrible loss."

"Thank you. I appreciate your kindness," Rapture replied.

There was a brief, solemn moment of silence. "Drink?" I asked. Rapture declined. I was taken back with how young she was, maybe in her late twenties, but with the poise and confidence of a woman far beyond her years.

Rapture glanced at me, and then back to Coyote. "You have something I want, Ms. Coyote. What do I need to do to obtain the map?"

"Just call me Coyote. It's easier. Friendlier."

"Fine. And the map?"

"Three million dollars paid in cash at the roulette table of your choice."

"Why the roulette table?" I asked.

"Public and private."

"Sounds like she knows what she wants," I said to Rapture.

"Listen," said Rapture, ignoring my comment. "This treasure is worth millions. Want us to sign you in for a percentage of the deal? We could."

"I am so sorry. All I want is the three million dollars in cash. Nothing else. If I do say so, my demands for the map are very small compared to the overall profit you'll enjoy for many years. Now, if I may be so bold to ask, in a polite Southern kind of way, you are interested in the map, aren't you?"

"Yes, we are," Rapture said, "But..."

My cell phone vibrated and I sort of waved a pause in the

conversation and pulled an earpiece from my pocket and placed it in my ear. I knew it was Sheri. "Go," I said.

"Fargo, Barnes left his hotel and is headed down the Strip in your direction. Oh, oh, he just turned into Treasure Island."

"Okay, I got it. Thanks." This was going to be a close one.

"Good," Coyote said. "I expect you will have a table especially reserved for the occasion."

"You take care of the details." Coyote stood up quickly. "If payment is not made in full, then I will have to find a new buyer for my half of the map. And I want cash, not chips."

"The map is no good unless they have my half."

"That's the buyers problem. Not mine."

"But I..."

"Fargo, how nice to have met you," Coyote said, extending her hand.

"Just one question, Coyote, if you please?" I asked.

"Yes," said Coyote, as she dropped my hand, but kept her eyes focused on me.

"How did you come about owning half of the map?"

"Poker, Mr. Blue. Just a simple good ol' game of poker," she said in her Southern drawl. "Cards can be so much fun, don't you think?" Coyote turned and disappeared.

"Well, I never," Rapture said.

"Interesting. Very Interesting."

"We need to know more about her," Rapture said. "She's holding all the cards. Ours are all face up and hers are all face down."

I nodded and left the table leaving the Sport's Lounge to enjoy

Rapture. I was concerned that Barnes would spot me with Rapture. I scanned the area and glimpsed Coyote as she threaded her way through the crowd. She was there, then gone, then there. Tricky to follow.

"Sheri," I said into the microphone phone attached to the earpiece.

"Boss?"

"What's your location?"

"I'm doubled park and just entered the lobby. Barnes is ahead of me."

"Keep on it, I'm headed in your direction. If you see me, don't acknowledge. We don't know who knows who and we don't know who's watching."

"Right, Boss."

I would love to have Sheri working a front tail with two-way communications, along with security, and the eye in the sky tracking us and giving us directions. Not to be, and made a mental note to work these kind of meetings with backup.

I did not know what I was going to do, or what exactly I was looking for, but when my client has three million on the line, I need to know more about the opposition. I first made a pass around the casino while working my way toward the front lobby. There was something that was true and to the point about Coyote's presentation of her offer. Rather then making an exchange at a bank in a nice, neat conference room, Coyote wanted the exchange to take place at the roulette table. Coyote already said she wanted cash. The casino would follow through with the normal paperwork for taxes since Rapture was cashing out a large sum of money.

Rapture would pass over what was left, around three million to Coyote, who could put it in some kind of bag and exit the casino. Clever, and crafty, I thought to myself. Could this be what Barnes is talking about? Money as a gift is still taxable. Coyote had figured out a way to put cash in her hands, with no record in the casino with her name on it. It was up to her to report the money on her taxes, but then again, there was no record. Sort of like waitresses and tips. Only a portion is ever reported. It was pure and simple. If Abby and I were walking in the Fashion Show Mall, and she needed a hundred dollars, and I gave her a hundred dollar bill, there would be no record of this being reported to the IRS. It was ingenious. Only this was being accomplished with three million dollars. Money laundering in a casino. This could be it. Barnes is interested in Coyote. Barnes is a smart guy to be on top of this one. If my suspicions were right, I'd have to hand it to him.

As I approached the lobby, Sheri and I walked right past each other brushing shoulders never giving away we knew each other. She was a real pro. Barnes must have missed me. I stepped out the revolving doors to the entranceway and scanned the parked limousines.

"Looking for me."

I turned at once, recognizing the southern voice. "Actually, I was."

"I expected as much," Coyote said. "I figured it would be better to talk, than you following me around Las Vegas."

"Maybe I wouldn't mind."

"Maybe."

"So tell me, do Coyotes run wild?" I said, smiling at her.

She smiled back. "That, Mr. Blue, I am not able to answer."

We studied each other. Her eyes told me that life was an adventure, and that she played the game out of love for adventure. "Do you really have the map?" I asked, studying the casual way should stood, the way she moved her head just a little bit to the side when answering a question.

"Of course I do. If I have learned one thing in life, that is to be honest and always follow through with my end of the deal."

"Not a bad philosophy in this town."

"Thank you," Coyote said.

"How do we know your map is real?"

Coyote laughed. "I do declare, Mr. Blue...."

"Call me, Fargo...."

"Fargo...you are a gentleman, but not a scholar of deals. In a deal like this, the map has to be real. If it wasn't...that would be like...cheating...and we girls of the South never cheat. Do you cheat, Fargo?"

I smiled. "Of course."

"Then I approve. An honest man is hard to find. But just so you won't be disappointed, I have something for you." Coyote reached into her small handbag and pulled out a transparent envelope with a slim piece of paper on the inside. I could see that it had the imprint of jagged edges on one-side. "I did anticipate your request and made a copy of the edge of the map. You will be able to take this and match the torn edge of your map with the outline on this copy."

"I'm impressed."

"My, you have not had a lot of experience with the South, Fargo. We're always prepared. Always."

"I'll remember that."

"You will never forget, I promise," said Coyote.

I studied Coyote. "I'll have Rapture check this copy against her map, and we'll see what she says."

"Such a nice young lady," smiled Coyote. "I know it will be a perfect match. I expect we'll be in touch before the game. I do love a good game of roulette, don't you?"

"Actually, roulette is not my game."

"How unfortunate."

"Since you'll be playing roulette, when do you want Rapture to pass the money to you?"

"Anytime during the game, or when the game breaks."

"Do you want to take possession in cash or chips?" I knew the answer to this but I wanted to hear it again. Was she the one that Barnes is after?

"Cash, of course."

"Very clever."

Coyote smiled. It was a warm smile that I would always remember.

"And the map?" I said bravely.

"You will get the map when I have possession of the cash."

"Then what...?"

"The road goes in two directions, Fargo. I'll take the one less traveled, and you'll take another."

"Poetry in motion?"

Coyote smiled.

"And that is the end of it?" I asked.

Coyote's eyes never wavered. "This is business. It's a way to make a living. This is not about ruthless deals that follow you into the night." A white limousine pulled to a stop behind Coyote. The driver got out and moved around and opened the door for her.

Coyote looked at me, and then nodded with an ever so slight smile. She turned and floated into the limousine.

Chapter Sixteen

I FOLLOWED THE WHITE LIMOUSINE with my eyes, and caught a rather haunting look; a stare that drilled right through me. At the last second, she turned and looked straight ahead as the window slid closed. I felt as if I was not even there. Expendable.

I thought about this as I made my way back through the casino and found Rapture at the high stakes roulette game. She had the prime seat with an easy reach to all the numbers. The casinos enjoyed the action on Monday nights when it was relatively quiet after a busy weekend. I moved up next to her and brought the piece of the map into view. Rapture's eyes lit up when she saw the torn edge clearly visible.

"It's the right size," Rapture said, excited. "I think it will fit perfectly."

"We have to make a huge decision," I said, sitting down next to Rapture in the one unoccupied chair at the table.

"And what is that?"

"Is the treasure really worth more than three million dollars?"

"Absolutely."

"How do you know?"

"My father told me it was going to be one of the richest treasures ever found."

"Going to be...?"

"Is..."

"How do you know that it is going to be worth over three million? What is buried there that would be worth so much?"

As Rapture laid out her chips, she talked. "In the late 1800s a Spanish Galleon sank. Most of the crew were rescued by a sister ship, but the Galleon went down. It was rediscovered in the mid-1900s, and a considerable amount of bullion and coins were recovered. But a large storm came up quickly and the entire salvage operation was destroyed."

"There must be more records of what has happened over the years," I said, trying to picture this large ship that was so valuable. Rapture watched the white ball fall into a slot on the spinning wheel and checked the chips she had placed on the numbered playing area. After only a few spins I figured that Rapture was playing the same numbers over and over. I did not know if these were "favorite" numbers, or were numbers selected to take advantage of certain runs on the board. I did not see any type of money management system in play as far as a doubling up system ala martingale, or going south after a certain amount of money had been won. But I was impressed with how confident Rapture was in her play, so I was betting that she had a game plan, and would stick to it.

Rapture turned to me. "Yes, we have quite a bit of history on this shipwreck. The map locates the original wreck. We will work from that location. There have been many shipwrecks and many recovery operations over the years. The exact location and notes are critical information."

"What good is a map going to do?"

"The map is the key to finding the treasure. With both pieces of the map, we'll confirm our suspicions on which ship, and also the location of what we're after."

"So what is down there besides some coins that makes this such a valuable effort?"

At seemingly the last minute, Rapture laid out a series of bets in a quick fashion, and a hand waved over the table signaling no more bets. You could hear the ball drop, and all eyes turned to see what magic number would decide the fate of the table. "Thirty-seven," said a voice that had the edge of interest. This was high stakes roulette and the croupier was paid to take an interest.

I glanced across the table and Rapture had seven chips stacked on the number. At 35-to-1 payoff, Rapture had just won a tidy some. This was a five hundred minimum bet game, and I had no idea of her chip buy-in value.

"How did you pick that number?" I said, changing the subject briefly.

Rapture turned to me and gave me a flash of a smile. "Dumb luck, I suppose, or a method I'm not willing to share with everyone." She nodded her head in the direction of the croupier, and I glanced up to see both the croupier and the pit boss with their heads cocked in our direction. They then glanced discreetly away.

I nodded my head in agreement, and watched the payoff. I wanted to know more about the treasure. That's the stake everybody was playing for. "What is it about this wreck that makes it so interesting?"

Rapture leaned over and whispered in my ear. "A cross."

"A cross! It must be some cross." I said a bit too loud.

"Rapture put her finger to her lips indicating silence. She whispered, softly. "It's a solid gold cross four feet high, and about three feet wide. It's inlaid with every jewel you can imagine in a way that can best be described as Byzantine. Private collectors have estimated the worth of this piece well over one-hundred million dollars."

"But what if it was already salvaged years ago?"

"I assure you it has not been discovered or salvaged. If it were, it would have found its way to a museum. This is almost passed museum quality."

"Are you familiar with the art world Rapture?"

"Yes, quite a bit in fact."

"Well, I have a passing interest in the arts, particularly gallery showings. I know of a very private art gallery in Northern California. Couldn't this be in a very private collection? I mean, it makes sense if it is, as you say, beyond museum quality."

"I know it's a possibility, but I also know that if they had brought it up, the world would have known. No question about that. It's there."

"But what if they did bring it up. What if they did? Your three million will be gone."

"I know for a fact it's there. The technology in the mid-1920s, when the last serious attempt was thwarted by the storm, did not have the capability to do deep excavations. Now there is equipment that makes this less difficult. The weight of the cross has caused it to sink deep into the mud. This makes the location and the excavation extremely difficult. It's there, Fargo. It's there."

"Excuse me, sir. You are welcome to sit there, but we have another guest that would like to play. Could I help you with your buy-in, or can we arrange a voucher slip?"

I looked up to find a rather thin man with a beard waiting to take a seat. He was somewhat edgy. I nodded toward him as I began to get up. As I did so I noticed his slightly frayed collar and cuffs. I got out of my seat and offered it to him, and he slid in as he removed his money from his pocket. As he did, several ATM withdrawal tickets fell to the floor. I retrieved them for him, and he accepted them back somewhat embarrassed, but nodding his thanks. Money was slid across the table, and play continued. I stood slightly behind Rapture at her elbow.

"Looks like it's time to play," Rapture said.

"One more question." I leaned over and spoke into Rapture's ear, smelling the whiff of perfume from her hair. "You have so much knowledge of this wreck, but you don't know where it is. Isn't three million dollars a lot of money for a lot of maybes?"

"Let me ask you a question, Fargo. You said you did some treasure hunting. Is that right?"

"Yup, in fact I go every chance I get."

"Where do you go?"

"I've got some spots, some here in Nevada and some in Colorado. I'd been scouting wrecks in St. Thomas when you called."

"Specifically, where are your locations?"

"Well now, I keep those pretty much to myself..." I caught Rapture's eye and realized I had been caught. "I see, treasure hunters don't tell other treasure hunters, and that basically is the key to this mystery. Everyone has kept it a mystery, except for this map."

"Right. This map is the last known positioning of the rig that spent three months over the wreck. And as you know, as time goes by, memories get weaker, and sooner or later, everyone forgets."

"And you don't have the three million to pay off Coyote."

"Yes. We've discussed that."

"And you are going to win the three million by playing roulette?"

Rapture smiled. It was a hopeful smile.

Chapter Seventeen

EARLY TUESDAY MORNING we pulled onto Boulder Highway and worked our way into the flow of traffic. Sheri was at the wheel of my Grand Cherokee and had the police scanner working. We had just left American Shooters Supply, which stocked some of the finest firearms in the West. We were lucky to have it here in Vegas. I had a conversation with Billy Mack about AK's that pointed me in the right direction.

"So Boss, what do you think is going on?"

"I keep telling you I'm not your Boss."

"Whatever you say, Boss."

I ignored her last comment and took it as an endearment. I also remembered the movie "Cool Hand Luke."

"Mornin', Boss," I mumbled to myself trying to imitate Newman's southern drawl.

"What?" Sheri said.

"Oh, nothing. Remind me to bring a movie when we hit the high seas again."

"Right, Boss."

I gave Sheri a hard look.

"So, where are we headed?"

"Well, Billy made a phone call and was able to set us up with an AK shooter who was heading out to the desert to fire off a couple of magazines. So, to make a long story short, we were invited along."

"Cool," Sheri said.

"Did you do a lot of shooting in the Coast Guard?" I asked, as

Sheri threaded the Jeep through traffic.

"I did when I was stationed in Astoria. Matter of fact, I shot as much as I could. The north coast of Oregon is great. Lots of places to go shooting. I even wore a sidearm when I was on deck."

"What kind of sidearm?"

"Standard Coast Guard issue 45."

"Big gun for a small lady like you," I teased.

"You know I can outshoot you any time," Sheri said. "And besides, all of me is not small."

I glanced over at her.

"Caught ya!"

"I was set up."

"Yeah, right," Sheri said, smiling.

"What kind of action?" I said, trying to change the subject.

"Drugs mainly. Or sea rescues. Always something going on. The Columbia River has a lot of large ships using the channel to move upstream to Portland. That means anyone can use it to enter the States or to bring in contraband. Or spies."

"Yeah, or terrorists."

"That too," said Sheri, reflecting on the tragic incidents of 911 and how America had changed.

"Must keep the Coast Guard busy," I said.

"Well, what really keeps the Guard busy is the weekend boaters who have a couple of drinks, and then try to cross the bar on the Columbia River.

"The bar?"

"It's where the outgoing river meets the incoming waves. It

creates a rough sea that has been sinking ships since Captain Gray found an entrance with his ship the Columbia in 1792."

"Remind me never to try."

Sheri was gifted. With her Navy experience, her work as a P.I., and her obvious good looks, she was always ready and could roll with the punches with the best of them.

"Did you ever go out with your attorney friend?" I asked. Sheri had met a young Las Vegas attorney by the name of David Alexander Albright, who was also a Professor of Law at the University of Nevada. His specialty was Criminal Law.

"Yeah, we've been out a couple of times. He's a nice guy and he loves my work. I want to introduce him to Uncle Leo. They'll have a lot in common."

"Good idea," I said. "He would make a perfect D.A. someday."

"How's that?"

"If he abbreviated his name it would be D.A. Albright."

"Cute," Sheri smirked.

"Are you good friends?"

"Yeah, maybe he's the right one."

"Really?"

"Maybe. Just maybe. Unless of course you want to date me," she said in a teasing way.

"Abby would kill me."

Sheri laughed. "...and then come hunting for me!"

Sheri continued to work her way through traffic while we listened to a popular Las Vegas oldies station, intermingled with police calls. It was a mild day with the temperature hitting the low 80s, a perfect day for a drive. It was strange to be going out to the desert to shoot an AK, trying to get a lead on the hotel murder. An AK was an awesome weapon. I remember when I was first handed one.

It was a horrible night in Hong Kong. The Vietnam War was over, but violence continued in many countries. I had a friend who was taken captive by pirates right off the dock near the Star Ferry. I was young, fired up, and ready to go. I boarded a Chinese speedboat with seven other kids who had background from gambler to drug runner, I later found out. We had all been sitting at the bar when a young lady came in and told us the story. Said there was a boat willing to give chase, but needed some bodies to throw at the Chinese Junk. In the rowdy way men can be, we all said sure, and ran down to the dock.

We were going after the Chinese Junk that was just out of the harbor. I was handed an AK-47 and a sling, which I threw over my shoulder. I counted the clips. I carried seven in all. On our way out of the harbor a sea-worthy smuggler gave us all quick lessons on magazine changes, and we all caught on fast.

It was quite easy, really. We swung wide and approached the Junk from the bow, and when the Junk made its move we swept along side with AK's firing. We had been instructed to take out the sails, but when the Pirates saw seven guys spitting bullets, they quickly threw our man overboard, and we recovered him. One Pirate tried to fire a handgun, but a blaze of fire from our boat ended the attempt, and a little bit more.

"Memories?" asked Sheri.

"Yeah." Little did she know. We were on an old desert road and could hear the sputtering sound of an AK somewhere up ahead. The road was rough but the Jeep was at home here. I opened the glove compartment and pulled out two Glocks. I handed one to Sheri. She chambered a round without asking, and made the Glock available to her by sliding it down next to the seat. She also carried a handgun in her purse. I did the same with the other Glock, but stuck it in the door side compartment. I was wearing an ankle holster, but I wanted the Glock for quick access if I were near the vehicle. We drove into a small clearing and noted a Humvee, which was desert ready. Cans of drinking water and extra gasoline were tied to the outside of the vehicle. There was a tall whip antenna on the back flying a small confederate flag at the top.

"Can I help you?" said a soft-spoken man who wore a faded blue denim shirt with red suspenders, and a straggly beard. "Derk is the name."

"Hi, my name is Fargo, and this here is Sheri." I shot out my hand and was met by a firm grip. "Thanks for meeting with us."

Sheri followed suit.

"Nice looking Humvee there. Don't see many of those."

"Yeah, thanks. Not many people recognize the difference."

"What's the difference, Fargo?" Sheri asked, as she compared her Jeep to the real deal.

"Hummer refers to the civilian models and Humvee refers to the military ones. Humvee comes from HMMWV, a military term for "High Mobility Multipurpose Wheeled Vehicle."

"Where did you get a military version?"

"They're around. Just need to ask the right question to the right people," Derk said

"What's with the confederate flag?"

"Doesn't mean what it used to. It's a symbol of independence for a lot of us."

"Maybe we can take a spin sometime," Sheri asked hopefully.

"No prob. Say, Billy Mack said you wanted to shoot the AK. Always glad to demonstrate how the AK's work. You on the force?"

"No. Used to be. Long time ago."

"Like to know who I'm talking to...know what I mean?"

"Understood," I said. "Anyway, Sheri and I wanted to find out the local gossip on AK's in and around Vegas."

"Plenty around, not enough for everybody, but enough."

"Easy to get?" I asked.

"Just takes money," Derk answered.

"What if you don't go through Fed checks the gun stores run on you?"

"Takes mo' money."

"How'd you get interested in AK's?" Sheri asked.

"Fell in love with them when I was in Nam. I picked one up on an LRRP mission, and used it whenever I had the opportunity. At times our whole team carried them. They were more dependable than the standard M-15 issue, and we could supply ourselves with unlimited ammo in the field."

"How?"

"Dead bodies, miss."

"Oh, Sheri" replied, somewhat embarrassed at the obvious.

"You were with the Rangers, I take it?" I asked.

"Yup. Get in. Get out. Two-to-five day patrols. No talking. Silent stalkers."

"Did you pick up the one with the collapsible stock over there?"

asked Sheri.

"Nah... got that right here in Vegas."

"And there is no trouble getting them?" Sheri asked again.

"How many you want?"

"So they're a real common item at the gun shows?" Sheri asked.

"Used to be that you could pick up these babes for eight-nine bucks a piece. Now we're talking some serious money. Might set you back a half a thou, but it's a hell of a weapon, fun to shoot, and does the job."

"I'd like to give it a try. Been a few years," I said.

"No prob," said Derk. He removed a mag from the AK and handed the AK over to me.

"You got eye and ear protection?"

"In the car," I said.

"I'll get it, Boss," said Sheri.

"I'll walk you through the weapon while she gets the gear," Derk said. We ran through the AK in a couple of minutes and it was almost like being at a gun show where dealers are only too proud to show off their latest find with a short history of the weapon, then go through the mechanics of how the weapon works.

After Sheri retrieved a gun bag from the car with ear and eye protection, I stepped forward and set up to shoot. Derk handed me the mag and I slammed it home. It had been a long time since I shot one.

"You of course have heard the rumors," asked Derk.

"What would that be?" I asked casually, as I tucked the AK under my arm and got used to weight. "This sure brings back some memories."

"AK's all have memories," Derk said. "This is a serious weapon and when you're trading bullets with the enemy, you're trading life long memories, no matter how short your life is going to be."

"What about the rumors?" Sheri questioned.

"Heard it was used in a hotel on the Strip. Took one guy down, and made a mess of the place."

"Yup, you're right about that," I said.

"The question is, how do you know...?" Derk asked, looking up at me.

I perched the AK onto my hip, and then pulled out my I.D. and flashed my badge. "We're both P.I.'s and we're working the case."

"Un huh." Derk gave Sheri a glance, stroked his beard and arched his eyebrows with new respect for Sheri.

Derk turned back to me. "I need to tell you something. We think the weapon was dumped in the desert. It's got the AK'ers upset. A good AK shouldn't be dumped."

"I agree." I said.

I pulled on my ear protection and turned toward the range checking left and then right. "I'm hot" I said to know one in particular as I threw the safety and racked the first round in. I raised the AK to my shoulder and shot off a short burst of three each. I then lowered the weapon to my waist, and fired off more short bursts until it was empty. The AK was solid and the acid smell of gunpowder hit the air.

I lowered the weapon, hit the safety, pulled out the magazine and checked to make sure there was no round chambered before I handed the AK to Derk.

"Nice. Real nice," I said. We all pulled off our ear protection, and I pulled off my yellow shooting glasses.

"This is a great AK, and I really like the folding stock."

"Top notch," said Derk, as he started to set up Sheri to shoot.

"Just one question, Derk. Can you put the word out that you want to buy the AK? If this is a local deal, then someone will know someone who knows where this AK is. If we can get a lead, we might get the guy, and you might have a chance to get the AK out of the wrong hands and into the right hands. A beauty like this one should find a good home."

"You betcha...not a prob. Glad to help. I'll spread the word. And I'll be careful about it. Looks like we got ourselves a bad apple out there. I kid you not."

Derk looked at Sheri who now was getting ready to shoot. She was wearing short white shorts and a bright yellow blouse that made the sun look like a shadow. With ear protection, glasses and a determined look, she gave us a nod, turned toward the line, and racked in a round. "I'm hot," she said. Both Derk and I faintly heard her laugh to herself. We glanced at each other and Derk raised his eyebrows again, just before the sound of the AK hit the blue sky.

Sheri pulled the trigger and let loose a blast that was awesome. She fired the entire clip in short bursts holding it at waist level. When the clip ended, she cleared the weapon and clicked on the safety like a pro. She held the weapon high with the butt balanced carefully on her hip. She was quite a sight.

"Miss, you can come out here and shoot any time. You make the desert look a whole lot better."

Sheri flashed her smile, and the world was a little bit safer.

Chapter Eighteen

SHERI ARRIVED EARLY TUESDAY AFTERNOON for the meeting with Morton at Las Vegas Metro. She was asked to sit in the small entrance lobby, which was also used as part of the inner office circulation. Consequently, police officers and detectives moved through the sitting area. Their holsters slapped against their thighs as they moved creating an image of authority and control. Each carried a file or a piece of paper, and looked like they were on an urgent mission. "Hello, Hi," and "Excuse me, Ma'am," filled the air as the desperate parade moved along.

Actually, they were checking Sheri out. She was dressed in a provocative manner: a tight fitting white low cut blouse, a white matching sweater and white matching short skirt. The whiteness of her outfit contrasted with the deep tan she picked up in the islands. Rumors persisted through the office that she was a P.I. and worked with Fargo. Those who did not know her wanted a first glimpse, and those who knew her wanted to see her again.

A leggy overweight blond walked up. "This way, Miss," she said, with attitude.

Sheri got up, feeling like she was a little school kid following the mean teacher to the principal's office.

"Greetings," said Morton, meeting her halfway. "Listen, they're moving a new filing cabinet into my office my so I thought we could just talk out here in the squad room...if that's okay?" He motioned to a chair in the center of the "Pit" as it was commonly referred to. He picked up a stack of files from Sheri's chair and placed them on an already over-stacked desk. He eyed them for a second to make sure they were not going to tumble, then pulled up another chair and smiled at Sheri.

"It's nice to see you again," Sheri said, as she took her seat. Her skirt slid up a bit revealing her tanned legs. She caught Morton catching a look, and then glancing innocently away. That innocent, guilty look. The hairs went up on the back of her neck, and she sensed that someone had moved in behind her. Double-teamed, she thought.

Sheri stood up, turned around and shot her hand out startling the detective that was number two to Morton. He was so surprised he actually jumped, spilling his coffee. She then noted that there were around eight detectives moving in slowly around her.

"I'm Sheri."

"Joe, Joe's the name." He offered his hand and they shook hands. Sheri never took her eyes off of him.

"So, Morton, is Joe joining us in this meeting?"

"Standard procedure."

"Standard procedure for what?"

"Standard interview procedure, Ma'am."

"Call me Sheri," she said as she sat back down.

"Okay, Sheri it is. Now, we just want to ask you some questions about your entrance into Treasure Island. Where were you coming from?"

Sheri scanned the room and there were detectives all around her, then she brought her gaze back to Morton. "I think Fargo told you we were coming from the islands. St. Thomas specifically. We were on vacation. Did you forget that?"

Morton avoided a question being thrown back to him. "Who is

the we?"

"Fargo, Abby and myself. We rented a thirty-eight foot cruising yacht that we sailed around the island."

"Two women and Fargo?" Morton said, as murmuring came from the team of detectives who had gathered in the background.

"It's not what it seems," Sheri said.

"It is what it is."

"What does that mean?"

"Well, in my years of law enforcement, the facts all generally point to a direction, and most often it is what it is. In this case, it appears that Fargo was having a great time."

Sheri ignored the obvious implications.

"Since when does Fargo know how to sail? He's more of a desert rat, isn't he?" asked Morton, as small laughter and chuckles emerged in the background.

"He knows his way around the dock. But I'm the one who was Captain of the ship."

"You?" Morton looked around the room and received support in terms of laughter. Sheri crossed her legs in a move that invoked pure confidence, creating a moment of silence.

"Yes. Me. U.S. Coast Guard, ten plus years."

"Oh."

"You should do better background checks. I hope this isn't a reflection of this department's ability in a case like this. Is Fargo an integral part of your investigation?"

"No." Morton shifted his weight, somewhat agitated.

"You're just interested in our vacation? I can get you some travel brochures if you can wait a few days." Muffled laughter rippled through the chorus of detectives.

Frustrated, Morton snapped back, "No, we're interested in your entrance into Treasure Island."

"Why did you ask where we were coming from then?" Sheri asked. She was playing with him, enjoying the encounter.

"Again, we're interested in your entrance."

"How does that tie into the murder at Treasure Island?"

"We don't know. That's why you're here."

Sheri hadn't moved during the entire exchange. "Well, if it is what it is, then look at these pictures." Sheri bent down to pick up her small hang bag, and Morton's eyes followed her chest, as did the eyes of the whole detective division.

"Listen guys," said Morton, just take it easy here...I know you got work to do." More murmuring came from the detectives. None of them moved, knowing just how far they could stretch Morton's patience.

Joe in the back looked on enviously. Sheri pulled out several photos of her and Abby onboard Noble One. They both appeared in the briefest of bikinis. Abby was quite light skinned, and not tanned, compared to Sheri who was deeply tanned. Both were obviously voluptuous.

Joe came around next to Morton, breaking the procedure.

"Do you have any suspects in this killing?" Sheri asked.

"We don't have a thing," said Joe, as he gawked at the photos.

Morton shot him a look, and Joe backed up realizing his mistake, drawing more rumbling from the gathering of detectives.

"Does Fargo have another client besides Rapture?" Morton questioned, as he tried to gain the advantage.

Sheri put her legs up on an opened desk drawer blocking Joe's retreat toward her back. Morton had to look around Joe to talk to Sheri. Meanwhile the detectives were all moving in and pilfering through the photographs.

"Fargo has lots of clients. Obviously I know who the clients are, but they're not my clients. You'll have to ask Fargo that question."

"Why are you hiding that?"

"I'm not hiding anything. I told you I know who they are. Why would that interest you?"

"Fargo's room was next to the murder. He made a loud and provocative entrance into the casino. We want to know if it's connected in any way to his current clients, other then Rapture of course."

"So, Fargo is a suspect?"

"In this situation, everyone who had opportunity is a suspect."

"You told Fargo he wasn't a suspect. Did you lie to Fargo?"

Silence. Morton and Joe looked at each other. More murmuring.

"Who was in the room on the other side?" Sheri asked.

"Listen," said Morton. "Fargo is not a suspect in the usual sense of the word. He just happened to be at the scene of the crime, and we have to check it out."

Joe was standing there thumbing through the photos of Sheri and Abby. There were two other detectives hanging over his shoulder, and several more wanting to take a peek.

"What about Fargo?" asked Joe.

"Fargo," said Sheri, "was not wearing a swimming suit." Sheri dives into her bag. "Hey, I think I have some photos if you're interested."

Joe dropped the photos of Sheri and Abby like hot potatoes. "No,

173

that won't be necessary," said Joe.

Sheri continued to dig through her purse. "Really, I think I have some in here." Sheri looked up. "You want to see everything, don't you?"

"No, Ma'am, no I do not."

Sheri looked at Detective Morton. "What about you? Do you want to see...?"

"Good God, no," Morton blurted out.

Sheri went back in her purse digging around. "WOW, here's one!" She whipped out a photograph and held it up in front of the detectives. They reacted like vampires to a cross, turning away, hands in front of their eyes. Sheri swung the photograph around the room and all eight detectives turned away and hid their eyes. Sheri looked at it, and then dropped it back into her purse. "Well, all you have to do is ask. Now, where were we?"

"I have no idea," Morton said, turning around. "Please, don't do that again."

Sheri glanced at Joe, who was once again thumbing through the photos. She turned and looked at Morton. "Are you checking Fargo out, or are you checking out Abby and me?" She nodded her head in Joe's direction.

Morton grabbed the photos from Joe throwing them on the table. "All right you guys, get out of here." The detectives all moved away from the desk.

"You know, if you want to see more of Abby, all you have to do is to check out the late show at the Trop. If you ask nice, I'll help you get front row tickets. As for Fargo, you're on your own there."

Both Morton and Joe looked awkward.

"As for me, you're also out of luck," Sheri said.

"No, we're not interested in checking you out."

"You didn't answer my question. Who was in the room on the other side of Fargo? Seems like they would have opportunity just like Fargo."

"We're checking on it."

Sheri was astounded. "You don't even know the name?"

"Yes, we know the name."

Sheri took out a notepad, and stared at Morton.

"Okay. His name is Dean Michaels. He was questioned and found to have no relevance. We have him on camera in the casino for most of the evening."

Sheri scribbled a few notes. "Did he leave the casino?"

"Don't know. Security at the casino is handling that," Morton said.

"Has he done time? Any ties at all? Does he owe money?"

"Listen," said Morton standing. "We are conducting the investigation, and these answers must remain confidential."

"So you have something, but are not willing to divulge it. I will pass that on. Is Fargo a suspect?"

"No," Morton said.

"Good." Sheri stood up. "Since Fargo is not a suspect, I take it that you really don't have any questions for me?" As she stood up, her sweater opened up and revealed a shoulder holster.

Both Morton and Joe became attentive. "Are you carrying?" Morton asked.

"You bet I am." She opened her light sweater to reveal a compact

Berretta Cougar snuggled under her arm. "You wouldn't want a girl like me to be unprotected, would you?"

Both Morton and Joe were mesmerized. "No of course not," said Morton. "Just surprised that you got in here with it. We usually pat everybody down if they're coming into the Pit."

Sheri held her arms out to her side and spun around. "Anybody want to take a shot?"

The room was silent. There was not a detective in the room who would not have given up carrying their Glock for a month to be given the chance to pat down Sheri.

Joe finally spoke up. "Well, if nobody's interested..."

"Get the hell out of here Joe," screamed Morton.

"Yes, Boss," said Joe as he backed away.

"Good line," said Sheri.

Chapter Nineteen

I WALKED THROUGH the casino at the Treasure Island Hotel and noticed what a good time the crowd was having. Bells were ringing everywhere, as slots paid out. After driving back from the desert where Sheri and I learned about the AK scene in Nevada, I had dropped Sheri off so she could ready herself for her interview with Morton. I stopped at my place, changed clothes and switched cars. Knowing she would come back with more information than Morton would get from her, I headed back to the scene of the crime at Treasure Island.

After parking my BMW in the garage, I entered the hotel and moved directly toward the elevators taking the first one available. I shared it with a couple that just looked at the carpet the whole ride. I didn't ask. I got off at the sixth floor where my old room was and found casino security standing guard outside the door where the murder had gone down. I flashed my P.I. badge, and the guard checked his clipboard as to who could have access to the crime scene. He found my name and waved me in.

"Thanks," I said, as he opened the door.

"No problem."

"Are you getting much traffic?"

"Nope. You're the first since the team left."

"Forensics?"

"Yep. It looks like a mystery to me."

"So it is," I said, as I entered and closed the door behind me.

Upon entering I was not surprised to see the entire room dusted in a black powder, the kind used to help lift latent fingerprints. First I turned and studied the lock on the door. The interior security latch was broken from when Tony and I had forced our way in. The door lock was a standard magnetic card system from the outside, and from the inside there was a dead bolt that was manually operated. I then turned and studied the connecting door that led to my room. This door was locked, according to the police. I knew my side was also locked so entrance and exit to the crime scene was impossible from this side. Walking across the living room I glanced out the window and confirmed my suspicion that no one could get through the sealed windows. There was also a sunken dining room with a round table that had the remains of a catered dinner. Looked like it had been for one person. No company that night, at least not planned.

Walking into the master bedroom I found more of the black powder on all the bureaus, switch plates and molding. The bathroom was in the same shape. Black powder everywhere including on the large oversize Jacuzzi tub and walk-in steam room with six spigots. In a busy hotel with different guests every few days there would be dozens of prints almost eliminating the possibility of finding the suspect. But the police had to try just in case they could come up with a match. I examined the connecting door and it was the same set up as the one in my hotel room.

This door was open, so I entered the next room and glanced around. Nothing unusual. I walked over to the door leading to the hallway, and studied the locking system. It was the same as on the door of the suite where the murder took place. I walked into the room where the murder had occurred, and just tried to imagine what had happened. A violent end to a life had occurred here. It was deliberate. No mistake about that.

I left the hotel room and thanked the guard. I was halfway to the elevators when I stopped and turned around. Something was bothering me, but I could not put my finger on it. I walked back and smiled at the guard and asked if he could open my hotel room. I walked around and sat down on the bed and listened. The door and wall were still shot up, and the room was filled with black powder like the rest. Utter silence. I got up and walked out to the security guard.

"How ya doing?"

"Been better, been worse," said the guard. "Not exactly the most exciting duty, but they pay me for it."

"I know. I did some security guard work when I was in school. Pretty boring."

"That's where I go next."

"Yeah, we all have to work them. Get as much education as you can. What's your major?"

"My declared major is psychology with a minor in police science. I figured it would be good background for police work."

"Good for you. Stay in school as long as you can. It's hard to go back."

"Thanks for the advice."

I pulled my card out and handed it to him. "Here's my card. Keep in touch. You never know when we might need someone."

"Hey, thanks."

"Listen, I wonder if you could do something for me."

"Sure."

"I'm going to step back into my hotel room and I would like you to go halfway down the hallway, and run past my room to the end of this corridor."

"Okay. Great. Something to do. Real fast, or real slow?"

"A moderate speed. You've got some place to go, but you're not going to race to get there. Go all the way down to the end of the hallway."

"Okay, I got it."

"Give me about ten seconds in the room before you start."

"Okay," said the guard, as he started to backtrack down the hallway.

I went into my old hotel room and stood exactly where I had been standing the night of the murder. I listened to total silence, and then heard the footsteps running past me. I was in deep concentration trying to compare it to what I heard on the night of the murder. It was the same, only different. I stuck my head out the hotel door and asked the guard to do it one more time.

One more time I listened to silence and then the running steps past my hotel room door. It was the same, only different. But there was something wrong, and I could not place my finger on it. I sat down on the bed and just thought. Suddenly, I stood upright and smiled to myself.

I burst open the hotel room door and thanked the guard as I left.

"Figure it out?"

"No, but I have an idea."

I proceeded toward the elevator banks and walked through the "wheel" that connected the different corridors where rooms were located. I spotted a maid's cart about half way down one of the long hallways positioned right in front of a room door blocking the entrance. Maid protection. I changed directions before I got to the elevators and continued on down the hallway and slowed up as I got close to the cart. Piled high were towels, magazines, keys, sheets and a large bin for storing the sheets. I studied her cart and memorized all the details. I turned and headed for the elevator.

Chapter Twenty

"FARGO, GLAD TO SEE YOU," said Gil Sanford, head of security for Treasure Island. "Come on in and sit down. Heard you had come by the offices a few days ago, but I was out. Thanks for your updates."

Dressed in a dark gray suit, white shirt and immaculately groomed, Gil could be mistaken for a corporate executive. True to Las Vegas, Gil had that polished, very rich, and in-charge personality. After my visit to the sixth floor, I walked around the casino trying to get a feel for what was going on. I came up with a couple of crucial questions that I needed answered right away, so proceeded directly to Gil's office.

"Thanks, Gil." I was keeping Treasure Island in the loop on anything I found out about the murder. I wasn't about to make a mistake that our Federal agencies were guilty of, which was not sharing information. The CIA and the FBI still liked to keep information to themselves. Sort of job protection blown out of proportion I guess. I sat down in Gil's office that had floor-to-ceiling windows facing the Las Vegas Strip. It was an impressive sight, and I always like to take a quick look at the ever-changing landscape of my town. "Just a couple of quick questions."

"Sure, no problem."

"Police have anything yet?"

"Not a thing."

"Have you been able to track the guest whose room was right next to murder scene?"

"We got him all over the hotel. We have him on twenty different

182

videos and he's covered through the whole evening. Security ran him and he comes up clean. Insurance agent out of Washington state. Seattle, I think."

"So he was here alone."

"Right. Until today, anyway. He attended a conference. His family flew in today and they're doing Las Vegas with the kids. Happens all the time."

"How deep did you go?"

"We pulled everything. I can tell you who was at his fifth grade birthday party"

"Good. I wanted this guy to be as clean as they come."

"He's clean."

"What ya got, Fargo?"

"Nothing," I said. "That's the problem. I just want to eliminate some loose thoughts floating around as I try to work through the details of this case."

Gil leaned back in his chair. "I will have to agree with you. This locked room is a real puzzler."

"But it happened, and it's my job to try and figure out how they put this together."

"We've been working on it, but frankly, nothing has surfaced."

"Any ideas?"

"None."

I shifted in my chair as I studied Las Vegas through the window. It was busy for a Tuesday afternoon. "What about the rest of the people on the floor?"

"We've gone through all their backgrounds. Not as detailed of course as the room right next to the murder, but we've checked them out."

"What about down at the end of the hall?"

"What have you got, Fargo?"

"Just ideas."

"What kind of ideas? I know you and how you work. You've got something. I can feel it"

"Don't know."

"You're following something up...."

"Just ideas. Something's bothering me. Can't put my finger on it."

"Care to explain?"

"I want to know who was on that floor at the time of the hit. Everybody."

"We've given Morton at Metro everything they requested. All the records of the guests who were staying on that floor."

"You check them out yourself?"

"We checked out everybody. They all proofed up. Nothing to write home about."

I leaned forward and put my elbows on my knees and clasped my hands together. "Lets look at this from a different point of view," I said.

Gil straighten his chair and met my gaze. "I'm ready for any creative input on this case."

"Everybody is asking the obvious questions. Who did it? Why did they do it? You know, the usual. Motive and opportunity. This is what everybody is thinking. But try this. What did we not find at the murder scene? What was not there? What's missing?"

Gil sat back and I could see the wheels spinning. I also sat back. I did not have an answer, but by trying to figure out what wasn't there, we might gain some insight into this crime.

"Well," said Gil, "we did not find the murder weapon and the killers left no sign of tools to gain entrance into the hotel suite."

"Right, they left no signs that they had been there except a dead body, and cartridges on the floor. Were all the slugs found?"

"No. Some of them went into the wall but were stopped by the exterior building material. Hard to get to. Others were too distorted for a positive match even if we did have the murder weapon. But they did leave the ropes hanging out the window."

"That always struck me as odd."

"Yeah, you're right."

"Why would you want to vault out a sixth floor window? You would be seen by someone."

"Fast escape?"

"Maybe... but why three guys to make one hit... who do you know sends out three people to make a hit?"

"Nobody," Gil said.

"Exactly. Let's say the ropes don't come into play."

"Decoy?"

"I think so. If we assume that the ropes are a decoy, then how did they escape?"

"By more normal means. But somebody did set the ropes, and they were used on the roof for something."

"Right, I know that. But if the ropes don't exist, then maybe we only have one target, not two or three."

"Possibly."

"I was in the hallway right after I heard the footsteps, which is right after somebody unloaded two magazines in the hotel suite."

"Two?"

"Right, two. I heard the magazine change."

"Wow. How do you know what that sounded like?"

"Hong Kong. Long story."

"You'll have to tell me sometime."

"When this is over. Anyway, there was a guy down the hallway in P.J.'s who was fast asleep. The police arrived a short time later, and nobody, to my knowledge used the elevators. If they did, they had a short window, which is when I went in with Tony to clear the room."

"Right."

"So that only leads us to one conclusion."

"The killer never left the hotel floor."

"Bingo," I said.

I left Gil's office after we had developed a new game plan based on the premise that the killer never left the hotel floor. Gil was going to obtain photos of everybody leaving the elevators right after the murder for a twelve-hour period. We were going to run these through hotel security that used a face I.D. system to try and come up with a match. If they were in the computer, we could attach a name and background to them. Possibly an alias, but still a name. While this approach was a hit or miss situation, we were also contacting all parties on the entire sixth floor, and asking them to account for their comings and goings from their hotel suites the night of the murder. We would develop a huge wall chart and check off each person as we traced when they entered and left their suites.

This might show us a pattern for the evening.

I swung open the doors that lead to the roof and was blinded by the Las Vegas sun. The roof had been cooking in the relentless heat for hours, and it was not a pleasant experience as I walked to the center of the roof. I gazed one more time at the side of the building where the three ropes had hung a few days earlier. I just could not get the concept out of my mind that this was the escape route used the night of the murder. Even though Gil and I had established a premise that the killer stayed on the floor of the hotel, I wanted to double back on my investigation and see if I could get some hits on this obvious escape route, even if it was a decoy. The ropes used were lightweight, and I guess that mountain climbers used this type of equipment. I pulled out my notebook and made a notation to run some checks on this idea. I imagined that the police had already been down this road, but I like to follow every path of my investigations, no matter where they lead. As I slid the notebook back into by jacket pocket, my cell phone rang.

"Fargo."

"This is Uncle Leo. Glad to have caught you."

"What's up?" I asked, as I walked from the center of the building to the edge, which I had examined a few days earlier.

"Abby just reported in by phone. Her trip downtown for her interview was uneventful. However, she said she caused quite a stir by appearing in her costume for the late show. She told them she was in rehearsal and didn't have time to change. She also handed out free tickets for tonight's show. It was quite a scene."

I laughed thinking about what a commotion it must have been. "Did she pick up any info?"

"No, not really. They were just doing the necessary interviews, running the numbers, talking to everybody. Abby did say that the police were absolutely baffled by the fact that the murder room was locked from the inside."

"I think I have the locked room figured from two different possibilities," I said.

"Really?"

"Well, let's say that I have some ideas floating around. I think there is only one suspect and the ropes are a decoy. The killer planned this attack in great detail. Once we are able to put together a timeline, it should help us figure out how the doors were locked. He didn't slip under the door with an AK and then slip out again. He walked through. That's where the police have made some serious mistakes. They keep seeing it as a locked room."

"You're right about that," said Uncle Leo. "I have to say that I've been seeing it also as a locked room. Break it down for me next time you're in the office."

"Will do. Anything else going on?"

"Nothing. I've a court appearance in a few minutes. Got to go."

I shut down my cell phone and placed it back on my belt. As I did so I caught a flash from down the street near the top of a building. This caused me to once again examine the lighting system covering the roof area. I pulled out my notebook and made a notation to find out how the lamps had been put out.

The heat was overwhelming as I turned and headed for the door leading back into the infrastructure of the hotel's maintenance system. I was thinking to myself that I sure would like to see photos of the ropes in use. That would tell me exactly what happened that evening. I stopped in my tracks and spun around. I was sweating, and could feel the sun starting to burn me from the sun's reflection off the roof and windows of the hotel rooms.

I walked quickly over to the edge of the building again and started to move back and forth along the edge. I spotted it, a flash from the top of the parking structure. I was betting it was a camera lens. I took note of its position, and once again headed for the door to escape the heat.

Chapter Twenty-One

I LEANED FORWARD on a comfortable high backed office chair in anticipation of what I was going to see. I was sitting in the security screening room of the Mirage Hotel and Gambling Casino. I had called John Weaver, an old friend, and told him what I needed. By the time I arrived in their state-of-the-art security control room, everything was set up.

"How long have you had the camera in this location?" I asked as I studied an impressive display of video surveillance equipment.

Weaver leaned up against one of the control tables that allowed them to target certain players from any angle. Modern surveillance rooms were about the same as television control rooms. The only difference was the ability to create productions. But they could follow somebody through the entire casino, capture it on video, and be able to replay it in sequence.

In the years since John Weaver had left Homicide, he had not lost his competitive edge, like that of a police cadet right out of basic training. A sharp dresser, he kept in style, and in shape. His tan slacks and Hawaiian shirt gave him the look of a tourist if he was working the floor. Give him a cup of coins and he could be an average guy from anywhere in the country trying to hit a slot to pay for his vacation.

"We installed it as the casino was being built. It serves to cover part of the roof area but it also covers the side and roof of Treasure Island."

"Yeah, I saw the...."

"Here we go," said Weaver, interrupting me.

The video operator worked his magic as Weaver and I leaned over his shoulder. The screen burst to life and we saw time code flash by on the bottom of the screen. These high tech security areas employed talented technical crews who could spot suspected card cheats and other casino improprieties. They also knew their equipment inside and out. The operator slowed the video as we got close to the chosen time.

"Wait," I said. "Roll it back a bit." I watched the tape roll back and didn't see anything. We rolled the video ahead and watched as one man, who we could not identify, opened a door and stepped out onto the roof of Treasure Island. He carried a clipboard and carried himself with the authority of somebody who was just doing his job. This is the same door I used the morning after the murder. The suspect walked out onto the roof, looked around, and then proceeded to walk directly to the pipe where we had found some blue fibers from a nylon climbing rope. The suspect bent down and worked on the pipe for a while.

"What's he doing?" asked Weaver.

"I think he's planting evidence."

"Interesting."

"Yeah. We found fibers around these pipes and several fibers on the roof." The suspect stood up and walked toward the edge of the building, and then every few feet his hand would drop to his side, and then continued to walk toward the edge of the building.

"What's he doing?" said the video operator.

"He's still planting evidence. He is making it look like the murderers left by way of this roof. We'll find out in a few minutes."

"Do you recognize him?" asked Weaver.

"Not in the least. It's interesting he is doing this in broad daylight, and not concerned with anybody seeing him. I will show this to Treasure Island, but I expect that they won't be able to I.D. him as one of their employees."

The suspect turned and walked across the roof, stopped, looked up at the upper levels of the hotel, and then went through the door closing it behind him. The video operator fast-forwarded the tape and we watched a blank rooftop. Because the operator had magnified the view, the image was grainy and somewhat distorted. As night came, we could see less and less.

"I heard they used an AK inside the hotel," Weaver said.

"Wow, really?" said the video operator.

"Yep," I commented. "Makes a real mess inside a hotel room." As the video slowed blinking lights appeared in the hotel windows as people entered and left their hotel rooms.

"There it is…slow it down a bit and back it up. Right there."

"Amazing," Weaver said.

The sixth floor window exploded outward and shortly afterward, three ropes were tossed out."

"Okay," I said, "the murder is just a few minutes from now." We watched the tape closely for about ten minutes and eventually a head appeared in the window. "That's me," I said.

"Nobody used the ropes," said Weaver.

"I think this was a huge decoy." We ran the video ahead and it slowly turned to daylight and the last thing we screened was Detective Morton and I on the roof looking for clues.

"Okay," I said. "That's it. I'm going to need a couple of copies to pass around. It answers a few questions. Shows that the ropes were never used."

"No problem," said Weaver. "You'll have two copies before you leave. How about Homicide, do they have anything yet?"

"Not that I know of. They'll be interested in the tape and so will Treasure Island. If it's true the suspect set up an elaborate decoy operation to lead the investigation in a new direction, then we have a very complex, carefully planned homicide."

"But you have to ask yourself," said Weaver, "why all these decoys? What are they leading you away from?"

"Good question. Really good question."

Chapter Twenty-Two

I SWUNG MY BMW INTO TRAFFIC and hit the accelerator. An all black car really heats up in the Las Vegas sun, even on this early Wednesday morning, but this car had an incredible cooling system that chilled the air to an extreme. Getting out of the desert heat gave me time to think. Ideas were floating around in my head based upon what was on the videotape. I felt like we had gone from searching for two-to-three suspects, to one individual on the roof. As soon as I was out of the Mirage I called both Treasure Island and Detective Morton and left messages about what I had seen on the videotape. My cell phone rang and I picked it up as I turned off of Boulder onto Tropicana.

"Fargo here."

"Fargo, it's Sheri. I'm in the office and we just got a call from Derk. He says an AK has turned up at Shooters Supply."

"Really."

"Yep. There's no way of knowing if this is the right AK. But it's a start. He said it was a nice one. Folding stock. It's been cleaned up, but they're handling it with care. Detective Morton is on his way over now.

"How did Morton find out?"

"Shooters Supply called him. They're holding the AK as he knows it might be a dirty gun. Evidently it did come up clean on the Federal check."

"Okay. I'm headed that way right now."

"So is Derk. He wants to see it."

I crossed over the Strip and headed toward Arville where I could cut across to American Shooters Supply. It would be a long shot if some usable prints could be lifted.

It took me a while to get across town. I ran into the normal traffic jam at four corners and with the construction in progress around the freeway interchange, it was a longer drive then usual. As I pulled in, Morton was just getting out of his typical plain-Jane car that detectives were given to use.

"Nice car," I said rubbing it in a bit.

"Same to you," Morton replied. "Be careful or I'll put the word out to have the city boys keep closer tabs on you."

"Actually, I got pulled over just recently. Failed to signal."

"Our tax dollars at work. So I see your net on the street pulled in an AK," Morton said, as we entered Shooters Supply.

"Either that or a coincidence. Check every possibility; who knows where it will take you?"

The first thing that happens when you walk into Shooters Supply is you smell the acid odor of fired guns mixed with a slight oil smell from the weapons. In the background you could hear the muffled pop, pop, pop from the firing range. My kind of place. It was a cop's hangout as well, with occasional visits by agents from Treasury and other Federal services.

They carried the uniforms, badges and general supplies that the boys working the black and whites need. It also had a thriving business in security guard uniforms. Some of the smaller shops didn't supply uniforms, but American Shooters Supply did.

At the counter was Derk dressed in his usual desert attire, which showed signs that he had spent a great deal of time outdoors. You could just look at his clothes and imagine the canyons and crevices he had crawled through looking for the illusive metal that men have dreamed for centuries of finding. Finding a nugget here and there was also Derk's passion that kept him going. They say the desert was getting rough for those who traveled off the beaten path; but when you ran into Derk in the desert, carrying an AK-47 and a complementary .45, you steered a wide path.

"Hi Fargo," Derk said. His eyes were bright, faced flush and apparently glad to see me.

"Hey Derk. This is Detective Morton. He's with Metro working the case we talked about."

"Glad to meet you," Morton said, shaking hands with Derk. For an old guy, Derk's hands were strong. It was like shaking hands with a steel vise. "I guess you're the expert in AK's around these parts. That's what I hear anyway."

"There's a lot of guys like me left over from Nam. They know as much as I do about these guns. Too much, in fact."

Just then Matt Flannery came out carrying an AK and wearing white gloves. Matt had a long history in Las Vegas dealing with all sorts of firearms. His one weakness was he wanted to purchase every firearm that came into the store. To him each firearm had a story, and one could only imagine what had happened. He laid it down on a foam pad for everyone to see. The weapon was bright and shiny. It had been cleaned but Matt wasn't taking any chances.

Everyone leaned over to look at the AK knowing that Detective Morton was going to have to impound it and run some checks. Sheri arrived, and after greetings were exchanged, we got down to the business of the AK.

Sheri studied the AK with great interest. "I just had to come down here to see this"

"Did you ever shoot one of these?" Morton asked.

"Did she ever. You should have seen her," said Derk.

"I bet it was something," commented Morton.

"Lit up the desert," Derk said, slapping his hand on the counter.

Sheri smiled. "What's the background behind the name?"

Matt turned the assault rifle over to where the serial number was located. "The rifle was first built in 1947 by Avtomat Kalashnikova, hence the designation AK-47."

"Oh, so simple."

"Just like the gun," Matt said.

"So who brought it in here," I asked.

"We got the guy on tape. I'm cueing it up now. He says he found the gun in a ditch in the desert. Said it was totally messed up, so he cleaned it up before he brought it in. He also fired some rounds through it. Said it was a beauty."

"We won't get prints now," I said.

Matt turned over the AK. "I'm afraid not. Not a chance in the world."

"Well, we'll check it for a bullet match," Morton said. "That's going to tell us if this AK was involved in the shooting at the hotel."

"How accurate are these?" I asked.

"It's a close-in fire fight weapon," answered Derk.

"Exactly what does that mean?" Sheri questioned.

"Well, it's like this. This is a close-in, fight and run weapon. Fire fights. Spray the bushes and run, or if they were advancing, they would put a wall of lead down that would be hard to get through. We would do a staggered retreat with two guys always firing, and then the rest changing magazines, taking their turns before the entire patrol turned and put down our own wall of lead, then disappear into the jungle."

"Good story," said Morton.

"Wasn't a story," said Derk.

Morton pondered a moment. "I understand."

"So they're not that accurate I take it?" asked Sheri.

"Their for rock n' rolling, not sniping. The Vietcong rarely used them as a sniper rifle. Sniping is long-range stuff. These are meant for fighting. We used them sometimes. I spent time as a sniper, and we used very special rifles for that."

Without question, I suddenly became a patriot of this man. There were a lot of untold stories still to come out of the jungles of Nam.

"Can you show me how to do that sometime?" Sheri asked.

"Ma'am, it would be my pleasure."

"You know," Morton said, "Metro has a special firing range indoors. What if we make some arrangements for you to come out and give our special ops team some of the benefit of your experience."

"Ya got yourself a thousand yard range in that itsy bitsy building out there?"

Morton realized his mistake. "Ahhh, well ya got me on that one."

"How about if you make it out to my place. We'll set up a shoot, and I'll tell your special ops team what I know."

"Sounds good to me. I'll also make it worth your while. We need

198

to work with guys like you."

"Okay, sounds good. I'll do it on one condition."

"What's that?"

"That this little lady also be included."

Sheri beamed.

"It's your range and your lesson. Deal."

I was hoping that Sheri was going to ask me. I glanced at her and she gave me a wink, and I knew I was in. "What about the guy?" I asked, bringing them back to the subject at hand.

"He's clean. All the proper credentials. Comes in all of the time. A desert rat named Alex White," said Matt.

"Hey, I know him," said Derk. "He's a good guy. Been bumming around here for years. Likes the desert and the solitude."

"Here's the tape. Take a look for yourselves." Matt clicked a remote and the TV mounted overhead jumped to life. It showed a color video with numbers running across the bottom with the time and date. A desert rat sort of a guy comes in carrying the gun wrapped in a blanket. He unwraps it and hands the AK to Matt, who clears it to make sure it's not loaded. After an inspection, Matt lays the rifle down on the counter and records the serial number. He then enters it into the computer. Stares at the screen, and then comes back to the counter.

"Any sound?" I asked.

"Nope, we just use it for I.D.'s when we need to."

"Can you track the gun?"

"Yep. That's what I was doing. It's clean. No record it was used in a crime. Also, no known owner."

"What happens to the AK when this is over," Sheri asks.

"If it was used in the crime it will end up in the evidence room. Then eventually it will be destroyed."

"Oh, that's too bad. I wanted to buy it."

"And I wanted to sell it," said Matt. "Looks like I'm out some money."

"Why not get the money back from Alex?" Morton asked.

"Naa. He was square with me. The weapon came up clean when I ran it, and I made the deal. He needs the money more than I do. And just maybe the AK will come back to me. This finely made semi-auto isn't guilty of killing anyone. It's as guilty as a guitar is when someone plays Lady of Spain on it. It's the guy who pulled the trigger that's guilty."

We all stood around and looked at the beautiful weapon. The guy who found the AK had meticulously cleaned it, and it seemed to glow in the light in the store. There was a moment of silence when they all realized that it would probably be destroyed. Another loss to the right to bear arms.

Chapter Twenty-Three

SHERI STARED AT THE REFLECTED IMAGE of Coyote in the Miracle Mile Shops at Planet Hollywood Hotel and Casino, formerly known as Desert Passage. It was a classic game of cat and mouse. They had been playing it for over two hours. Only Coyote didn't know she was being observed. Or did she? Sheri had followed Coyote by taxi to the Bellagio Hotel. After over an hour of shopping, Coyote slipped across Las Vegas Boulevard and enjoyed a short walk before entering the famed Miracle Mile shops.

The Miracle Mile Shops were special indeed and reflected the glitz of Hollywood that people love so much. The concept of a "total environment mall" was at the very heart of the Miracle Mile Shops concept to entrap the visitors by transporting them to tinsel town, and bringing out the romance and adventure of Hollywood. Sheri had enjoyed many an afternoon exploring the riches of over 130 specialty shops.

Fargo wanted to track Coyote at every opportunity. Uncle Leo and Fargo were convinced that Coyote was under the same dangers as Rapture because she held the other half of the treasure map. Fargo gave Sheri the assignment to stay with Coyote and watch for trouble.

Sheri was ready when Coyote exited the Venetian Hotel early Wednesday afternoon. Sheri carried a large shopping bag. It was a reversible handbag, and inside she carried an assortment of reversible hats, scarves, eyeglasses, and complete change of wardrobe if necessary. This gave her many options in changing her appearance as she worked the target's path.

Coyote had chosen the main entrance of the shopping complex off of Las Vegas Boulevard and was lingering in front of one of the shops. Sheri moved into the classic "front tail" operation working the reflection of Coyote as she window-shopped from store-to-store.

Sheri and Coyote shopped their way through the Miracle Mile Shops with Coyote stopping for a short time at Jacqueline Jarrot, and then on to Tommy Bahama.

Sheri maneuvered herself behind a center kiosk and set her bag down. She quickly removed her sunglasses and switched them for a different pair; white rims instead of black. Then she took out a different hat, reversed it, and put it on in place of the one she had been wearing. She quickly donned a light jacket, then emptied her bag and reversed her handbag, placing the items she just took off in the bottom of the bag, and bringing to the top possible items for another change. She then walked past the nature photography shop and moved herself in a position behind Coyote. If Coyote continued in the same direction, then Sheri would now be tailing from behind Coyote. If Coyote reversed direction, she would be front tailing her out of the Miracle Mile Shops. Just as expected, Coyote continued in the same direction working her way through and around the shopping mall.

The Miracle Mile was laid out so that it circled the center of the Planet Hollywood Hotel and the gambling operation. From various exits along the shopping complex, you could enter the casino and be subjected to spinning wheels, cries of victory as numbers were hit and profits realized. Fortunately, winners were noisier than losers and the glamour of Las Vegas was perpetuated no matter where you were.

Sheri watched Coyote exit the shopping arcade and she decided to take a chance. She moved to the left of Coyote through a bank of slot machines around the steps leading to the escalators. She rose quickly up to the mezzanine level, saw two or three tables empty, sat down, and ordered iced lemonade with mint. Sheri knew she had taken a chance, but she waited patiently until her drink was served, pulled out some travel folders, and began to study them.

Sure enough, she was rewarded for her foresight. Out of the corner of her eye she spotted Coyote arriving on the mezzanine level via the steps, which Sheri had just passed. Coyote spotted an empty table near Sheri, and sat down and also ordered an iced soda water. Sheri snuggled into her brochures that made her a tourist for sure.

Coyote tipped very generously and received a gracious thank you from the cocktail waitress when her refreshment arrived. Coyote's phone rang. "Hello," said Coyote. "No, that won't be necessary. I will be here for about two more days and then I fly to Alaska for the convention before I head to Japan."

Sheri did not stir as she switched folders and continued to listen to Coyote. She reached into her handbag and pulled out a pen and marked up her travel brochures, but in reality she was making detailed notes of Coyote's conversation.

"I don't think that we'll have to worry about this much longer," said Coyote. "This operation will be completed in a matter of days. It is essential that I remain solo for the time being. We'll meet tonight at the Palms. Front entrance. Be there at eight," and then Coyote hung up the phone. She sipped the last of her drink, and then gathered her packages and exited down the stairs moving quickly through the registration area.

Sheri was checking her makeup when Coyote left the mezzanine area. As soon as Coyote disappeared, Sheri picked up her packages and left. She exited via the escalators on the level above the mezzanine. She descended into the registration area, and headed for an exit of the hotel.

As Sheri left the Planet Hollywood Hotel, Coyote stepped out of the shadows of a magnificent column and tipped her sunglasses down so she could see over them. She watched as Sheri disappeared out the door. Coyote turned and left the hotel through the shopping arcade with a slight smile on her face. It had been a classic cat and mouse game. This time the mouse had won. At least she hoped so.

Chapter Twenty-Four

"FARGO, HERE," I ANSWERED, leaning back in my desk chair. I had spent a few minutes at my desk working out details and making my case notes from the previous day's investigations. It was important to document all my conversations and go over my notes. We investigators are a meticulous breed.

"It's Sheri, Fargo."

"How's Coyote?"

"She just spent hours and hours killing time. It just appears to be senseless wandering. I don't get it."

I leaned back further and lifted my feet on the desk and studied the law books that surrounded me. "She has money to spend. She is wealthy. She does not need to work, so it seems. What's so unusual about that?"

"Coyote is too smart just to wander around. If she is that rich, I can imagine a lot of other ways to spend time. Meeting with people who are on her social circuit. Something. But she does nothing. She's a loner."

"Maybe she's turning this into a vacation?"

"It's a Wednesday. I don't get that impression from following her. She's waiting for something."

"I see your point," I said.

"Get this," said Sheri. "She's meeting somebody tonight at the Palms. I was able to overhear a phone conversation and here's the gist of it. The operation will be completed in a matter of days. She's to remain solo for the time being. Coyote said, 'we'll meet tonight at the Palms.' "

"That's it."

"Yep."

"I wonder who?"

"Don't know."

"I am more bothered by the part of remaining solo for the time being."

"Yeah. What do you think it means, Boss?"

"I don't know. It might have nothing to do with Rapture and her map. But then again, it could have something to do with the map, and that Coyote has a team member we don't know about."

"Think they're setting Rapture up?"

"No," I said. "Do you think Coyote was on to you?"

"Not a chance."

I stared at my monitor and thought about this for a few seconds. What was Coyote up to? Who was her partner? What about going solo? I needed to know more about Coyote. One thing remained a question. Coyote was the only person who had a real motive to go after J.T. and Rapture. I could not overlook this fact for too long.

"Boss. You still there?"

"Sorry, Sheri. Just thinking about Coyote. Has it ever crossed your mind that Coyote could have a motive for killing J.T.?"

"You mean like, she has the other half of the map."

"Yes."

"Then why is she still around?"

"Good point. Decoy maybe. Everyone is a suspect until it's over."

I saw Uncle Leo stick his head in the door and I waved him in. He took a careful look around as he entered and noted the stacks and stacks of files I had placed on all the chairs. I was responsible for my own files, but it was Sheri who kept me organized. Uncle Leo removed a case file from a chair and sat down, carefully placing it on the floor.

"I'm sure Morton would love to get a hold of that piece of information," said Sheri.

"I was thinking the same thing. I'm not going to look too good hiding these facts from the casino and Metro if it ever comes out."

"You always look good, Boss."

"Try me with cold vertical steel bars in front of me and a roommate named Bubba."

"You'll look good to him, too."

"Thanks."

"Can I drive your BMW?"

I laughed. "Of course, Sheri. I would not want it any other way. However, you're my partner on this case...so...."

"You wouldn't turn me in, Boss."

"Of course not."

"You don't sound as positive as you did a few moments ago," she said.

"Hey, next to Abby, you're my best friend."

"Thanks, Boss."

"Okay...you're going to have to go to the Palms tonight and see what you can dig up."

"I'm half way home now," said Sheri. "Going to get dressed up a bit and then head out. I don't think we can let this pass by us. I'll give you a call when I pick up Coyote."

"You got any contacts at the Venetian?"

"None."

"I was thinking of trying to pick her up there, but if they said the Palms, let's go with that and see what happens."

"Okay. I'll be in touch."

I hung up the phone and looked for a reaction from Uncle Leo.

"Sounds like the two of you have been pretty busy," he said. "And just let me say, I will not represent you if Metro is going to press charges against you unless you put a very large sum of money in an account I can draw from against my invoicing which will be large and continuous."

"Where's the faith?"

"Lost in a dark courthouse full of unjust prosecutions."

"I'll keep a light on."

"Cute. And what, may I ask, out of extreme curiosity, are you not telling Homicide?"

"About Coyote."

"Ahhh," said Uncle Leo. "As I expected. "Withholding information from the police can produce expected problems."

"What would you suggest I do?"

"As your attorney, or as your friend."

"As my friend."

"Don't bring it up, and if it comes up, tell them that you never connected the two. Play it as dumb as you can."

"As my attorney, what would you say?"

"First, you're assuming that I am your attorney."

"Yes, I am," I said. Uncle Leo and I always played this game. I knew that he would always be there to defend me, but Uncle Leo always liked to play it that he had a choice in the matter. It was his way of making a point.

"I would tell you to turn over what information you have to Homicide. The police can always play the 'obstructing justice' card for allegedly withholding information."

"They play that one a lot."

"Sure they do. It's their card. But how can it hurt you? So they want to interview her. Big deal. If Coyote has something to hide, then it's her problem."

"This might ruin Rapture's chances at buying the map from Coyote."

"Might, might not," said Uncle Leo.

"What if I told Security at Treasure Island what I knew about Coyote."

"It might help," said Uncle Leo. "It would show that you did something with the information that you were able to obtain from your client. Your client, Rapture, is involved in this, and I expect has been or will be interviewed by the police."

"What if Rapture does not tell Homicide about Coyote....,"

"That is between Homicide and Rapture."

"True."

"Did she tell Homicide about Coyote?"

"No, not that I know of, but I don't know for sure."

"Then Rapture is withholding information from the police," said Uncle Leo.

I twisted in my chair trying to work the details out in my mind.

"If Rapture did not tell the police about Coyote, then she is not giving Homicide the lead that they might need to find J.T.'s killer. Does that make Rapture an accessory to murder?"

"Only if she knew that Coyote was going to make the hit."

"Okay. I see your point. Of course Rapture is trying to protect her deal with Coyote."

"Separate issue," said Uncle Leo.

"But I know that Rapture would want the police to know any information to solve the murder of J.T."

"So, pick up the phone and call Security at Treasure Island."

"Right now?"

"Sure, why not? You get rid of information that would not look too good to withhold, and can continue with your case."

I reached over and picked up the phone eyeing Uncle Leo. He was always right. I would have gotten around to it but sometimes I circle the problem instead of stepping up to the plate and taking a swing. Other times I just start swinging. I punched a button and I was on my speakerphone.

"Good afternoon. Treasure Island."

"Gil Sanford, please," I said.

"Thank you. I'll connect you."

"Security," said a pleasant, but official voice.

"Hi, this is Fargo Blue. Is Gil Sanford available?"

"Just a minute, Mr. Blue."

I glanced over at Uncle Leo and he was eyeing the law books that circled my office hunting for missing volumes from his library. It was a routine that Sheri and I were used to."

"Fargo. Gil here. What can I do for you?"

"Hi Gil. It just occurred to me that a young lady who Rapture is doing business with might have been at he hotel sometime in the past. I thought I would run it by you and also let the police know."

"What's her name?"

"She goes by the name of Coyote."

"Oh yes. Morton mentioned her."

"He did? You know about her?"

"Sure. The police cleared her yesterday. Morton said so himself. No problem there."

"Really!" I blurted out. Rapture must have said something about her as a business associate, I thought to myself.

"Got a call from Morton and he said that Coyote has been cleared of any connection with J.T.'s murder. Said that he got her name from Rapture. He had called here to see if we had her on tape to collaborate her story."

"Which was...?" I asked.

"Let's see. Rapture was a business associate that she was going to meet on the morning of the murder. So we checked it out and we have Coyote on tape approaching the elevator door, being stopped, and then leaving."

"Did they interview her?"

"Apparently so. Had a solid alibi."

"Okay. Thanks. Looks like Homicide is one step ahead of me on this one," I commented.

"No problem. Let me know what you find out."

"Thanks Gil, I will," and once again punched the button on the phone to clear it. "Well, that surprised me," I said to Uncle Leo.

"Morton is sharper than you give him credit for."

"I know Morton doesn't miss a trick," I said. I picked up the phone and started to punch numbers.

"Who's it going to be this time?" said Uncle Leo.

I punched the speakerphone again.

"Morton."

"Afternoon. It's Fargo."

"Tell me that you have the murderer in custody, and that I can come by and pick him up," said Morton.

"Not that easy. Question. When did you clear Coyote of an involvement with J.T.'s murder?"

"Yesterday afternoon. I dropped by the Venetian and talked to security and also Coyote. Very pleasant and cooperative."

"Really?"

"Yeah. I also viewed the security tapes at Treasure Island just before we interviewed Coyote. Her story checks out. But you know how it goes, everyone is a suspect until they're cleared."

"Right. Thanks. I was just checking in."

"Let me know if you find anything else out."

"Right," and I punched the phone and the speaker went dead.

Uncle Leo got up from his chair. "Lots of people know lots of things. You can't know everything all the time. But at least this cleared up your questions on what to do, and you aren't withholding information."

"Rapture must of told Morton about Coyote. I will check it out."

"Doesn't matter. You know the routine. You worked Homicide.

212

You ask a thousand questions. You get a thousand answers; then you follow up on everything. Morton does a good job."

"Yeah, he does," I said. "He was in the department while I was there, and he always baffled everybody because of his ability to ferret out details."

"A rare ability," said Uncle Leo.

"Sixth race at Arlington this afternoon. Looks like Dancing Lady is going to post with good odds."

Uncle Leo looked at me with a slight amount of suspicion. "How do you know these things?" he asked.

"Hey, this is Las Vegas. It's a small town."

"Your money is down?"

I pulled two tickets out of my pocket and waved them at Uncle Leo.

"Okay. Thanks for the tip," said Uncle Leo, and headed out the door with a sense of urgency in his stride.

Chapter Twenty-Five

SHERI WALKED THROUGH THE LOBBY and registration area of The Palms and marveled at the open, spacious feeling of wealth. If The Palms was striving for a feeling of the young and the restless, with money and lots of it, that's who they were attracting. Even for an early Wednesday evening it was busy. It was Vegas' new "in" spot, the place to see and be seen.

Sheri had been in the casino before and knew her way around the hotel. One of the routines that Fargo always demanded of his operatives was to walk through all the new casinos from time to time. Get an idea of the layout. Study how the traffic flow was set up to always guide guests back through the casino. Learn all the exits and the parking garage structure. Learn the locations and attractions of the different cafés and eateries the hotel offers and know which entrances to use that would not allow your target to spot you as you entered the casino.

This was always a tricky assignment especially if the subjects are careful about how they sit in a café. If their backs are up against the wall, and your job is to watch them, it makes it difficult because they have a clear view of all activities around them.

Fargo and Sheri occasionally played a game when meeting at a casino location. The first person there had to spot the other person as they made their way to the meeting. It kept both of them sharp. One time Sheri had climbed over the railing at one end of Wolfgang Pucks at the MGM Grand, and walked behind Fargo and asked him if he needed any service. Fargo was totally surprised since he was sitting with a full view of the entrance.

This evening Sheri was at least an hour early, and had set herself up close enough to the front entrance where visitors disembarked from their limos and cabs. She figured Coyote for a cab, and wanted to catch her coming into the casino. This way she would not have to second-guess which way Coyote was going to head. Sheri's cell phone rang.

"Sheri."

"Fargo here. Any sign of Coyote?"

"None. I am an hour early. How long before you and Rapture show up at Carluccio's?"

"At least an hour," said Fargo.

"I'll be there as planned."

"Thanks," said Fargo and hung up the phone.

Sheri folded her phone and put it in her handbag. She pulled out her notebook to make some entries. Like Fargo, she recorded all observations, times and events in her file. She would later compile these into case notes. Now all she had to do was wait for Coyote to walk through the entrance and observe the who, what, when, where and how, the basics of surveillance. If something significant developed, she would stay with Coyote and let Fargo know that she would be late to Carluccio's.

Just then she happened to glance up when she heard the sound of high heels. Coyote walked past her and out the exit of The Palms. Sheri, for a second was stunned and caught off guard. She never expected Coyote to be exiting the Palms. She placed her notebook back in her handbag and walked out the front exit and saw Coyote leaving by way of a taxi. Several airport vans pulled into the entranceway blocking her vision. Coyote's cab made the light and Sheri knew she had lost her. The old adage of "follow that cab" wasn't going to work. Surveillance was a lot more complicated than what was portrayed in the movies.

Chapter Twenty-Six

I MADE A RIGHT TURN off of East Tropicana onto Spencer followed by another right and eased into the parking lot of Carluccio's Tivoli Gardens, which also shared the parking lot with Liberace's Museum. Mr. Showmanship himself used to hang out at Carluccio's. He designed the piano lounge and used to drop by and entertain the diners. The parking lot was crowded for a Wednesday, but I lucked out with a space right up front. The locals came to Carluccio's to eat, relax and have a good time. Las Vegas residents tend to favor the local casinos, such as the Orleans or Sam's Town. If you found them on the Strip it was because someone from out of town was visiting.

Rapture sat beside me and literally glowed in the moonlight as we eased to a stop. She was dressed in all black, which contrasted with her fair, lightly freckled skin that was so common with redheads.

"Ever eat here?" I asked.

Rapture leaned back in the seat. "Never. Didn't even know it was here. I know about the Liberace Museum but would never have come out here to eat. It's nice to see the rest of Las Vegas."

"You're right, and you'll like it here. It's busy, noisy and quiet all at the same time. Good Northern and Southern Italian cuisine. We can lose ourselves in here for awhile." I got out and walked around the car to open the door. Sitting on the edge of the lot was a gray Lexus with the engine purring. Inside sat Sheri. I didn't know the outcome of the Palms' investigation and would just have to wait. I nodded toward her but couldn't really see anything because of the dark tinted windows.

Sheri was a pro. I had arranged for her to tail us tonight. I wasn't taking any chances. Rapture got out of the car and we made our way to the front and through the double set of doors.

I recognized the hostess. "Hi Sally, good to see you."

"Fargo," Sally said. "Good to see you also." She leaned over and gave me a kiss on the cheek. "We have a table all ready for you and your guest."

I glanced at Rapture and she raised an eyebrow.

"Friendly place," I said as we moved past the others that were waiting.

"I'll bet. You're sort of Mr. Showmanship yourself."

I shrugged in response. We received some ice-cold stares that made me feel good and bad at the same time. There was always a wait at Carluccio's Tivoli Gardens even if you made a reservation. But I ate here so frequently that I could pull all the strings when I had to. Normally, I enjoyed a glass of wine in the bar before eating.

We slid into a corner booth in the middle room, which was somewhat isolated from the rest of the restaurant. Water was poured and our server took our drink orders. We decided on a bottle of California Merlot from Parducci Wine Cellars in Mendocino. Abby was the true wine expert of our group, and she had told me about this wonderful red wine. The grapes of Mendocino were giving the competition a run for the money as wine connoisseurs loved the coastal blends being produced.

As I gazed across the table at Rapture I was constantly reminded of how beautiful she was, but at the same time I realized that she was carrying a great burden. The death of her father, and then the death of her father's partner was a big load. On top of that she was risking everything to go after the gold. It was both admirable and chilling at the same time.

"How are you holding up?" I asked.

"Actually, quite well given the situation. I just can't understand why all of this happened."

"Buried treasure can bring out the worst in people. It's about greed. Some people are willing to kill for it."

"But J.T.?"

"The intruder thought he had the map, and was willing to kill for it. Something probably happened in the scuffle in the room. Maybe the murderer was unmasked. Something happened to force the intruder to open up with the AK."

"J.T. always carried a gun."

"Really. Did he hold a valid CCW in the state of Nevada?"

"I would expect so, but I really don't know. He did go by the book though."

I leaned back in my chair and glanced around seeing if I recognized anybody as I pondered what Rapture had just revealed. So J.T. had a gun. I expect that is what brought about the firing of the AK. I wondered what had happen to the weapon. "What color was it?" I asked Rapture.

"Silver."

"Did it have little holes near the barrel?"

"Yes."

"Shiny?"

"Yes."

"It was most likely a .38 police special. I will inform Metro of this, if you don't mind."

"Of course not."

I pulled out my notebook and wrote a reminder to forward the information to Morton. We both swirled our wine for a few seconds. "You know, in a free society, the bad guys always get to take the first shot," I said.

"How terrible...."

"But true."

"Yes, but we get to shoot back," said Rapture.

"I tipped my glass. To us, the good guys."

She raised and tipped her glass and never took her eyes off of me. "I really do believe in dreams coming true, and I believe the treasure is there, waiting for me."

"What if it isn't?"

"It's there. I can see it."

"What do you mean?"

Rapture absently glanced around the room as she thought about her answer. "I can visualize it in my mind. Some people call it positive thinking. I don't. What I believe is people set their own destinies with their mind."

"I think I understand." As we talked we glanced at the menu. I knew it by heart, but I just wanted to see what hit me tonight.

"Have you ever known someone that had everything, but every time you talked to them they had a major problem, and couldn't even begin to take advantage of the opportunities in front of them?"

"As a matter of fact, I do. The daughter of a doctor who had everything, but had nothing. She never amounted to anything. Yet, out of all of us in our group, she had more opportunity than anyone."

"That's what I am talking about," Rapture said. "Most people deal within their own reality. Yet, the movers and the shakers constantly step out of their own reality and ask the questions. Can humans fly?"

"So those that ask are those that can visualize, and in the end experience their dreams."

"Right. The Wright brothers asked the question, and then went on to show that everyone who said they were crazy, were wrong."

"So that's what keeps you motivated in this quest for the gold?"

"What it really does is to carry on the dream of my father."

Our server appeared out of thin air, an old Las Vegas trick, and we suddenly went through the universal struggle of what to order. After some debate between us, we both started with a salad consisting of chunks of Roquefort over crisped salad greens, with a hint of a balsamic wine vinegar and olive oil topping. For the main selection, Rapture went with Chicken Marsala and a side dish of their famous pasta, and I went with Crab Stuffed Shrimp. Enough French bread was brought to the table to feed an army, and we were left to await our meal.

"So, I need to ask this one question."

"Ok." Rapture tore off a piece of French bread and started in on the butter.

"How do you plan to win all of this money playing roulette?"

"I'm good at it. And, I am hoping for a lot of luck."

"But the odds are against you."

"So, help me even the odds."

"How?"

"I don't know."

"What about a system?"

Rapture took another piece of French bread. "I've read about them, but really do not have any ideas."

"Okay. I know an old vice cop that has worked in the city for years. He's retired, and if anyone knows of any system, it's him."

"See, thinking outside the box works."

"I don't know about that," I said. "But I do know I want you to have the best shot at your dream."

"Okay. Where do we start?"

"I'll give him a call. His name is Bennett and lives out by the lake." Just then my cell phone vibrated indicating a text message. I looked down and saw the message – Geronimo. It was the code word for danger that Sheri and I used. Oh, oh, I thought; something's going on.

"Looks like you're wanted," Rapture said. "Go ahead, don't worry about me. I've got all this French bread here to keep me company. Go detect or whatever it is that you do."

"Thanks. It will just take a minute. I need to make a call in the bar, if you don't mind. I hate it when people in restaurants talk on the phone." I stood up checking to make sure my phone was still at my side.

Rapture raised her wine glass in agreement. I gave her a wave as I flipped on the cell phone. I left our table and moved into the main part of the dining area, which was next to the entrance. The entire room had a red glow to it, and each table was set in their own, almost private area, for guests to enjoy their meal.

"Fargo, Fargo is that you."

I looked toward the voice and there was Barnes walking toward the bar area.

"Barnes," I said in shock.

"Nice to see you Fargo. Thought I would grab some dinner.

Someone at the hotel recommended this place and I thought I would try it out. So, are you out for the evening?"

"Ahaaaa, yes. You said someone at the hotel recommended this place? They usually recommend the Strip restaurants. I thought you had a condo here in Vegas."

"You're right. I do have a condo. But I get tired eating alone. I love Italian and I really like pizza. Have it delivered all the time. But I was at Treasure Island and thought I would ask. I wanted something out of the way where the crowds don't go. So, here I am. Are you here with a group?" He looked over my shoulder as he settled into one of the small tables located in the bar area.

A very youthful and fit looking waitress approached us and asked for our drinks. She probably went to UNLV that was just down the street, and ran ten miles a day. If you want to feel old, hang around a campus.

"I'll have a Scotch, straight up," Barnes said. "Fargo, anything for you? Or your group?" He again looked over my shoulder.

"No, no thanks. I already have a drink." I'm thinking fast. I'm here with Rapture I didn't want Barnes and Rapture to get chummy. Rapture was my client and I try to provide privacy for all my clients. There was no reason for them to know each other. Why was Barnes here? Did Barnes follow me? What was going on here? I had an uncomfortable feeling that I was being followed. I would have to address this, but this wasn't the place. I was plotting ahead, thinking, projecting consequences, calculating, trying to run ahead of the pack.

"Listen, normally I would invite you to join us, but tonight is kind of special, if you know what I mean?"

"Oh, hey no problem. I don't mean to intrude. No problem. I eat alone all the time."

"In fact I need to get back to my table."

"Go ahead. You don't want a pretty woman sitting alone in this place."

"Yeah, yeah you're right." I wonder if he saw Rapture, I thought.

At that moment, Sheri walked in. Can this get more complicated?

"Sheri," I said surprised. Now this was a bold move. Who's following who?

Sheri reacted as if surprised. "She leaned over and gave me a kiss on the cheek. Under her breath she whispered, "I'm here to save you, Boss."

Sheri then turned toward Barnes who stood up. Sheri extended her hand in a greeting of hello. I got the better deal on that one.

"I decided to treat myself to dinner tonight," Sheri said.

"I need to get back to my table. Sheri, Barnes is also eating alone. Why don't you join him for dinner? The two of you can exchange information."

"Or maybe just stare at each other," Sheri said, reminding everyone of their first encounter.

"Oh my, I don't want to impose on you. Please, don't worry about me." Barnes was somewhat uneasy. The mood had changed. Now it was him who was being controlled.

"Hey, why not," Sheri said. "Maybe I can find out about the Treasury Department. Maybe they can use someone like me."

"Listen, I've got to get back. You two work it out, and I'll see you in the morning." I reached over to shake Barnes' hand and he reluctantly grabbed my hand giving the impression he had been somewhat defeated, or at least outflanked. I then gave Sheri a kiss on the cheek. She didn't say anything, but I noticed just the hint of a smile. Just a little. I knew I would never hear the end of it. Somehow this was going to cost me.

"Thanks. Nice seeing you, Barnes." I gave Sheri a squeeze on the shoulder and left.

Then I turned and went back. I had to address this issue with Barnes. I didn't like being followed. Barnes and Sheri were sort of staring at each other. "Say Barnes, I need to talk with you about something. How about meeting me for breakfast tomorrow morning?"

"Sure, name the spot and time."

"How about the Angel Park course, say about nine a.m.?"

"Sounds good. I can find it. I live close to there."

"Want me to pick you up?"

"No, I'll see you there."

"See you then." I left and headed for the hostess area.

"Listen, Sally, the two singles in the bar have just joined up. One of them is Sheri. I need a big favor. Make sure they're in a different part of the restaurant. I don't want them close to my table." I pressed a hundred-dollar bill in her hand. Their dinners are on me; the rest is yours.

"This really isn't necessary. I'll take care of you," Sally said.

"I'm in the green room, around the corner."

"Consider it done."

I quickly made my way back to Rapture who had just started on her salad.

"Is everything okay? You looked so stressed when the message came through."

"Thank you for asking. Yes, everything's okay. I get a lot of interruptions in my line of work. And I'm looking forward to dinner with you even more. How's the salad?"

"It's on my list as the best of the best," smiled Rapture.

Chapter Twenty-Seven

I SAT BACK AND WATCHED the golfers on the undulating course as I waited for Barnes to finish his phone call. He had received a phone call shortly after ordering breakfast, and had gotten up and moved to the side to have some privacy.

The Angel Park clubhouse overlooked the splendor of the eighteenth hole as it followed a slightly bending dogleg path to end up with an elevated green surrounded by four massive traps and an inviting looking pond. Thursday mornings were always busy as people tried to beat the heat and the crowds of weekend golfers. It was man made and truly beautiful. I thought about last night's dinner at Carluccio's and my meeting with Sheri afterwards. I had to smile when Sheri made her announcement about Coyote.

"Boss, I lost her."

"It happens."

"Not to me, it shouldn't. I was waiting for her arrival and she just walked out."

"Sometimes it's better to let them get away and pick them up later, rather than blow your cover. Besides, as it turned out, I needed you to be at Carluccio's and that turned out to be very important."

"Thanks."

"You going into the Treasury Department?"

"Not in a hundred-million years. No freedom, too many bosses. It sounded like they have Barnes on a leash. I just can't see myself working that way. I had enough of that in the Coast Guard. I like the private sector."

"How was Barnes?"

"You owe me big time, Boss."

"Yeah, you're right. I owe you."

"I can hardly wait to settle up. I'm getting closer to being your partner everyday."

I ignored her completely. "So tell me, what happened?"

"You're ignoring me, Boss."

"Yep, I am."

"Okay then, I was sitting in the parking lot flustered about losing Coyote, and a car engine started about twenty feet in front of me, turned on its lights and moved up the aisle toward a parking spot. I almost fell over when Barnes got out. That's why I couldn't give you much warning."

"Were you compromised? If I remember right, I nodded toward you as I walked around the car, all so briefly, however.

"We'll never know for sure, Boss. But I don't think so. You were on the opposite side. After I spotted him when he got out he never looked toward my direction. But he is a trained agent."

"What happened with you and Barnes?"

"Nothing. We talked about his role at the Treasury Department, but he was edgy all evening."

"What happened after I left the bar?"

"We were seated in about fifteen minutes and he didn't like it. He ended up with his back to everyone so he couldn't see people coming and going. Man was he edgy about that. He couldn't see a thing. Sally orchestrated the whole thing. Told Barnes that there was a draft in the seat he wanted, and I would be more comfortable with my back to the wall."

"That was a smart move on Sally's part. I noticed the same thing when I had that first early meeting with him in the buffet at Pirate's Cove. He really likes to watch who's around him."

"Right. I know he wanted to see who you were with. He even asked me, and I told him I never asked, wasn't my business, and that you and Abby were a thing. How is Abby by the way?"

That was Sheri's way of asking me how the evening with Rapture went. "Just fine. Just fine. How is your lawyer friend?"

"Touché. Very good, Boss. Very good. Anyway, if he was tailing you, then he already knows you were with Rapture. Depends upon when he picked you up. But he just couldn't get up and go see, as it would have been too obvious. Sally was pretty firm as to what was available. And thanks for dinner."

"My pleasure."

"By the way, after you left, and after you kissed me good bye, Barnes made a remark about how friendly we are."

"Oh?"

"Yeah."

"What did he say?"

"He asked if we get it on?"

"So how did you reply?"

"I kicked him!"

"You kicked him?"

"Yep, I nailed him under the table. Got his leg. Good thing he wasn't sitting any closer. Then I said I was sorry. It was an accident. I think he got the message."

"You kicked him?" I said again in disbelief.

"He'll be okay."

What a dinner that must have been. Sheri and I ended the conversation and I thought about the unfolding case. It was getting more complex. Sometimes being a detective is a lot of waiting. You put a list together, and you start checking off the boxes. Then you add more boxes and keep checking. Sometimes a box leads back to another box, and you start all over again. It's all that police training. It's very procedural, but it works and it's necessary so that every detail no matter how small is covered. This is particularly true with the forensic guys who see a crime scene through a different set of eyes than regular people.

"Must have been day dreaming there, Fargo. You looked like you were on a desert island, with no problems," Barnes said, returning to the table.

"Sometimes I wish I was. Life would be a lot simpler."

"Fargo, I really didn't mean to bust in on you last night," he said sitting down.

Just at that moment our breakfast was served. The basics. I had scrambled eggs, hash browns, sourdough toast, and bacon. Barnes went with biscuits and gravy, a side order of bacon, and a side order of hash browns. Coffee had already been served.

Barnes dug right in after our waitress had disappeared. "I mean of all restaurants in this town, I had to pick that one. And thanks for picking up the tab."

"No problem. I hear you had an interesting dinner."

"Well, it sort of started out as a staring contest. But I would of lost that..."

I laughed out loud.

"What's so funny?" asked Barnes.

"Everybody loses against Sheri."

"I could have guessed that. We just used the time to exchange info. You've got a pretty smart partner there."

"She said I was her partner?"

"Nope. Sheri said she wanted to be your partner."

"Yeah. I know. I hear about it every day. So tell me, how is your case here going? How long do you expect to be in town?"

"Forever it seems like. That's why they call us field agents. We live on the road."

"It can be good and bad. It's what you make of it."

"As far as the case is concerned, we're still tracking the subject. Waiting to see what turns up."

I took another sip of my Bloody Mary. "Frustrating I'm sure. Why can't a local guy handle this instead of pulling you out of D.C.?"

A foursome just walked off the green after shaking hands. In the distance another golfer stood ready to take his shot. Dressed all in white he stood out from the lush green foliage. Lawrence of Golf was ready to take his shot.

"It's how the Agency is set up. We are assigned based upon the operation profile, not by geography. Besides, the local guy is known, and I'm not." Barnes studied the golfers and sipped on some coffee. "Do you think that guy can hit the green," Barnes said, as he motioned to the lone figure dressed in white.

I looked at the golfer in white. "Well, let's see. If he did get there in one, he's a long hitter. If he was there in two he probably would be in the fairway even if he was a slicer. At least on the edge. I would say that Lawrence there, that's what we'll call him, is going to go for it. A long hitter can't, or someone who thinks he is a long hitter, just can't play it short and safe. So I would say he is going long, but will end up in the pond. How about you?"

"Boy are you analytical. You should have a check up. But, I would say you're right. But he'll play the shot to the far right and end up on the edge of the green."

"I agree. But overcorrecting actually increases the chances of a slice. It's the pond for sure."

"Bet?"

"You're on. Breakfast. We'll call it a fifty."

As we talked Lawrence went through the process of lining up his shot. It was obvious he had some training. First he approached the ball from in back of it, and studied its proposed flight. Looked like a pro so far. He stepped up to the ball and did some practice swings. After a moment of concentration, he took the swing. We had a perfect view as the ball exploded off of the club and started out to the golfer's left, and then started to slice to the right. It hit the green, took one bounce and ended up in the pond.

Barnes got up smiling. He took a fifty out of his pocket and it floated onto the table. "Fargo, I'll give you ten-to-one odds that Lawrence there has never seen the left side of this course. Nice call. Thanks for the invite. No hard feelings. I've got to run."

I gave him a thumbs up. "No, it's me who must thank you for breakfast. I'll catch up to you later."

Barnes left and I took the fifty and put it in my shirt pocket, and sat back adjusting my sunglasses. Lawrence's group by this time had made their way to the green. The man in white saw me sitting on the balcony and gave me a wave. In Las Vegas, one of the first things you have to do is to hedge your bet. Lawrence was a long time friend that I often played golf with who wanted to go pro. His slice kept him off of the tour.

I picked up my cell phone and dialed Abby.

"This is Abby."

"He's on his way out. Did you get the job done?"

"One black box under left fender. He's just pulling out."

"Good job, Abby. I'll see you tonight."

"Deal."

I hung up the phone, and smiled. I would be able to track his car either in my BMW or Sheri's Lexus. Just another hedge in Sin City.

Chapter Twenty-Eight

WE WERE ALL SEATED AT THE ROULETTE WHEEL. Rapture sat closest to the wheel, Uncle Leo was sitting next to her and next to him was an empty seat for Coyote. Abby, who had Thursday night off, sat at the end, and I sat on her right facing Rapture, Uncle Leo and the empty Coyote chair. We were at Bennett's house, located near Lake Mead off of Lakeshore Drive. This was a magnificent house located high up on the Las Vegas side of the lake that offered a spectacular view of the city at night, with easy access to the lake by day.

Sheri was following Barnes at a distance thanks to the bug Abby had planted while Barnes and I had breakfast at Angel Park. The bug would let her stay well behind Barnes. Hopefully, Barnes wouldn't get any ideas if he drove past the Spy Shop on Tropicana to stop and scan his car for bugs.

We were planning our attack on the casino very carefully. Abby and Uncle Leo were going to act as shills so we wouldn't have any strangers in the game when we hit Treasure Island. Besides, it was always nice to have your attorney with you as a witness.

Bennett was a collector of gambling equipment and tables. He had a full size roulette wheel, plus blackjack, craps, pai gow poker and traditional poker tables. He even had a table for baccarat, which was my favorite game. Bennett was the father of Officer Bennett who had stopped me for a ticket. After retiring from the force he became engrossed in systems play, and spent his time running systems via computers and actual table play on the various games. He was also looking for ways to spot the table cheats that proliferated the casinos, and as a consequence, consulted with some of these casinos. Bennett even had overhead hidden video cameras set up the same way casinos do so that play could be evaluated. This was Bennett's way of keeping active during his retirement years. Most people stop living when they retire, but it was clear that Bennett was as active as ever.

We were casually dressed and ready for the long evening. Bennett had an odd request. He said that in order to sit at the wheel everyone had to wear a baseball cap of some sort. So there we were all having a great time each wearing a different cap. His reasoning was to lighten up the group a bit so we wouldn't be so nervous. It took the edge off and was a clever way to bring everyone together. Rapture sported an NYPD cap while Uncle Leo wore a UNLV cap to support his alma mater, the University of Nevada Las Vegas. Abby wore a black cap that said "Topless or Bust." Show girl humor at its best. I sported a khaki Makarov cap. Nice, small dependable handgun.

We had just finished a meal and were enjoying the view that overlooked Las Vegas. This magnificent site was worth the long drive to Bennett's house. I had made a deal with Bennett that we would bring dinner and he would teach us about roulette. On the way out I stopped at Metro Pizza on Tropicana near UNLV. It was one of my favorite pizza hangouts. Top of the line pizzas and something for everyone. Abby and I had spent more then one evening in the bar with a bottle of wine, a salad and one of our favorite pizzas.

"So, you're here to lose," Bennett said.

"No, we're here to win," Rapture responded.

"Lesson number one. Everyone, over a period of time, loses in Las Vegas. Everyone. The casinos have the advantage of time. The longer you gamble the more it increases the odds you will lose your money."

We all nodded in agreement. Caps were bobbing.

"So, based on lesson number one, what is the best bet in the house?"

We all had moved into the classic teacher/student roles and kind of looked at each other. Abby took a shot at it. "I say it's the crap table. I've been told that if you take odds, you can get an advantage."

"True, very good. But even then, with an odds bet, they still have an advantage. They will beat you in the long run. Even in blackjack the house will have some advantage. If you count cards, you can lower and sometimes get a small advantage in certain situations. But counting takes work. And if they catch you, you're out of there. But it still isn't the answer to the question."

We all looked at each other for a while. "We give up," I finally said.

"The best bet in the house is one bet on any game."

"One bet?"

"Yes. One bet. And the reason is that you give the casino only one shot at your money. With one bet, if you win, you turn and walk. If you lose, you turn and walk. It means the casinos can't take any more money from you."

"Okay. That makes some sense," I said. "But people travel thousands of miles to get here. They're not going to make one bet."

"Right, so it's even more of a reason why the casinos have an advantage. In fact, what casinos want to happen is for you to arrive, play a little at your favorite game and win. Preferably they want you to win big on the first day. Then you will spend the rest of your trip playing with the hope of another win because you think you're up. You're a winner. And what happens is, you lose. You make dumb decisions. You play games you don't know, move to a larger betting unit, or make long-shot bets to impress the crowd. And when you start to lose, you play even more so you can catch up because in your mind you're a winner. And you continue to chase your money until you go home."

"Broke." Abby said.

"Right, most people go home broke. But they go home feeling like a winner. They won big, and then they chased it. They get their meals comped, a free show, maybe a free room. But they go home thinking they're winners, but they're broke."

"So, what is the best way for me to make some money?" asked Abby.

"Invest. That's my recommendation," said Bennett.

"He ought to meet Sheri," Uncle Leo said, which sparked some laughter.

I explained that Sheri was invested better than anyone of us.

"She even wins in down markets," Uncle Leo said, shaking his head.

"But you're here to win at roulette. Right?"

"Right," we all mumbled.

"Rapture is here to make a killing at the game," I said. "As I explained, it's complicated but it's part of a plan. We need to get the very best opportunity to win a large sum of money. But we need to do it legally. That's why we're here."

"Okay. Lesson number two, and the only one you really need to know. Roulette wheels have no memory but will favor a certain part of the wheel."

"Who was the first one to figure that out?" Uncle Leo asked.

"Actually it was a British engineer at the end of the last century. He and six colleagues tracked a wheel at Monte Carlo, and then took them for a sizable sum of money."

"But everyone knows about it, right?"

"True. Even though the state gaming board comes through and balances the wheel, a wheel can easily go out of balance. It doesn't take much, just a little bit will create a situation where one part of the wheel is favored."

"So, what's the first step?"

"First we identify the part of the wheel that is being favored."

"How do we do that?" Abby asked.

"We establish a counter. Someone who stakes out a wheel and records every spin for at least two days."

"Impossible," Rapture said.

"Not really. I can have that done," I said.

"How? That's just not feasible," Rapture said.

"No, I can take care of that. Once I get all the details I will make the necessary contact."

"Who might that be?" asked Rapture.

"Uncle Leo shot me a look and I got the message. No one knew about Bobby Lawrence being an undercover at Treasure Island, I thought. My ace in the hole is going to come through big time. It's best sometimes not to have all your cards on the table. "I'd rather not say. But I will say, dependable, reliable, concise and loyal. I'll have the information when we need it."

Rapture nodded in an understanding way. "But, isn't keeping track of the wheel illegal?" asked Rapture.

"Good question," Bennett said. And the answer is yes, and no. Casinos welcome system players and you can sit there all day and record numbers. What they don't want is you using a computer during the play to project a winning number."

"You mean someone has tried that?" Abby said.

"Yes, in spades. They've brought in disguised computers, and they've brought in links to computers. Almost everything has been tried."

"I bet it's getting harder with all of these smaller computers and communication devices."

"Yes. It's very difficult for the casino."

"What's the next step?" I asked.

"We're looking for patterns. The big money is of course a single number, which pays thirty-five to one. That certainly is important. But we also have patterns such as red and black, odd or even, high numbers or low numbers, first, second or third dozen and rows. There are also adjacent number considerations, meaning numbers that are adjacent on the wheel. By recording numbers we should be able to determine a pattern. Since we also are trying to determine the part of the wheel that is being favored, we eventually can come down to a group of five to seven numbers that are red and odd in a certain part of the wheel. Then you bet and cross your fingers."

"This isn't going to be easy is it?" I said to no one and to everyone.

"Nope. If it were easy then everyone would be doing it. The tendency is for people to try to cheat and beat the house, and that in the long run, will get you in all kinds of trouble."

"But what about copying down all of those numbers?" Abby asked.

"It's like the ponies," Uncle Leo said. "You can sit there all day long and handicap every angle, but in the end, it's still a horse race. That's why so many roulette games have the numbers flashing in front of everyone as to what were the last twenty or so numbers. As Bennett said, they want the systems players."

"Right."

"So we're basically handicapping a roulette game," I said.

"Exactly."

"So, just out of curiosity, how does one cheat at roulette?" Rapture said.

Bennett picked up the little white ball, gave the wheel a spin, and then spun the ball in the opposite direction. "Being a dealer is an art. If you have done nothing else for twenty years but spin this little white ball, after a while you start to get bored. And what do the dealers do but start to play games with themselves. They say, let's see if I can get the ball to drop in a certain portion of the wheel. I mean, these guys and gals are totally bored, so now they have something to do, something that makes their job a little bit more exciting. And the best part is no one knows they are doing it. It's their secret little game."

"You mean they actually can control where the ball lands."

"Right. An experienced dealer can control the area that the ball hits. Not every time, but consistently enough to make a difference. For example, right now I'm shooting for numbers six, eighteen, thirty-one, nineteen, eight and twelve. So one way to hustle the house is through an inside job with a partner. It's almost impossible to catch and just requires a little luck."

"Is that the only way?" Just then the ball came to rest on number thirty-one.

"Wow," Abby said.

"At thirty-five to one, I would have made a tidy sum. But there are other ways such as last minute bets, blocking the dealers view, chip stealing, magnets. A million ways and new ones everyday."

"It's like picking the horses. It's a science and it comes down to physics," Uncle Leo said.

"Exactly. And if you ever want to test this theory, just go to the Big Six Money Wheel, which is also known as the Wheel of Fortune. They have them in every casino, usually near the entrance where you can easily pull out a few bills and make a quick bet. Ask the dealer spinning the wheel how many years they have been doing it. When you get one that says they have been spinning for twenty years or so, place a bet for you, and another one for the dealer. Ten to one he'll hit it right on the nose."

"Wow," Abby said. Everyone was shaking their heads at Bennett's logic.

"So, what we're going to try is to do it legally, right?" I said.

"Right. The casinos will take the position that anything you do that gives you an advantage is not something they like to see. But it happens all the time. You note a lot of number cards on several hands of

Blackjack, so you reduce your bet until the pack is richer. You're playing slots and you see someone dump a ton of money into a progressive machine that doesn't pay. So you follow their play and play knowing you are closer to a jackpot. You notice no elevens have been thrown for thirty or so rolls of the dice, and even though dice have no memory, you play it because there might be a chance, however small."

"But what about using a computer to analyze the numbers. Isn't that illegal?" asked Uncle Leo.

"During play, yes. But the system player that records the numbers, goes home and runs them through a computer looking for a combination, they can't stop that. But this game is going to be watched carefully with the amount of money being bet. I expect a big crowd, and every pit boss in the place is going to watching our every move."

"So, what's next?" Uncle Leo continued.

"I think we need to determine which wheel and start to record some numbers. Next we have to decide how we'll bet, and when we'll bet."

"What about game limits?" I asked.

"We'll have to make arrangements. We don't want to be in the high roller's part of the casino on the second floor because we can't record numbers there. So we'll need to reserve a table for our action."

"I'll take care of that," I said.

"Before we start to learn the play at the table, let me demonstrate a technique used by the bad guys," Bennett said. "Let's move around a bit. Abby, I'm going to have you spin the wheel and place the ball in the game. So you come around here. Rapture, you slide over and let Uncle Leo be next to the wheel. Can I call you Uncle Leo?"

"Sure, everyone does."

"Including the entire jail population at Metro," I said, creating a lot of laughter.

"Great. I want you to be here," Bennett said pointing to Uncle Leo and motioning to the now vacant place next to Rapture. Rapture, you're the block, so when the ball starts to bounce and find a home, I want you to stand up and lean over to see what number comes up."

"If I was wearing the right outfit, no one would ever see the board," Rapture said.

Bennett smiled. "Right. It's the gambling secret known as cleavage. I'm going to take the place next to Abby. Fargo, you stay where you are."

Everyone moved into place.

"Okay, now let me have a private word with Uncle Leo." Bennett and Uncle Leo moved away from the table. After a very short conversation, they came back and took positions at the end of the table next to Rapture.

"One last thing, the only bet on the table is going to be one chip bets that are scattered around the table. Everyone has chips in front of them so place your bets."

"Okay, everyone ready?" Bennett said. We all nodded.

Abby gave the wheel a spin, as our hearts beat a little bit faster. She then launched the ball in the opposite direction. Everyone waited and eventually the ball dropped. Right on cue Rapture got up to lean over to see the number. Everyone followed her gaze. The ball hit, and then everyone looked at the board to see where the number was located. To their surprise, there was a huge stack of chips sitting there.

"Unbelievable," I said.

"But true," Rapture said, finishing my thought.

"How did you do that?" Abby asked.

"It's all about misdirection. Uncle Leo signaled me what the number was, and when Rapture leaned over she acted as a block, preventing the dealer from seeing me. Then I leaned over and moved a pile of chips onto the number."

"Wow, so that's how it's done," Abby said.

"One more time," Abby said. They did it again, and again the chips magically appeared in the selected square.

Bennett then moved over to a monitor and rolled back a tape. From three different views we watched the last two spins of the wheel and how Bennett slid over the chips under the concealment of Rapture while Uncle Leo gave the signals on where the ball had landed. It was an impressive demonstration of talent.

"Okay, now we can get down to business. I have recorded twenty-four hours of spins on this wheel. I was working the numbers before you arrived and it looks like we have a wheel that is favoring the numbers between twenty-four and eight. It also looks like we have more blacks coming up than reds, and more odds than evens. It also looks like the wheel is favoring the top half of the board. That means we have narrowed the numbers down to these three."

Bennett masterly laid out the approach and started to coach Rapture in making the combination of bets needed to win.

As I looked on I thought of the risk of the play that Rapture was making. To win would mean to win the map, and winning that map would take her to the treasure she wanted to find for her father. I was there to help. I'd promised myself I would find J.T.'s killer, the person who made Rapture's life spin in a new direction. A promise is a promise, I thought. A promise is also a dream and a measure of a man.

Chapter Twenty-Nine

I FOCUSED MY EYES ON THE TOTE BOARD at the Sports Bar in Treasure Island. It was just after noon on Friday. I had arrived about ten minutes ago, ordered a draft beer, and was taking a few minutes to relax. I was going to place a call to Sheri but casinos did not allow you to use cell phones if you were betting the ponies. People did, but sometimes they were asked to stop. Never know when they had somebody with inside information at the track, and were phoning it in.

Even though Uncle Leo was the real sports bettor of our office, I never resisted a chance to sit back and watch a few ponies run. I had been watching the horses being led out to the track and noticed that the number one rated horse threw his head back twice. I thought of what a trainer watches for after he takes the bandages off a horse's legs, and has the groom put a shank on him, taking him out for a cold jog. If the horse is lame in front, then his head pops up when he walks. This is called nodding off. If he is lame on his rear legs, his head will be pulled down when the sore leg hits the ground.

It appeared to me that the favorite showed a twinge of being lame in the front legs. But usually a horse is warmed and ready to run by the time it hits the track. When they're warmed up, the horse will not be nodding.

I watched the board and did not see any of the numbers change. Reasonably sure what I had saw, I moved up closer to place a bet in the last few minutes before betting was closed. I was able to get a bet down on the second rated horse with a minute to spare. I watched and saw no stable money hitting the board. I sat back and enjoyed a hell of a horse race. The number one favorite broke clean from the start and set the pace all the way through the backstretch, and the number two favorite kept the pace and was always challenging for the lead. Sure enough, as I expected, the favorite pulled up lame as they were coming out of the turn toward home. The second won cleanly, and paid $3.60 to win. My twenty-dollar wager netted thirty-six dollars and life was good once again. There's nothing like walking out of a casino a winner.

"Pocketing some pretty good cash there, Fargo."

I looked up to see Bobby Lawrence swagger up to the bar and sit down. "All in a day's work in Vegas," I said. "How's Treasure Island?"

"Hopping," said Bobby, as he signaled for a beer. I took a look at the tapes and there is nothing that is going to tie us to the perp. We got one guy though, room 6380, two doors down from you. We don't have him on tape anywhere, and the casino is looking. Could be who you're looking for."

"Any other way off the floor?"

"You can take the stairway. If you know the hotel layout, you can make it to the street without too much of a problem. Play the tourist who drank too much and work your way through the maze and out the side entrance. You can also go down to the third floor, find your way into the new wing, and then exit into the casino, or take the stairway to the basement and head for the street."

"No cameras on those, I suspect?"

"Nope, there are only ones in the main part of the casino. None on individual floors or in the elevators."

"Got a name on this unknown?"

"Ted Smith."

"Sounds about as phony as it comes."

"No doubt. Paid cash for two nights. He refused to have a credit card on his account."

"I thought all hotels needed to have credit cards these days?"

"Sometimes they let them in. A story always goes with it. Wallet just ripped off and his cards are frozen until he can find out if they have been used. Hotel will deactivate the pay-for-view television stations so that no room charges can be applied."

"Okay. Well, it would be nice to get some in depth info on this guy?"

"I'll do what I can," said Bobby, taking a sip of his beer.

"Thanks."

"Hey, the police are doing a walk through 'show and tell' of the murder room. Interested in attending? In about fifteen minutes."

"Count me in."

"Good."

"Also, I've got another assignment for you."

"Keep them coming."

"Roulette, know the game?"

"Yeah, spin the ball and lose your money."

"That's the one. It's like this. This Saturday night I gotta hit the table for six million."

"Huh?"

"You heard me."

"Yeah, right. I heard you. And I got an uncle who thinks he's

Darth Vader, but that does not make me a space cadet."

I looked at Bobby, and he looked at me, shrugged his shoulders, caught the bartender's eye and ordered two more drafts. "Well, count me in for a million," Bobby said with a smile.

"Here's what I want you to do. There are three tables we have targeted. I want you to run a number check on all three wheels. At least three-hundred numbers for each wheel. More if you can."

"You're kidding?"

"Nope. This is serious business."

Bobby laughed out loud. "And you're going to take this information and beat the wheel. You're going to beat Las Vegas? This town is crazy when the locals start to dream the dream of dice, cards, naked woman and a streak of luck," laughed Bobby.

"Hey, that's my life you're talking about."

Bobby held up both hands to stop me. "Hey, I got no problems about your dreams. Go baby go. That's my motto."

I shook my head thinking that Bobby was probably more realistic then I was.

"How long have you been in town Fargo? You got a math degree and are going to find a trend and bet the hell out of the trend and win? You got to be kidding? You'll be taken to the cleaners for a bundle. You'll have the worst rep of any dick in town. I might have to stop hanging with you. Don't wanna ruin my rep...know what I mean?"

"I got the picture, but that's the plan."

"Man, you gotta take a vacation. This is professional suicide."

"Just a long shot. Part of the case I'm working on."

"Ya know, I got some pull over at Mandalay Bay. They have a

high roller suite there that's about five thousand square feet. It's beautiful, all done in warm colors with multiple levels and four bedrooms. Plush carpet, oriental rugs and hardwood floors. Walk in steam room, shower for about twenty people, all the food you want, anything at any time, the best view, pool table, Jacuzzi, fireplace and everything that goes with it. They even have a butler to take care of you. I can get you off the street and you can take it easy. Get your senses back."

"I'll pass, although it sounds tempting."

"So, next you're going to ask me to rig the wheel. I don't do that, Fargo. Ole Thumbs Louie is going to dig me a grave in the wide open places...know what I mean?"

"Just count the spins, record the numbers, plus the reds and the blacks. Looking for variation. Any slight variation will do. I also want it watched between nine and eleven in the evening. One more thing. Watch the dealers. See if you can pick out the dealer who has been at it the longest. Has a set routine. He glances at the wheel when he spins. Those are the ones I'm looking for."

"It's true then? A dealer can spin the ball to a certain part of the roulette wheel?"

"It's been rumored that after several million spins the dealer has a certain amount of control over the results. Very small, but it's a factor."

"You didn't tell the casino did you?" asked Bobby, looking over his shoulder.

"They're going to know all about it."

Bobby's shoulders slumped. "Man, this is really bad. I hope you don't mention my name. I got enough people interested in my bod with out having to have Treasure Island upset."

"You'll be fine. I'm sure you'll only get a couple of years if...."

"What...?"

"Nah...just playing with ya...."

"You know, Fargo, you're playing detective just a little bit on the wrong side of the spinning wheel."

"Yeah, kind of makes it more fun."

Detective Morton and two other detectives appeared along with Gil from Security.

We both stood up and shook hands all around.

"Hi Fargo, glad you could make it," said Gil, smiling.

"Always like a good mystery," I said. Morton and his cronies did not smile.

"Fargo, this is Baker and Smith. New to the department since you were there. They're along for the ride, and they both know I always spring for coffee."

We shook hands and were off to a good start. Bobby and I finished our beer and we all headed toward the elevator.

"He never buys coffee," said Baker, the taller of the two. I could tell by looking at his dark blue eyes he'd seen a lot of crime in his days on the force. They all get that hardened weathered 'I can't believe anybody would do that' kind of look. It's why I got out of the force.

"Bought me one yesterday," said Smith, as we all entered the elevator and punched the button for the sixth floor. Baker gave Smith a quick look. "Just kidding," said Smith.

We arrived at the sixth floor, the doors slid open and we headed toward the crime scene. The room was still taped on the outside. Gil opened the door and we kind of slid under the tape. The guard was no longer in sight. I closed the door and we all stared at the lock.

"So," said Morton, ignoring Baker and Smith, "when you were outside, the deadbolt was opened by security, and the metal arm was down preventing entry."

We all stared at the metal arm, which had been ripped from the door and was hanging by one lose screw.

"Right, I said. I used a metal mirror to peer inside the room. I could see the body sprawled over there." We all turned and looked at the outline of the body at the end of one of the couches.

"So you then popped open the door?" asked Morton.

"Right," I said. "I followed the security guard into the room. I cleared the bathroom, we examined the body quickly before checking out the rest of the suite."

"Going back to the metal bar lock," said Smith. "You're sure that it was connected?"

"Oh yeah," I said. "Take a closer look at the bar." We moved forward and examined the metal arm latch. "Note that it's still connected to the rack that is attached to the molding of the door. The bar did not give, but the screws were still attaching the rack to the molding. It took a pretty good pop to get it open."

"The killer never came out through this door, and never exited via my room, which is right next door."

We moved over and examined the door connecting to my room. "Everybody agrees that this could have not been an exit point," said Morton. "Fargo was inside, and checked this door when he and Tony entered."

"The glass curtain wall is out, so that only leaves the connecting door from the second bedroom," said Gil. We've been through this process a few times. All the exits are locked."

"Yeah, but you want to clear this room of the crime scene, and we've got to make one last check so I can sign it off," Morton said.

"I know. The powers that be want to clean up this room and get it back into circulation," Gil said.

We wandered through the suite and I watched closely as Baker routinely swept the room with his eyes. There was a good bet that he could have given you an inventory of the entire room. We went through the process of examining the locked connecting door, and it was explained that four people could swear that it was locked from the other side, and also the front door to the connecting room was locked.

"What you're telling me is that there was no way for the perp to get out of this room after he murdered the victim. Is that right?" asked Baker.

Gil said, "That's why we're having this party. Nobody knows how he got out of this suite. Fargo here was in the hallway seconds after the bullet slammed into his room. He was here when my two security guards showed up. How long Fargo?"

"About fifteen seconds after I got into the hallway," I said.

"And you saw nobody else in the hallway?" asked Baker.

"Nope. Some heads sticking out, and I talked to one person. He was basically asleep."

Baker turned to Gil. "Has he been ruled out? The person down the hall from Fargo's room?"

"No, not yet. We're looking at him. Checked in, paid cash, no credit cards. Fargo saw him."

Barker turned and looked at the suite. "Boy, there has to be a key to this someplace. Locked rooms can always be opened."

I spun around and studied Baker, but said nothing.

Chapter Thirty

I WAS JUST DRIVING OUT OF TREASURE ISLAND when my cell phone rang. A lot was happening and I was anxious to get back to my office for my Friday afternoon shot at the paperwork. I also needed to coordinate our gambling session for tomorrow evening at Treasure Island.

"Fargo here."

"Fargo," said Sheri. "I'm sitting on Coyote in front of a magazine store off Sahara. Right next to the old Smith's."

"I know it," I replied as I started to change lanes moving my way to the right so I could get to the Strip and head toward Sahara. "What's going on?"

"Not sure. I followed Coyote from the Venetian and I expected her to turn into Treasure Island, but she continued. Right after I got here, another car pulled in just outside the shop where she is. I thought for sure that the driver put some glass on Coyote in the store."

"Where are you parked?"

"I'm well in the back of the parking lot."

I turned onto the Strip and headed toward Sahara. "What exit do you think she will leave by?"

"She pulled in off of Sahara and is parked past Smith's facing out toward Maryland. If she is going to head back toward her hotel, she might go down Maryland, or turn right on Maryland and then a left back onto Sahara. She could also take a right on Sahara."

"I spun a quick right on Sahara and knew I was not far from Sahara

Towne Square. "She's going to be going down Sahara I would expect. It's too hard to make a left out of the Smith's complex onto Maryland." I flew past the parking area for the Sahara Hotel and was gaining. I eventually crossed Maryland. "What's happening to the follow car?"

"He's just sitting there. I got the plate numbers but it's a rental."

I pulled into Smith's and hung an immediate right and worked my way around the backside of the lot. I spotted Sheri right away, and she was well back of our target car in front of the magazine store. "Wonder why Coyote would go to this store?" I asked Sheri.

"Don't know. But it struck me as unusual. She pulled right to a stop, so I expect she has been here before. She knew where she was going. Here she comes."

"I got her," I said. I put some glass on her and sure enough, there was Coyote walking toward a slick looking white jag. "Nice wheels."

"She doesn't appear to be worried about money," Sheri said. "You should see her shop. She must own a bank."

"Must be nice."

"So, what's the plan?"

"You stay with Coyote and I'll watch our suspect car."

"Want me in front of the suspect car or behind it."

"Let nature take its course."

"Got a start up on the suspect vehicle."

"Buckle up," I said, strapping my own seatbelt around me more securely. I reached over and pulled open my glove compartment. My two 9mm Glocks fell into view. I left the door open since they were both holstered into the glove box, and I could reach over and pull them out if I had to leave the car early. Both Glocks had a round chambered.

Coyote placed two small bags in the trunk of her Jag, and then opened the driver's door. She stopped, turned and looked toward Smith's, and then entered her own car and closed the door. "I think she is thinking about some shopping," I said to Sheri. "Roll past her and take a right on Sahara. See if you can set up a front tale on her. Keep your face away from the follow car."

"Gotcha," and I watched Sheri move across the parking lot take a left and drive in the lane closest to the strip mall. She was just about to where Smith's complex started when Coyote started to move. She swung out into the parking lot and made a small U-turn and entered the same lane Sheri was in. "I see her, Boss," said Sheri.

"Go right. She's going to go right. Too hard to make a left."

Sheri took a right and fell into traffic. She had timed it so that when Coyote arrived at the driveway, there was also room for her to enter the flow of traffic. Right on cue, Coyote turned right. I returned my gaze to the follow car, and it backed up slowly and moved into the lane next to Smith's following the path of Sheri and Coyote. "I'm going to be right behind you, Sheri. Follow car is making a move on Coyote."

"Wonder who it is."

"Don't know." I watched as the follow car crossed the front of Smith's, and then inched toward Sahara. Another car was trying to cross in front of the follow car, but this was a cool customer in the follow car, as it sat politely and waited for the car to pass. It then moved up to Sahara, watched the traffic and entered the right hand lane following the white jag. I then made my move, as I did not want to get behind the follow car until it was out of site. I turned onto Maryland, taking a right, got lucky, moved right up to Sahara and turned right again. I was immediately able to spot the follow car and the Jag. The handless cell phone mic came in handy. I could drive and talk at the same time. "Sheri, how ya doing? I'm eight cars back."

"We're working our way down Sahara. We've got Bruce Avenue coming up. I wonder what kind of store she's hunting for?"

"Who knows."

"What's important here?" asked Sheri.

"What?" I said, wondering what Sheri was thinking.

"Well, is it important to know where Coyote is going, or who the follow car is?"

Sheri was like that, always cutting to the point of what we we're doing? "To find out who the follow car is" I said. "Coyote is a mystery, but we have no idea who is in the follow car."

"Exactly," said Sheri. "So storm the castle and let's see what happens."

Okay, I thought to myself. Sheri once again solved all the problems and put things into perspective. The longer we followed the follow car, the sooner we would be spotted and the follow car would break off the tail. "Okay, I got the idea," I said to Sheri. I tightened the seat belt just a bit, glanced at my two Glocks, and moved up closer to the follow car.

"I'm going for it," I said to Sheri.

"Listen," said Sheri, "If we want to lose the Jag what about if I pull closer and snap a couple of photographs as he drives by."

"Okay, give it a try." I used this time to move up to within striking distance of the follow car. We proceeded down Sahara for about two minutes.

"I'm parked," said Sheri. "Give me seven seconds and I'm set."

"Okay," I said. I counted off the seconds as I moved slowly up on the follow car. When I hit seven, I moved up within three inches of the follow car, honked my horn. I wanted him to think I was a tailgater. I could see mirrored sunglasses looking in the rear view mirror. We flew by Sheri and she panned on the follow car. I knew she used a pro Nikon 5 with motor. She probably got fifteen pictures of the driver. I watched the rearview mirror of the driver, and he kept looking at me and watching the traffic in front of him. He jerked his head to the left. I looked to the left, than looked back, and he had disappeared. He must have turned onto a side street.

I braked hard, but flew by the side street. It was a neat trick. He looked left, and turned right at the same time. I looked left, and then looked back and he was gone. I had traffic right on top of me and had to go another fifty yards before I could pull into a used car lot. I grabbed my cell phone. "He took a right on Bruce Avenue and I can't get to him."

"I'm coming up on Eastern," Sheri said. "Traffic is heavy."

I tried to inch my way into the used car lot looking for an exit onto the side street.

"Want to sell your car? Take it over to Fred?"

I looked up and there was a salesman with the loudest suspenders I have ever seen. Nobody would forget him.

"Yeah, I know they're loud, but nobody forgets Suspender Sam...."

"You're right about that. I want an exit onto Bruce. Kind of in a hurry."

"Can't from here," said the used car salesman. You'll have to back out or go around the building"

"Thanks," I said. I leaned over my car seat to back out. I was looking at two cars behind me. I was trapped.

"Boss, I'm on Eastern approaching East Karen, and there's no sign of him."

"Yeah, he did a good job all right. Really good." I sat there drumming my fingers on the seat looking at used cars. The great ace detective meets Suspender Sam.

Chapter Thirty-One

MY OFFICE HAD A VIEW OF THE COURTYARD and of the fountain. A gentle wind blew through the open windows as I reflected on the last several days. The hot desert sun was sometimes quite forgiving in the late afternoon. I always tried to catch up on my paperwork on Friday afternoons unless I was on an assignment. Sheri came in carrying three Starbucks® Frappuccino's® with caramel and whipped cream. She set them on the desk and plopped down in a chair and sort of curled up in her usual way. Just then Uncle Leo arrived and took a seat next to her.

"Perfect," I said. "That was very thoughtful. Thank you, Sheri."

"So, how's the firm's star detective?" Uncle Leo asked as he reached for a Frappachino.

"I don't know, why don't you ask her?" I replied.

Sheri laughed. "See Boss, you need to make me your partner."

"I know. I know."

Uncle Leo took a sip. "So Fargo, how's it going?"

"This is one complicated case. There are all sorts of twists and turns."

"Well, add this to the pile," Uncle Leo said. "Sheri, tell our detective friend here what you found out."

"I got an e-mail from Metro. There was a man recently killed right on the Strip, and it turns out he was a U.S. Treasury agent named David Holden."

"You're kidding." I picked up the report and read it quickly. "I drove by a scene that struck me as being odd about two days ago. They said the guy was an accountant, according to his business card."

"Does it say what Holden was doing here? Was he involved in any incident?" Uncle Leo asked.

"Nope, the report says he was just out here on vacation," I said.

"A lot of Treasury agents floating around this town," Uncle Leo commented.

"I wonder if Barnes knows him?" I said out loud to no one as I tried to absorb this new information. "He must know him." I pondered this new wrinkle in the case.

"It's a big world and a small world," Uncle Leo said. "I remember walking into a hotel in Hong Kong and meeting some people I knew and hadn't seen in over ten years. There they were, just standing waiting for the elevator."

"There is no such thing as a coincidence."

Both Uncle Leo and Sheri stared at me like I had completely lost it. Uncle Leo shifted in his chair. "What's your point, Fargo?"

"If it's a coincidence, then it needs checking. Sheri, who's your contact at Metro?"

"Routine inquiry. Remember Barnes' partner, the one who was double teaming you at Treasure Island when you met Barnes?"

"Yeah, I remember."

"We were going to run a check on the guy, and that was one of my inquiries."

"Do you think Metro suspects anything?"

"Not the way I asked the question. They're not connecting Treasure Island and this Treasury agent. At least not right now."

"Do you think it's the same guy?"

"Well, if it is the same guy, then that provides a certain slant on this case. If it isn't that guy, it takes on a different twist."

"Okay. We need to find out if it's the same guy," I said. "Sheri, why don't you track this guy Holden down through the coroner's office? Talk to Bernie over there. They'll have a photo. Maybe I can I.D. this guy."

"Sure enough, Boss. When I finish this case you're going to owe me a fortune."

"Thanks."

"I also wonder if this guy was really on vacation," said Uncle Leo.

"Now there are more questions to answer. But we know that Barnes is clean," Sheri said. "He comes up squeaky clean every way I run him through the system."

"I don't know. Something's funny about all of these agents floating around here," I said.

Uncle Leo took a sip of his Frap. "According to Barnes they have quite an operation here. And Barnes being the point man, he should know what's going on."

"That would make some sense. If Barnes is the guy in the open, then it probably means they have some people undercover. And you know Barnes is not going to tell you everything. Someone is going to be in deep cover," Fargo said.

"Possibly six-foot deep," Sheri said.

Uncle Leo and I stared at Sheri who probably had spoken the truth.

"Tomorrow night is the big game. Sheri, I think we need to go a little bit deeper into Barnes. I think we need to do a little snooping."

"I'm with ya, Boss."

Uncle Leo nodded in agreement. We all sipped our Fraps as we thought this through.

"Sheri, do we know where Barnes is staying? I know he lives in Summerlin, but I don't know where." I asked.

"Nope." She looked at her computer monitor and brought up the case notes. "The only thing we have is his unlisted telephone number. He gave it to you when you had the first breakfast meeting."

Uncle Leo got up. "You boys and girls have a good time. I've got a date."

I smiled at Sheri who gave me a wink back. "Have a good time," Sheri yelled after him.

I moved over to Sheri's computer screen and took a look at the notes. "Well, it's possible to get an unlisted number. We'll try to pretext the operator with official business."

"And risk being busted big time," Sheri said.

"You're right. We have to be careful. You hungry?"

"Fargo, you know me. I'm always hungry."

"Okay, why don't you order up Metro Pizza and have it delivered. I think we need to spend some time to prep for this investigation."

"Okay, Boss." She picks up the phone and dials the number. "The usual?" she asked.

"Yep, that'll be fine."

"Right, Boss. I'm on hold...okay, yes, I'd like to place an order... yes...telephone number is..." Sheri read the telephone number. "Right... yes, same location...I would like one...."

I spun around and looked at Sheri who continued talking and

placing the order.

She finished up and put the phone down. "What's up? Why the wild look?"

"What did they ask you?"

"The usual, asked me if I'm at the same address."

"When we were at Carluccio's Barnes said that he loved pizza and had it delivered all of the time."

Sheri sat there with a puzzled look on her face, and then it brightened up. "Fargo, you're a genius."

"Get out Barnes' number and let's find pizza places that deliver in the Summerlin area."

Sheri grabbed the telephone directory and did a look up. "Okay, here we go. There are four of them."

"Let's give it a try."

Sheri hit the dial and handed me the phone.

"Yes, I would like to place an order for delivery...phone number is..." I read the number off and waited. They asked if I was at the same location. "...ah...what do you have listed...yes, that's it...ah wait...I'll have to call you back...thank you."

"We got him on the first try!"

"Fargo, you're something else."

* * *

I turned off the car engine and sat motionless near Barnes' condo. Sheri was with me and we were dressed in all black. Nice enough to hit any of the 'places to be seen bars' on the Strip, but casual enough to do some snooping.

"What's your plan?" asked Sheri.

I had been pondering this thought on the ride out here. It was early Saturday morning and we were both tired. Sheri had met me at my condo at 4:30 and we took my car. It was still dark, but the skies were starting to lighten. We had picked up the beeper on Barnes' car, and it was located in the garage of his house. We were sitting in front of his condo, which the records said was owned by the U.S. Treasury Department. Apparently, they moved their field agents in and out of here when they needed someone in town and didn't want them at a hotel where people could ask questions. It also avoided the intrusion by a hotel maid coming in every day to straighten up.

"To get as much information on Barnes without breaking the law," I said.

"Isn't putting a beeper in Barnes' car illegal?"

"Technically, sort of. Yes. Maybe. Depends."

"Oh, you would be good on the witness stand."

"Which side?"

"My point, exactly."

"But it's done all the time. Police tend to look the other way because we're on their side."

"What about the tree falling in the woods bit?" questioned Sheri.

"I give up. I'm not even going to try and figure that one out."

"Remember the old adage is, if a tree falls in the woods, and there is no one there to hear it, does it make any noise?"

"Are you implying that if we push the law a bit, and there is no one there to catch us, did we really break the law?"

"I didn't say that."

"You should be ashamed of yourself."

"Makes sense. Speaking of Barnes, I've never seen a guy so clean."

"I think he's clean. But I get suspicious when someone is too clean. When I had breakfast with him, he seemed like a good guy. I mean, he seems like a decent guy. I actually kind of like him, and we share a lot in common. But, I'm a homicide detective. It's all I've ever wanted to be, and the first thing I learned was to check and recheck. So, for the sake of Rapture, my client, I'm going to check a little bit deeper. We need to gather some information."

"How?"

"Dumpster diving."

"Garbage archeology."

"Cute."

"Thanks."

"Isn't that also illegal?"

"Yes and no."

"Great."

"Do you want the first-year law student's answer?" I started the car and headed down the block.

"Give me the CliffsNotes® version."

"Basically, it comes down to this -- breaking the law to catch someone else breaking the law doesn't hold up in court as it infringes on the rights of the other, whose rights we are trying to protect by being P.I.'s in the first place. So, as private detectives, we're going to stay within the boundary of the law."

"Come on Fargo, where's your backbone?"

"There are exceptions to the law."

"Way to go, Fargo."

"Basically, make sure that the crime you are trying to catch someone in, is much bigger than the crime you are committing. And God willing and the creek don't rise, you might have a chance as long as the judge was born on the right day with the moon in an A.O.K. position."

"What does that mean?"

Cross your fingers and hope for the best." I turned right and then another right and started back down the backside of the condo, which was used as the service entrance. Each condo had a niche used for their garbage as well as one extra parking space. I came to a stop several feet short of the rear of Barnes' condo and turned off the engine.

"Now what?" Sheri asked.

"Stay here. I'll be gone for about thirty seconds. I need to check for surveillance and alarms." I got out and softly shut the door. I moved parallel to Barnes' unit and using a small flash light was able to identify the security system that included two video cameras covering the back of the house. I climbed back in.

"And...?"

"Basic security. Alarm and two video cameras. We should be okay out here."

"So we wait?"

"Right."

"For what?"

"The garbage truck."

"How do you know it's coming?"

"I called."

"Oh." She slumped down in her seat and was asleep in seconds.

Not exactly a testimonial to proper surveillance techniques, but at least one of us could get some sleep. After what seemed like a long time, a garbage truck pulled right in front of us. I tapped Sheri on the arm and she woke with a start.

"Time to rock n' roll." I got out and moved toward the back. Sheri moved a bit slower as she was stiff from sleeping.

The alley was antiseptic compared to other alleys in the world. A garbage man working the shift by himself jumped down from the passenger side and walked over to the wooden garbage enclosure that was painted to match the adobe colored stucco. He eyed us suspiciously as we leaned against the trunk of the car.

"Morning," I said.

"Morning." He lifted the lid of the enclosure and pulled out three bags and threw them into the back of the garbage truck.

I walked up and flashed my badge. "We're private investigators and would like to lighten your load a bit." I pointed to the three bags.

"Hell man, knock yourself out."

I pulled the garbage bags out of the garbage truck's bin and pulled them over to the back end of my car. I then walked over and slipped the guy a twenty. "For your trouble."

"Hey man, thanks. You can follow me around the neighborhood any day of the week." He started back to the passenger side. "Hey. Why didn't you just take the garbage and leave? Why the truck bit?"

"Makes it legal." I replied.

"Oh, I see."

"Thanks."

"Hey, does that make me a witness?"

"Yep."

"Right on. I've always wanted to be a witness. Name's Doyle. Doyle Townsend." He gave me a wave and jumped up and moved down to the next condo.

I lifted the trunk lid and took out several very large plastic bags with cinch ties and loaded the garbage into them, since it was already starting to stink. We double bagged them and threw them into the trunk.

"What's next, Boss?"

"The next part is trickier."

I pulled out a small rubber ball about ten inches in diameter from the trunk. I was wearing gloves, as Sheri was, but I wasn't going to take any chances. I took out a handkerchief and rubbed the ball in order to smear any fingerprints. Sheri and I then moved over to the wooden gate that served as a rear entrance. We tested it carefully. It was locked. I moved over to the garbage container and whispered to Sheri.

"Here's the plan. It's still a little bit dark. I want you to climb up here and observe the rear of the house. I'm going to throw this ball high in the air in the backyard. If there are any motion sensors, we should find them. But keep low because of the cameras."

"Fargo, you sneaky old dog you."

"Ready?" I backed up while Sheri hopped up on the garbage container.

She gave a thumbs up. I let the ball fly and the backyard erupted in a light show. Sheri ducked down.

"We're out of here," I said in a whispered voice. We both made for the car, and climbed in. I turned on the engine and we stole away into the early morning hours.

"It figures that they would have those lights. What a suspicious bunch of people those Treasury Agents are."

Sheri laughed. "They had four lights, two up, and two down. Think the cameras got us?"

"No, not unless those are really expensive cameras. They won't get anything in this light."

"What about the ball in the air?"

"That, they got. But you were out of range and were hidden."

"What now?"

"Now, we're going to go to my place and go through the garbage."

"To see what we can see?"

"Right."

"So, I assume by taking the garbage out of the public truck, it was legal?"

"Right."

"Tell me more Holmes."

I moved the car onto Decatur and headed toward my condo. "Federal case law is clear but subject to interpretation. There is no expectation of privacy if the garbage has been thrown away. The key word is expectation. However, trash within the curtilage of the house is not public."

"Curtilage?"

"Meaning the enclosed space or grounds immediately surrounding

271

a house."

"Like the garbage bins?"

"Exactly. Basically, if you throw something out for public pick-up, there is no reasonable expectation of privacy."

"So, when the garbage man moved the garbage into the truck, it was now public refuse."

"Right. Basically, that's our defense in the situation."

"Boss, where does one learn this kind of stuff?"

"CIA. FBI. Uncle Leo"

"Oh, I see."

I drove and we talked. Sheri loved everything about being a private investigator. She and I made a good team, and Sheri knew that I knew it. But part of me was fiercely independent and part of me was a kind of guy totally dependent on someone like Abby. I knew that I probably should have Sheri join me in my practice, but if I was really her Boss, then maybe things would be different.

I backed into my driveway, popped the truck lid and killed the engine. We unfolded very large sheets of painters plastic drop cloths and placed them double thick in three different areas of the garage. Then I took each bag and placed it in the center of each piece of plastic.

"So Sheri, let's start with one bag. You sit here and take notes, while I call out the items. We want a complete inventory for the record. Items of interest will be set aside, and the rest will be bundled up and thrown out."

"Boss, I'm so glad that you're the Boss and I'm the one over here taking notes. This place stinks."

"Yeah, it's not a very glamorous profession now is it?"

"Things to write home about. But, why the inventory?"

"It would help us in court, but it also might help establish a timeline if we find things with dates. Then we can get a chronology of the contents that could tie into other timelines."

"God you're deep."

"Thanks." I started in and opened the bag and called out each item. If it was a keeper, I placed it in a pile; if not, I placed it in another garbage bag. We worked steadily though the material. By now it was mid-Saturday morning, and I knew we had a big day in front of us. But we were making progress. It's when you least expect it that you strike gold.

"One memo from Treasury Department Inter-Correspondence." I held it aloft in the form of victory.

"All right. What does it say?" asked Sheri as she jumped off her chair and moved next to me.

"It's hard to make out." I looked a bit further in the bag. "Here's another one. In fact, here's a whole pile of memos."

"All right."

"This should keep us busy."

"What does the next one say?"

"They appear to be Internal Memos regarding Field Assignments. These could get kind of juicy."

"No pun intended." Sheri laughed at her own joke.

"Funny girl. Funny girl."

"Hey, I'm tired, and I stink."

"This is the last bag. Let's finish up with the inventory and get this trash out of here. Then we need to clean up and get some sleep. We're going to need it for tonight."

"Maybe we can take a look after we've gotten some rest."

"Sounds good to me. We will need to take each of these memos and establish an order to them. It's going to take a couple of days of work."

"I'm exhausted. I could use a shower. This smell goes right through me."

"Sure, you can crash here if you want."

"Naaah. But I will take you up on the shower. Then I'll go home and catch up on some sleep and get ready for tonight."

"Abby's got some clothes you can wear. You probably don't want to wear those clothes home in your car."

"You got that right. I'll throw them into a bag. Are you sure that Abby won't mind?"

"She would only mind if I didn't offer."

I bagged the garbage while Sheri took a shower. I threw out the garbage in the dumpster along with the plastic drop cloths. My garage was clean as ever. Left over was a stack of notes and memos and faxes about two inches high. It looks like someone had cleaned their desk and threw everything out.

Sheri was ready to go. I gave her a hug and off she went. After that I took a shower and decided I was hungry. So I whipped up an egg omelet and sat down. I passed on the coffee because I needed some sleep and decided on V8® juice.

As I sat there my curiosity got the best of me. I thought I would scan the documents. I knew it was going to take a very close read of every piece of paper, and if there were any thread of suspicion against Barnes, I would have to build a very careful timeline.

After finishing my breakfast, I pulled on a set of rubber gloves to protect the existing fingerprints if we needed to go that far to establish a lick with Barnes. I was working my way through the stack when I turned over a piece of paper that caught me completely off guard. I was stunned.

Chapter Thirty-Two

THE LOUNGE AT TREASURE ISLAND had a view straight down the Strip that offered a magnificent show of the lights, action and constant pulsating thrust of what is Las Vegas. It was Saturday night and the town was alive. Money was in the air. As I sat at the bar, I straightened my black tie in the reflection of the mirror behind the bar. Movement caught my eye and I saw the reflection of Rapture behind me as she entered from the elevators. It was nearing game time and we had agreed to converge in the lounge area to discuss last minute game plans.

I turned around and slide off the bar stool. "Rapture, you look wonderful."

She swirled around in her emerald green gown that was cut low in the back and even lower in the front. "What do you think?" she said.

"No one's going to be able to keep their mind on the game," I said, and she smiled at me in a bashful way.

Just then Uncle Leo entered with Abby in tow. Uncle Leo also wore a black tie and looked as if he owned the casino. He cut a handsome figure with his lean frame and gray hair. I asked him once how he kept so trim and his reply was it had to do with losing all the money handicapping the horses. It kept him from eating a lot. It took me a while to figure out it was his sense of humor.

My constant love, Abby, looked sensational. She wore a white gown that sparkled in the dim light. As a Tropicana line dancer she knew how to put it all together. She had gotten the night off and was ready to enjoy our romp in the casino.

I gave Abby a kiss on the cheek so I wouldn't destroy her make-up.

"You look wonderful Ab," I said using my nickname for her.

"Thanks. But this dress is pretty tight, I might need some help in getting it off tonight."

"I am at your service," I responded with a bow. Rapture smiled and Uncle Leo shook his head.

Just then Bennett and his son entered. The son was the officer that had stopped me on the Strip. "Officer Bennett, good to see you," I said as I shook hands with him. "At least this time I don't see you in my rearview mirror." He laughed. Officer Bennett's father was behind him and we shook hands. Everybody respected his years of experience and I really enjoyed his company. He was the mastermind of this attack on the casino. The senior Bennett notched his head toward his son. "Just call him Doug. I thought I would bring him along. He might come in handy. He can stay in the background as security."

"Great idea," said Uncle Leo as they shook hands.

I introduced them to Rapture and to Abby. We moved over as a group and sat down in front of floor-to-ceiling windows with a picturesque view of the Strip. The couch and chairs were wine-colored leather, the kind that once you sat down in them, you didn't want to get up.

"Where's Sheri?" asked Rapture.

"She is also going to be working security behind the scenes."

"So we'll have a team of two in the background," said Bennett. "Sheri and Doug."

"Right."

"Do you expect any trouble?" Rapture asked.

"No, not at all." I gave Uncle Leo a look. I had called him that morning about the paper I had found. I also had called Sheri after her nap and we had a three-way conversation. I had found a Treasury Department document that indicated that David Holden was a direct report to Barnes. The report indicated the start of an internal investigation of what went wrong on the field assignment they were conducting. Sheri was furious that the agents were connected because it means Barnes is covering something. We discussed it and decided as soon as the evening's game was over, we were going to find Barnes and confront him whether it was midnight or two-o'clock in the morning. I had put in a call to him and left a message. We couldn't tell him and "oh, by the way, we were going through the garbage last night and found the memo you accidentally threw away." But we were going to indicate we received some information from Las Vegas Metro and wanted to know what was going on.

I smiled a big smile. I must lead with confidence, I told myself. But we're going to be in a very high stakes game. We need to be careful. If everything goes as planned, we'll be exchanging the cash for the map.

A cocktail waitress appeared ready to take our order, and we all ordered drinks.

"I think this should be as far as drinks go," said Bennett. "This will take the edge off, but we'll need to be sharp during the game. We'll accommodate the casino with one round of drinks. But this is a serious game."

"Have we narrowed down the wheel?" asked Rapture.

"Yes, I retrieved the numbers from Fargo at about noon today, and ran them through the computer. Here is what I want us to do. I want

Fargo, Abby and Uncle Leo to bet normally. I will be doing the same. Even though this is a private game, if you go bust, buy in again. We don't want to lose our positions at the table."

"I'll cover your losses," Rapture said. "The casino would welcome any player that they could get into the game. We don't want that to happen."

"Sounds easy enough," said Abby.

"But it gets trickier. At some point Rapture will need to make her play. But this is only after she has won enough to make the one bet or combination of bets that will be the big hit. Only Rapture will know the signal to make that play. So we'll play the game until the right time. I will determine that, and give her the signal."

"Then we sit back and cross our fingers," Abby remarked.

"I would take it a step further. I'd cross your fingers, throw sea shells on the floor, recite Seth, meditate, and do whatever you do to get some good luck going," Bennett said.

"Seth?" Rapture repeated.

Abby smiled. "I will tell you about Seth. Just keep thinking positively. It'll all work out."

"Rapture, why don't you and I move over there so I can explain how we will do this." Bennett said.

"Why keep it a secret?" Doug asked.

"Because we want everything to be as natural as we can make it."

"Is this illegal?" Abby asked.

"No, not in any way," Bennett said as he got up. "Only if we had a computer in the casino and we were using it to determine a number."

"I agree," said Uncle Leo. "There is very little successful litigation in this area."

Bennett and Rapture moved across to another table. Rapture looked beautiful in her emerald green gown.

"She is a very beautiful lady," I said to Abby.

"You're right. She has real beauty. The kind you can't buy in this town."

Abby and I had a good relationship. I would marry her in a second if I could, but she was married to dance, to the lights and drama of the stage. Tonight would be another form of drama; we would dance at the roulette table in the lights of the casino. Stories about this would be passed on for years. Some pressure here, I thought. Some pressure.

Chapter
Thirty-Three

THE SIX OF US EXITED THE ELEVATOR as a group and headed toward the casino gaming area. We struck quite a scene in our tuxedos and full-length evening gowns. I had Abby on my arm and Uncle Leo did the same with Rapture. People actually stepped aside as we came through the casino. Officer Bennett and his father followed, with Officer Bennett melding into the crowd when we were about halfway to the gaming area.

As we neared the roulette table I could see a dealer and two pit bosses all standing at ease awaiting us. A pit boss stepped forward to greet us, and parted the velvet rope barrier that had secured this private game.

"Welcome Mr. Blue. Treasure Island welcomes you and your guests. My name is Wendell Rush and I am at your complete service this evening."

"Thank you Wendell." I turned toward Rapture. "I would like to introduce our group. This is Rapture."

Rapture stepped forward and extended a gloved hand. I introduced Uncle Leo, Abby and then Bennett Sr.

"Your dealer for the evening is William Parks." Parks nodded toward us. "Everyone calls him Parks."

"How long have you been spinning the wheel?" Bennett Sr. asked of Parks.

"Thank you for taking an interest. I have been doing this for over forty years at various casinos on the Strip."

"That's why we selected Parks for tonight," Wendell said. "Experience."

"My, you must have seen quite a bit over the years," Abby said.

"What's the one thing you remember the most?" Uncle Leo asked.

"I was at the Sands when the Rat Pack played. They spent money like it was going out of style. Sammy, Frank, Joey and Dean! What a combination! They favored blackjack, but they occasionally spent some time at the wheel."

"Oh my, what an experience," Abby said.

"Yes, it certainly was. But I must say for all the drinking that the Rat Pack was famous for, Dean was the one that made sensible bets. It just looked like he was out of control."

"A history lesson right here in the casino," I commented.

"Please everyone take a seat and we'll get started. Parks gracefully motioned to the waiting stools.

"You have requested a no-limit game. Are you sure that you wouldn't be more comfortable in our private gaming area upstairs where we can easily accommodate your every wish?" Wendell asked.

"No, I think this will be just fine." We all moved to our positions as we had practiced. Rapture closest to the wheel with Uncle Leo at her side. The next stool was empty awaiting the arrival of Coyote. Bennett Sr. took the last position with Abby at the end, and I took the inside corner.

"We are waiting for one more player," I said.

"Why don't we accommodate your buy in?" Parks said.

"I'll start with twenty-five-thousand," Rapture said.

"Will thousand dollar chips be your desire?" Parks asked.

The gallery behind us stirred as the amount was whispered through the crowd. Our group had created an aura of excitement and anticipation, and now there was a gallery forming all around the table.

Uncle Leo bought in for ten thousand and Bennett the same. Abby and I followed; one thousand each of us. As the chips were being pushed toward Uncle Leo, I heard a commotion from the crowd.

"Excuse me," someone said. The crowd parted and there she was. Coyote had arrived.

We all stood up and Rapture was the first to greet her with cheeks brushing cheeks. Introductions followed with handshakes. She was a very attractive woman full of confidence. Her black sparkling dress was spectacular highlighted by a string of pearls dangling seductively. She created quite a stir with the gallery.

"Fargo, how nice to see you" Coyote said, her eyes sparkling.

"Thank you and you look simply wonderful this evening. I take it the desert weather agrees with you?"

"Very much so," Coyote said, smiling. Her gaze stayed with me longer then usual. She started with fifty-thousand dollars. There was something here, something different.

Everyone settled themselves back into their seats and the buy in was completed. All of us knew what the stakes were, and why we were here. Except, of course, for the casino, who had simply accommodated us for a high stakes game.

"Shall we start?" Wendell asked.

Everyone nodded in agreement, and Rapture leaned forward to place her first bet. With her rather low cut gown she created quite a scene.

She placed the thousand-dollar chip on red.

We all placed several bets and the wheel was spun and the ball put into play. At a certain point Parks the dealer waved his hand across the table signaling no more bets. Wendell and another pit boss stood off to the side with their hands crossed watching everything.

"Red, nine," Parks said as he put the marker down on the number. A blue chip rested on it and I looked around and saw that Abby had hit the thirty-five to one bet. Rapture also won as she had her money on red playing the even money bet.

As the losing chips were swept aside and the winning chips were moved to Abby and Rapture, the crowd sort of gasped. Abby won seven hundred fifty dollars with her twenty-dollar bet. Rapture had a thousand dollar chip on red and had won even money of one thousand dollars.

Rapture looked at me and I nodded at her. We were off and running. We both looked at Bennett Sr. who nodded back. The clear message was to keep on betting; moderation was the key, and wait for Bennett Sr.'s signal.

The game of games continued. We all made our bets and said our prayers as all gamblers do, but I watched Rapture's play carefully. Her bets were increasing and she was winning. She would increase with every win, and then drop down to her base when she lost. The more she won, the larger her base bet became. Coyote played with a handful of chips. She was here for a different reason, to collect on the purchase of the map. There was true emotion in this game as Rapture was betting her future on the spin of a wheel. As the bets became larger, the crowd grew in size and intensity. The Wild, Wild West, I loved it.

Rapture continued to win. Drinks were served but we were

careful to observe Bennett's rule. We kept it light, and continued to work the game. I had lost my original stake of one thousand and bought in for another thousand. Abby had doubled her money while Uncle Leo played very conservatively. Bennett Sr. also played conservatively but seemed consumed in thought. He hardly said a word.

I glanced at the crowd and picked up Officer Bennett who nodded at me, and then disappeared back into the crowd. I wondered about Sheri, but I was sharply brought back into the game when the crowd moaned.

I looked and saw Rapture had just dropped twenty thousand on one bet. It did not seem to faze her as she placed another five thousand on the next spin. She won. Roulette is like that, you are up and down and all around. It is a tough game requiring money management, luck and the fortunes of deep pockets.

We had played for about forty-five minutes. I glanced at the number board that towered above the table that reflected the last twenty spins of the wheel. There was an odd pattern. There were a lot more blacks then there were reds. I mean a lot more. The last seven spins had been all black.

Bets were being placed and Parks was just about set to spin the wheel. He was on the casino clock – the more spins, the more there is a chance for the house to take their percentage.

Bennett Sr. then announced in a very loud voice, "Parks, this bet is for you. I wish you all the luck in the world." Bennett Sr. then placed seven chips down all across the board on numbers eight, ten, twelve, nineteen, twenty-five, twenty-seven and twenty-nine. Parks knew that Bennett Sr. was playing with one hundred-dollar chips and stood to make thirty-five hundred dollars on the next spin.

"Bets for the dealer," Parks announced in a loud voice and turned toward the pit bosses.

Wendell nodded toward Parks. "You have a bet."

Parks turned back to Bennett Sr. and smiled. "You are very generous, sir, thank you very much."

As Parks waited for the rest of the bets to be placed he straightened the chips located next to the wheel. I saw him take a long hard look at the wheel. Puzzled, I wondered why. I glanced at Rapture and she was also studying the wheel just as Parks spun the wheel and launched the ball in the opposite direction. Rapture kept her eyes on the wheel.

Then, it happened. Rapture moved a stack of chips toward the board. "Two-hundred thousand dollars on number twenty-nine."

Coyote smiled.

The pit boss dove for the phone. Nobody had ever seen Wendell move so fast.

The ball was spinning. Parks glanced over his shoulder at the second pit boss who was frantically using his cell phone. The ball was spinning and they couldn't stop the game.

"You have a bet, Miss. Two hundred-thousand on number twenty-nine," Parks said, protecting Bennett's bet for himself.

Rapture then placed fifty thousand on black, fifty thousand on odd, fifty thousand on the high-numbers, fifty thousand on the top one-third of the board, and fifty thousand on the center row.

I totaled it up and Rapture had four hundred and fifty thousand dollars in play on one spin of the wheel.

The crowd went crazy. The entire casino stopped and there

were people around the wheel twenty deep. The bet of bets was being communicated throughout the casino.

"She's got two hundred thousand on one number," someone shouted.

"More then that," somebody else yelled.

"She's throwing it all away," cried another.

I looked at Bennett and he nodded. This was it. This was the play. Everyone in the room that could see the wheel kept their full attention on that little white ball that sped around and started to go slower and slower and slower. Rapture had covered her move with back-up bets. As I studied the table I realized that if she hit number twenty-nine, she would win every bet. But if she lost, there was a good chance she would win another bet and still be in the game. Plus she had about ten thousand in front of her that she had not bet. There would be enough money for another run at the table.

Suddenly, it all made sense to me. Bennett Sr. had studied this wheel with the numbers we had provided. He knew part of the wheel was favored as it might have been a little out of whack causing the ball to work uphill and then come speeding downhill. Bennett's bet for Parks was a signal to Rapture to play the middle number twenty-nine. Ingeniously, Parks had been doing this for over forty years and now had an incentive to hit those numbers. An honest situation had been created, where Parks, with his years of experience, actually targeted that part of the wheel. There was no collusion. It was an honest bet. Parks was no dummy; he wanted that thirty-five hundred. Rapture's bets had been placed after Parks had launched the ball.

The ball started to slow down. I glanced up and I saw security moving into the area. The ball went slower. The pit bosses had both edged over to the side of the wheel where they could get a better view. The ball went slower. Parks waved his hand across the table signaling no more bets. The ball went slower. We were all standing and leaning over toward the wheel trying to spot where the ball would land. The ball went slower and then took a bounce. There was a huge gasp from the gallery. The ball danced on the numbers; red and black, red and black and then slowed down bouncing a little bit lower each time before finding a home, a number to rest on.

Chapter Thirty-Four

MY HEART WAS PUMPING so fast I almost felt faint. The gallery was going crazy with people shouting, "What is it? What is it?" Then the ball took one more bounce and landed carelessly on a number.

"Twenty-nine, black. We have a winner," Parks shouted very loudly.

The casino went crazy in a huge rush of excitement.

"This table is closed," Wendell yelled.

Rapture collapsed on the table and Uncle Leo was at her side. Abby moved around and held Rapture in her arms.

"How much did she win?" came a shout from the crowd.

"Someone answered, "Over seven million dollars."

Coyote smiled.

Rapture had done it. We had all done it. We had won the game of games.

Security completely surrounded the table. Two more pit bosses showed up as well as management. Parks had stepped back from the table and Wendell had taken control of everything.

"Ma'am," Wendell said. "You have won a great deal of money. You understand we had to close the game."

"Cash me out, if you would please."

"Yes, no problem. But we need to sort all of this out." Counters had arrived at the table and were counting the chips. "We will need to move to our private offices so we can arrange the paperwork and establish an account here."

"No, I don't want to go to an office. I want to be paid here."

"Pardon me, Ma'am."

"I want to be paid here. I want to be paid in cash."

"In cash?"

"Yes, is that a problem?"

"Well Ma'am...that's highly unusual."

"Call me Rapture. This is Vegas. You should expect the unusual."

"Ma'am," said one of the counters. "It looks like you won seven million dollars with another three-hundred fifty thousand on top of that. And you still have your original bet plus about ten thousand that you didn't bet."

"Oh my, dreams do come true," Rapture announced.

"Yes, Rapture. Ahaaa, this is highly unusual," Wendell said repeating himself.

"Are you saying you don't have the money?" Rapture questioned.

"No, no that's not the problem."

"You said earlier that you could accommodate our every wish."

"Yes Ma'am...I mean Rapture."

"So what's the problem?"

"It's one of security. I really suggest that you consult with an attorney to arrange for proper handling of the funds."

Uncle Leo stood up. "I am her attorney. Her request is legitimate."

I stood up and flipped my badge. "I represent Ms. Rapture as a private investigator, and will take care of security."

"I see," Wendell said looking around. The gallery was twenty deep as they watched the beautiful Rapture who had just experienced what all of them dreamed about. He glanced above the crowd and could see that the other five roulette wheels were totally filled as everyone tried to win their fortune. The publicity alone would create enough buzz to recover the money in a number of days even though today's books were going to have a pretty big hit against them.

"Very well. This amount of money will mean fifty percent of your winnings will be retained and paid to the IRS on your behalf. That means you will be carrying a little over three million dollars."

"Fine."

"Very well," Wendell said as he turned to another pit boss. Gus, please advise the count room to prepare several parcels with her winnings minus the money we will have to hold for taxes. Have security bring the money and the required paperwork to this table. And call Gil. Let him know what's going on."

"What do I bring it in?"

Wendell's voice went up several octaves. "Use your head. Go to the gift shop and get some tote bags," Wendell said a bit edgy.

Gus stepped back to the table and started to talk into the lapels of his jacket, which hid the microphone of his two-way radio. Some of the pit bosses were connected to the sky above, and the main cage.

Wendell then proceeded to pay Parks his thirty-five hundred in chips. "Why don't you take the rest of the night off, Parks. You deserve it."

"Thank you, Sir. And thank you Ma'am."

"Rapture."

"Yes, of course. Rapture. Thank you very much." He offered his hand and they shook.

"And thank you very much sir for placing the bet for me," Parks said to Bennett as they also shook hands. He then turned and left.

A cocktail waitress showed up with another round of drinks. We sat causally around the table waiting for the pay off. I had slid my stool around to the other side and we were in a group. The casino bosses were on the opposite side having their own discussion. We were surrounded by casino security.

"So Coyote. I suppose this means that you'll be leaving," I said.

"Yes, once the transaction is done, I will be on the next plane out."

"Where to?" Uncle Leo asked.

"A place far away. A place where I can gather my thoughts."

Bennett Sr. and Abby were involved in their own conversation, and Abby was excited as she herself had won over two thousand dollars.

"So, do you have the map?" Rapture asked Coyote.

"Yes, right here." Coyote pulled out an envelope and then pulled out the leather map and started to lay it face up, and Rapture grabbed her arm. Coyote looked at her quite stunned.

"Security," said Rapture. "The eye in the sky."

Coyote nodded and silently mouthed the words, "Thank you," as she realized the video cameras above them would be rolling and would have photographed the map. Coyote then laid the map face down on the roulette table. Rapture also pulled the other half of the map out of her purse and unrolled it and placed it upside down next to Coyote's map.

"A long time ago the maps were cut in a jagged pattern. It's a perfect fit," said Rapture as she carefully scrutinized the jagged edges, which fit together like a jigsaw. "But I need to view the actual map to make sure of continuity."

"Here, let's just slide them down between us for a quick peak. I'm sure they will match." They both took their own map and very quickly matched them below table level.

"They're perfect," Rapture said. She took them both and put them back into the same envelope and set them down on the roulette table between the two of them. Just then the crowd around the table started to divide and seven security guards arrived carrying eight bags with the logo of Treasure Island stitched in gold. They placed the bags on the table in front of Rapture.

The security guard opened up a bag. "Each bag has a half a million in it. The smaller one has the balance of three hundred and fifty thousand plus your original bets."

"How do I know the count is accurate?"

"Ma'am, I can assure you that it is very accurate. We have video tape of the count and of packing the bags as well as video of the bags being carried here."

"Very well."

"If you could sign this paper work and provide us with the proper identification for the IRS, we can conclude the transfer, and provide security out of the casino."

A clipboard was pushed in front of Rapture and she penned her name on several forms and provided the identification. She was given copies.

"Thank you," Rapture said, as she stuffed the paperwork into her small handbag. She moved six bags over in front of Coyote.

"Thank you Rapture," Coyote said.

"What's this," Wendell said in a surprised voice.

"I'm paying her some money I owe her."

"You owe her three million dollars? You can't do that here."

"Why not," Uncle Leo said.

"Well, I don't know. But I don't think you can do that."

"You took out the money for taxes, and this is the cash that is left over. You transferred the money to her and she signed the papers. You have no authority over that money."

"But I do," a familiar voice said. We all turned and looked.

Chapter Thirty-Five

BARNES stepped in with Treasure Island security all around him. He flipped his badge at everyone in a slow arc all around the table so everyone could see it.

"Barnes, U.S. Treasury. I am here to secure the money for tax evasion."

Now there was a roar from the crowd and instead of moving closer to the table, they all moved back. Treasury agent. Internal Revenue. Plague.

"What do you mean by that?" Rapture screamed.

"Barnes, what's this all about?" I said.

Barnes then reached over and took the envelope with the two maps and stuffed it into his coat jacket. At the same time the guards lifted all the bags off the table. "I am securing this for back taxes and as evidence in an ongoing investigation. You will be contacted by the Internal Revenue Service."

"What back taxes?" screamed Rapture.

The crowd that surrounded the table was following every move. Back taxes, they thought. Finally, they get the rich person. There was no sympathy for Rapture.

"The back taxes you owe. Now that we have recovered the funds you will be entitled to an appeal. But you will lose."

"What...?" said Rapture. "Fargo...!"

"And I wouldn't go to Fargo for help. He's been working undercover for me assisting in the recovery of these funds. Here's his contract in case you don't believe me." Barnes pulled out a folded contract and threw it on the table.

Rapture picked it up, stunned. I put my hand on her shoulder. "I can explain."

"You'll never get the chance. When my attorneys get through with you, you'll be working Fremont Street for handouts. This is a conflict of interest. You double crossed me!"

As Rapture was yelling, Coyote moved over to where Barnes was standing. "You've got my money there. She paid it to me."

"Doesn't matter. She owes it and I am taking it for the IRS."

"Why take the maps?"

"Evidence."

"Evidence of what?" Coyote said. She was unbelievably calm.

"Assets. If there isn't enough money here, then we go after hard assets."

"You're pretty sure of yourself."

"In this business, you have to be. Here's the paperwork." Barnes threw down some papers. "You will be contacted with the amount after the IRS does the account." He immediately turned and left and the crowd parted easily as if he were contaminated with a horrid disease.

Coyote yelled after him. "Barnes?"

Barnes stopped and looked at her. "What?"

"I'll be in touch."

"Missy, you don't know what's up, or down. What's right or wrong. I suggest you mind your own business."

"It is my business now."

Barnes flipped Coyote off. The crowd sort of gasped.

As Barnes disappeared Sheri came into view.

"Sheri, stay on him," I said.

She nodded and was gone.

Rapture turned toward me. "Fargo," she screamed. "I'm going to sue you for every dollar you ever made in your life."

Uncle Leo had been watching everything very carefully. "Rapture, if I may. Let's try and piece everything together. Have a seat here while we assess the situation. Fargo, you've got Sheri on Barnes?"

"Right. And Bobby as well."

"Good. Now, what's your take?'

"Do we really know what is happening? Right now, it's in the hands of the IRS."

"Peculiar, don't you think?"

"I'll say. I never heard of the IRS taking money at a table."

Chapter Thirty-Six

SHERI MOVED THROUGH THE CROWD of well wishers with authority. As in any casino, when someone wins big, there is always a crowd of winner want-to-be's. They visualize themselves in the winner's seat and what they would do with the money. That is what Las Vegas is all about, the visualization of the happiness they believe money will bring.

Sheri pressed her handbag against her and felt the comfort of the Glock handgun in her concealed carry purse. As she neared the outside of the crowd, Bobby Lawrence joined up with Sheri.

"What's up?" Bobby asked.

"Looks like Barnes stepped in and used his U.S. Treasury badge to take the money and the map. Fargo wants us to follow him. Something's not right."

"That has a false ring to it. Did he check out?"

"He's Treasury all right. He checked out clean."

As they moved through the casino it was obvious that Barnes was headed toward the parking structure located on the second level. It's accessed via a huge escalator that delivers people directly onto the casino floor. The temptation of seeing the casino was too much for many people. Even if you were arriving just to enjoy a meal, you still had to pass rows and rows of slot machines and video poker machines.

"Contact Bennett and fill him in."

"Right, I met him a little while ago." He keyed his mic. "Bennett, this is Bobby," he said as they walked.

"I copy," Bennett Jr. responded.

"We're following Barnes who just helped himself to a very large sum of money in the name of the Internal Revenue Service. At least that is what we think right now. We're to watch and report. They're headed in your direction."

"Roger that."

They moved outside and followed Barnes who moved toward a parked car. Barnes opened it and the two guards threw in the bags. Barnes flipped them several bills and they turned and walked away. Sheri and Bobby looked at each other. It was then that Barnes spotted them.

"Is that how the Treasury department usually collects on debts?" Sheri asked.

Bobby had walked around to the back of the car and was copying down the license plate number, which Barnes observed.

Barnes approached Sheri. "Look little lady, you don't know what's going on here. You don't know nothing," Barnes said in an angry voice. "You're just another two-bit detective wearing a skirt."

"So do you always throw a couple of bills to your partners, or is this just kind of a hit and run exercise? Like you were back in the academy taking lessons" Sheri said, stepping forward, facing Barnes.

"Go back to your boyfriend and take some more lessons," Barnes said.

"Hey," Bobby yelled walking up. "Take it easy. You have no reason to talk that way."

"I can say anything I want. I am tired of young, want-to-be detectives, pretending to be in the business. I have top security clearance in a number of government agencies, and I'm tired of dealing with amateurs in the field." Barnes turned to Sheri. "You need to earn those stripes. You need to be dropped into foreign countries, forgotten about, and see if you can find your way out."

"I'm not in your department, and I don't care to be with agents like you," Sheri said. "I do a good job for my clients."

"You don't know nothing," Barnes repeated in an increasingly angry voice.

"Where are you taking this money?" Sheri questioned.

"Wouldn't you like to know?"

"Actually, I would."

Bobby stood slightly behind Sheri backing her up. Sheri never gave an inch.

"Little lady, how are you going to follow me?" Barnes said pointing to his waiting car and holding his keys.

Sheri extended her left hand, which held her keys. She held it very dramatically and pushed a button. A Lexus four slots over rumbled to life with the headlights coming on. "And your every move is going to be reported to your agency, and a few more just to keep your name in the loop."

Barnes just stared at the purring Lexus. As he turned back toward Sheri he brought his fist up and caught Sheri completely off guard and hit her squarely on the left eye, and followed it with a round house to the stomach. Sheri went down cutting herself on the concrete. Barnes then kicked her in his rage, and at the same time pulled a gun on Bobby.

Bobby's reaction was to start to pull his handgun, but realized that Barnes had the drop on him. He knelt over Sheri who had moved into a fetal position to protect herself, and hold her side. Barnes backed away, climbed in his car, drove forward thirty yards, blew out the front two tires of Sheri's Lexus, and headed for the down ramp in a squeal of tires and burning rubber.

Bobby pulled his cell phone and established contact with Las Vegas Metro to file a 'shots fired' report.

Sheri raised herself to a sitting position. "I'm going to get the bastard," Sheri said stiffly through her bleeding lips.

"That I would bet on," Bobby said.

Chapter
Thirty-Seven

I WATCHED RAPTURE who was furious, bitter and agitated. "You owe me those maps, Coyote!" Her voice was loud, and filled with fury. She pounded the roulette table where they were still sitting. Casino security surrounded the table as they tried to sort out the situation. In back of them were the winner want-to-be's shocked that the money had been taken for back taxes. She pointed a finger at Coyote.

"I can say the same thing. Where's my money," Coyote responded.

"I gave the money to you. You took possession when I passed the money to you."

"No, I never took possession. I was given the opportunity to take possession. There's a difference."

Rapture looked hard at Wendell. "You promised me security until the money got out of the casino."

Wendell was beside himself. "Ma'am, I'm afraid that we have done what you asked us to do. When you signed the receipt, you took possession of the money. I didn't know you had tax problems."

"I don't have tax problems!" Rapture turned away in frustration.

I moved closer to Rapture. "Rapture, we need to think this through," I said. "Time is running short. Do you have any tax problems, or does your company or father have any tax problems?"

"None. We're clean," Rapture said as she started to regain her composure. "The company uses the best accounting firm. Our books are ultra conservative. We conduct an independent audit annually."

"That's what I thought."

"Why?"

"Well, I don't know. That's not how the IRS works. Something's not right."

Sheri stumbled into the roulette gaming area holding her stomach. She was leaning on Bobby who helped her take a seat at the table. I moved quickly to Sheri's side. She had really been ruffed up. Her head, neck and arms were bleeding. Her jacket had dirt marks all over it and was spattered with blood. Her eye was swelling and she had several cuts on her face. Sheri pulled up the side of her blouse under her jacket and revealed a nasty black and blue kick mark that was swelling rapidly. She immediately collapsed in my arms. Abby was there in an instant. Uncle Leo and Bennett Sr. were there, but still silent. Uncle Leo was watching the unfolding moments like a hawk.

"What happened?" I asked.

"It was Barnes," Sheri said weakly. "We followed him to the parking structure and watched him pay off his security guards, and then throw the money in a car."

"He paid off his security guards?"

"Yeah. That's not normal," coughed Sheri.

I glanced at Uncle Leo and he indicated that he wanted to talk to me. I nodded back. "What happened next?" I asked Sheri, who was regaining her strength.

"He saw us, came back and talked, and eventually took a swing at me. I was so surprised I never moved. I went down, and he kicked me while I was down. He then turned and left."

I looked at Bobby.

"After he took a swing at Sheri, I jumped toward him but he had already pulled a piece. I backed away."

"And security was already gone."

Abby wrapped herself around Sheri who was still crying. Rapture was a mess and Uncle Leo was sitting there on the cell phone.

"It's getting worse," Uncle Leo said, with his hand over the phone.

"What now?" I stood there watching Abby take care of Sheri. She looked up at me and tried to smile. I took a deep breath, and looked at Uncle Leo.

"It's Treasure Island Security. They just reported that Bennett Jr. tried to stop Barnes. He was hit at the bottom of the ramp."

Bennett Sr. jumped up. "Where is he?"

"On his way to Las Vegas Emergency Center on the West side."

I nodded at Bennett and we both moved toward the door. I looked back at Uncle Leo and held up my cell phone, and he knew I would be in touch. I looked at Rapture.

Rapture was still furious at me. "You and me are done. You're a two-timing, low-life detective. My lawyers will be in touch." She turned and left.

I was sitting in the meeting room at Treasure Island Security. About thirty minutes had passed since Barnes had lifted the money. Things were moving fast. Sheri had been taken to the hospital in an ambulance. Bennett Sr. had gone to see his son. Uncle Leo had returned to the office to coordinate the phones. I had just finished viewing the tapes of Barnes taking the money when Rapture was escorted into the room by Treasure Island Security. I had asked them to bring her down from her room as I knew she wouldn't see me in her room. I thanked them as they closed the door. Now it was just the two of us. On one wall we had the view of the entire gaming floor. But it was thick insulated glass so we couldn't hear a thing. Better yet, they couldn't hear us.

"What's this all about," Rapture said angrily, "and why did you have them bring me to security?"

"We need to clear up this misunderstanding."

"What misunderstanding? It's pretty clear you were playing me for a fool. A big one at that."

"That's not true. I took the assignment in good faith. I provided a service, a good service. And you have no reason to question my competency."

"What about this?" Rapture pulled out the contract from her purse that Barnes had thrown out on the table. "It says right here in your Fargo Blue Investigations contract that you are were engaged by Barnes to follow me."

"Where?"

Rapture slid it across the table. "Read it yourself."

I picked it up. I used standard contracts for each engagement, which became part of the case file. Uncle Leo reviewed each and every one before they were presented to the client. That way, everything was consistent and our records were in order. Sure enough, this was the same contract. Flipping to the second page I saw that Barnes had inserted his own clause about me following Rapture. Didn't look good. I looked up at Rapture who was fuming. "I can explain."

"Yeah, I bet you can."

"Okay. I understand that you are mad. I'm mad too. But give me a chance. Just hear me out."

"Why should I?"

"To get your money back."

"Okay. Shoot. It better be good. I've already called my attorney in San Francisco and left him a message. It's too bad they shut down the island. It would suit you perfectly."

"What island?"

"Alcatraz."

"Nice view of the Golden Gate from there."

"Cute." She brushed back her hair and folded her arms, waiting.

"I pressed the intercom. "Okay. We're ready." The light in the room dimmed as Gil Sanford walked in and closed the door.

"Rapture, you remember Gil Sanford. Head of Security for Treasure Island."

"Yes. You in on this too?"

"Gil, why don't you talk us through the video."

"Okay." He gave an order through the intercom, and the monitor flashed to life. "We shot this from above. Actually we have several different angles showing the same thing. This is the point where our security crew arrived with the money and it was placed on the table. Next you can see Barnes arriving with Treasure Island Security."

"Okay. Big deal. Nothing new. I was there."

"Right, except there's one problem. Those aren't our security guards."

"What?" Rapture got up, and then sat down again.

"They don't work for Treasure Island. Worse yet, after the shooting we went back to the videotape and observed several people, the same ones in this video, actually take off their shirts and dispose of them as they left the property. Sheri also saw them being paid off. They got in their cars and left. This was just as Barnes was leaving and shot Bennett Jr."

"What does this mean?" She turned toward me. "Fargo, what does this mean?"

"Well, here's what we know. Barnes is with the IRS as a field agent. However, it appears that he absconded with your funds. It looks like you were set up, and that he has taken your money and the map and is on the run."

"Oh, my God." Rapture's mood changed. "So it had nothing to do with taxes?" She said to no one in particular. She was calculating, thinking. "Fargo, I am sorry."

"No problem. But I have more. Last night, Sheri and I did a garbage run at Barnes residence."

"A what?"

"A garbage run. Sheri and I collected his garbage and went through it piece by piece."

"You're kidding."

"No. Anyway. Here's what we found. In all of our investigations of Barnes' background he came up clean. But when David Holden, who was shot earlier this week in front of Treasure Island, turned out to be a Treasury Agent, that was too much of a coincidence. I found a stack of Treasury Department memos that tied Holden and Barnes together on an operation here in Vegas. But the thing was, one of the last memos said that the Agency thinks that Holden was killed by an insider. Barnes was told to report for questioning back at the Treasury Department yesterday. They were taking him out of field duty. I think he's our guy. I think he was after your maps. And I think he took the money as part of his plan."

"He wants the treasure?"

"Yes. That's what I think."

"Why?"

"My guess is Barnes is a disgruntled Treasury Agent, someone that goes bad after seeing so many people with so much money."

"What can we do now?" Rapture said.

"Go to the islands, and investigate."

"Well, I have a copy of the map. And I bet you Coyote has a copy of her half. If we can get it, we can go after him. At least that's a starting place."

"Yes, that's what I hoped you would say."

Rapture stood up and walked over to the glass-walled window that overlooked the roulette wheel where she had won all of the money. She turned toward me. "I apologize profusely. But what about that contract?"

"Barnes stopped at our offices several days ago and insisted that he engage me in an assignment. It wasn't to my liking, nor Uncle Leo's, but he threatened that he could cause us a world of IRS grief if I didn't comply. I discussed the situation with Uncle Leo and we decided it was better to play along than to be on the outside. So we took the assignment and ran deep background checks and he came up clean. The contract with Barnes was to provide some background intelligence on anything unusual happening at Treasure Island. Nothing more. Nothing less. It didn't conflict with my assignment with you, and I advised Barnes that if there were any future conflict I would have to back off from my assignment with him. He took the contract and inserted your name, which I had never told him."

"So if he knew who I was all along, that means he had been following me for a while."

"Right. And by hiring me, it simply got him closer to anything that might be going down. I was actually his spy on the inside. But I didn't know it."

"What about Treasure Island?"

"I've had an ongoing undercover assignment there with Gil for the last several months. That's why Bobby was on the scene. I don't know if Barnes knew I had an assignment, but I wasn't going to tell him until I found out what he was after."

"You had it covered three different ways."

"That was the way it happened. Everyone had a different interest."

"What about the Treasury Department?"

"Uncle Leo is making contact with them now. We are going to bring them up to date on what is happening, and hope they will provide us with more information."

Rapture turned toward Gil. "I am sorry. Really. I behaved like an idiot."

"No you didn't. You behaved like someone who had all of her money stolen."

Chapter Thirty-Eight

THE WHINE OF A LEAR TORE AT BARNES' EARS, but he walked straight out of his limousine onto the waiting Jet, gripping four large bags tightly in his hands. The limousine speed away, disappearing into the night. As soon as Barnes was onboard, the steps were pulled up, and the Lear moved slowly down the tarmac for take off.

Barnes sat down, quietly placing the bags next to him. A pilot appeared and moved toward him down the short aisle of the empty plane.

"Good Evening, Mr. Barnes. We have contacted flight control, and have permission to leave for St. Thomas. We would like to make a fuel stop in Florida before venturing on to St. Thomas. If that is all right with you?"

"Actually it is not," said Barnes. "I requested a straight flight to St. Thomas. Is there a problem?"

"Might be. Weather is kicking up a bit, but we'll be monitoring the situation all the way."

"Good. If at all possible, I want to go direct. Please let me know if there is a change in plans."

"Yes Sir. There are cocktails aft, Sir. It's sort of do-it-yourself on this evening's flight."

"No problem," said Barnes. "I have lots of work to do. You're heading right back tomorrow morning I take it," said Barnes, trying to befriend the pilot, who he had no real interest in knowing at all.

"Agency is short of pilots right now," said the Captain. "They keep us moving quite a bit."

"Well, sorry you can't stay for a couple of days. Get some sun, check out the island hot spots, if you know what I mean."

"Yes Sir. Been there a few times myself."

"Listen, can I use my cell phone until we take off?"

"No problem, Sir. Give us a call if you need any assistance."

"Thanks, I will." Barnes smiled as long as the pilot was in sight. He then dropped his artificial pleasantries and pulled out his cell phone. He checked the area around him one more time, and then dialed a number from memory.

A light voice answered with a slight Spanish accent. "Bueno."

"Smith here," said Barnes, speaking in a seemingly different tone of voice.

"They're up to something, Sir. I followed them to their office but I cannot see what exactly is going on. I spotted the young one carrying out two duffel bags and throwing them into a car."

"That would be Sheri. They're packing up. Follow them and let me know where they're headed. You can leave messages on my voice mail. I'll pick them up enroute."

"So, you headed to Mexico, like you planned?"

"Yeah," said Barnes posing as Smith. "You still going to meet me in Mazatlan?"

"Yeah. I expect it will take a few days to drive down there."

"Well, enjoy the trip."

"If the treasure maps were for the Caribbean, how come you're headed to Mexico?"

"Asking a lot of questions, aren't we Pedro?"

"Just curious," Pedro responded.

"How do you know of treasure maps, Pedro?"

"You mention one day..."

"No, I didn't, Pedro. You're pretty sharp, aren't you?"

"No Sir, just trying to learn the business."

"You do as I tell you and you'll learn the business."

"Yes Sir," said Pedro.

"Just because the maps say St Thomas, it does not mean St. Thomas. Understand."

"I understand, senor. I..."

"Want to know where the treasure is buried?"

"Oh... I sure do, senor...I am very excited..."

"Off the Baja Peninsula. There's an old shipwreck there. We're going to meet in Mazatlan, and then make our way back up and down Baja. By that time nobody will know where we are and we'll be freely dividing up millions and millions of dollars."

"That is pretty clever. I have to admit."

"Listen," said Barnes. "I want you to call me one more time and leave a voice mail message. After that, throw the cell phone away as it will no longer be of any use."

"Yes Sir."

"Do you know the number by heart, Pedro?"

"No, I have to look at the card you gave me."

"Okay. Before you cross the border, you have to throw that card away. You understand. Under no circumstances must you keep that card."

"I understand. I should not let anybody know that I work for the U.S. Government."

"Absolutely. Under no circumstances. You're a spy, Pedro. And spies don't go into foreign nations with information of who their employer is. Understood?"

"Yes, destroy all the information."

"Thanks, Pedro," said Barnes. "I will contact you in Mazatlan. I will find you. You go on about your normal family routine and don't even think about me. I might be there watching to see if anybody followed you into Mexico. When it's safe, I will contact you and we will be rich for all time."

"Yes Sir. We'll be rich. Do all spies become rich in America?"

"All spies, Pedro. See you in Mazatlan.

"See you there," said Pedro.

Barnes hung up the phone and held his head in his hands. How he had gotten mixed up with Pedro is beyond belief, he thought. He dialed another number and destroyed his voice mail system. When Pedro called he would be calling into a dead mailbox. Even if police where to get his voice mail number, there was no record of who owned the voice mail. It would be a dead end. He felt that Pedro was a loose end that might have to be tied up someday, but Pedro knew only as much as Fargo, Uncle Leo and the hotels.

Everything was going so well, and now he regretted hiring Pedro. Even though Barnes was on official business in Las Vegas, he had his own agenda and had to hire some local help to keep tabs on people. All agents typically pick up local field help that are basically dead ends. It was a practice that started years ago and was exposed somewhat during the

Watergate Hearings. Nobody wanted to be caught with dirty hands, so cheap help was bought off the streets for break-ins and routine "sit and watch" assignments. It became standard practice to keep various agencies' hands clean when involved in fieldwork.

These select few could be miss-directed and lost in the shuffle of life or killed depending upon the situation. These cutouts would not be missed. All Barnes did was spot Pedro in a bar off of Freemont Street, and then called Pedro from his car. He asked for the Mexican guy at the end of the bar, and hired him for a few routine "stakeouts" which he performed quite well. Barnes followed Pedro and watched his work, and then let Pedro know the "agency" was watching him. With Pedro's help, Barnes was able to track when and where Fargo and Sheri moved around Las Vegas.

Fargo Blue, of course, was also part of the local help. Barnes' surveillance on Rapture had lead to Fargo who was easy to set up.

"Prepare for departure," said the Captain over the speaker system. "We're rolling." Barnes felt the surge and was jammed against the back of his seat as the Lear rocketed down the runway.

Barnes knew this was his last ride on a company jet. Word would be out soon that he had removed three million dollars from a table in Las Vegas, picked up pieces of the map, and was presumed to be conducting a further investigation. Barnes reached up and pushed the call button.

Almost immediately the co-pilot appeared from the cockpit.

"What can we do for you, Sir?"

"Listen, I would like to go into St. Thomas unannounced. I was wondering if on your flight plan you listed my name as a passenger?"

"I called in our flight plan myself," said the co-pilot. "Your name was not mentioned. Standard procedure, besides, we're headed for Mexico."

"Ahhh...you're one step ahead of me."

"Yes Sir. We never file for our true destination. We will have to file a change in route destination in about an hour."

"Thanks. What about your pick up order?"

"We've had a pick up order at this location for twenty-four hours. Confirmed by your I.D. number."

"What about on landing in St. Thomas?"

"Just going through customs, Sir."

"What about on your arrival at your next stop?"

"No reports are filed with the FAA, if that's what you mean?"

"You do have my I.D. number," said Barnes. "I could be identified by that."

"That is true, but it appears on limited paperwork."

Barnes stared at the co-pilot and the whining sound of the Lear gaining altitude was all they listened to.

"It is possible," said the co-pilot, "that these numbers could be... changed...if you know what I mean..."

"That is possible," said Barnes. "But I could not ask you to do anything that would cause problems down the road, Sir?"

"Of course you never asked," said the co-pilot smiling. "All in a day's work for the company."

"On that note," said Barnes, "I just might have a light drink and toast the company."

"You do that, Sir," said the co-pilot, returning to the cockpit. The co-pilot turned and looked back. "We'll make our toast when we're safely on the ground."

Chapter Thirty-Nine

"WHEN'S RAPTURE ARRIVING?" I asked Sheri, who was checking her briefcase full of electronic gadgets. We had just crossed Tropicana on the way to McCarran Airport. I took a quick look at her to check on how she was recovering. One eye was puffy, and a bruise had formed where Barnes had hit her. She had scrapes on her arms where she hit the pavement, and massive bruises on her side, which were taped up to ease the pain. But she seemed in good spirits.

I was glad that Bobby Lawrence stepped in when he did. We both had grabbed our overnight bags from the office and threw those into Sheri's jeep, but Sheri wanted me to drive while she checked out a few items. I noticed an electronic bug detector, and an electronic jamming device had been slipped into her foam-lined case with her laptop computer. I was carrying some high-powered binoculars, plus some communication equipment.

"Rapture has already got the Lear warmed up and onto the tarmac."

"We're missing a few things," I said as I turned into the airport.

"Guns?" said Sheri, who was dead series.

"Going to have to make arrangements with the owner of Noble One for some hardware," I said.

Sheri dialed Uncle Leo on her cell phone. "Uncle Leo I need you to outfit us with some protection. Have them stored aft in Noble One." Sheri listened for a few seconds, and then clicked off the cell. "Done, Boss. Hardware will be taken care of by Uncle Leo."

"How is he doing?"

"Having a great time. He's at home on his ham station and making all the arrangements for us via his radios, then he confirms by landline. He's also working with the Treasury Department and has given them a complete report. I've got two portable radios and we'll be able to talk to Uncle Leo whenever we need him."

"Good. One more thing. Call the control tower and ask if there have been any charters filed for St. Thomas."

"Right."

I knew Sheri had the number for the FAA Tower and was able to get right through. I listened to her talk. She met my eyes, and shook her head no. She broadened her target area to where Barnes might be going, but still came up with no charters for the islands. When Barnes attacked Sheri in the parking lot, and then shot Bennett Jr., the game had changed. Everything fell into perfect focus. Barnes had disappeared. Once again Sheri shut down her cell phone.

"No go, Boss."

"Yeah. They filed for another destination and are going to re-file after they're airborne for a couple of hours."

"I'd do the same thing," said Sheri.

I looked ahead and spotted Rapture's Lear, and her limousine parked off to the side. As we came to a stop, another limo pulled up. Coyote climbed out and we all met. Coyote had brought the copy of the map that we would match with Rapture's.

I smiled to myself. I was headed back to the islands. Good or bad, it was still the islands.

Chapter Forty

UNDER A SCORCHING SUN, Sheri, Rapture and I cruised in Noble One. It was hot and humid, but it was good to be back on board. Sheri was at the helm topside, and feeling better. She was taped up so she was able to move more easily. She was ready to go. Rapture was astern focusing binoculars on the ocean. Both were dressed in bikinis. I was sitting in the galley area studying charts for this area of the islands. I missed Abby. I was alone in the forward cabin, and it didn't seem right that she was not aboard, but this was far from a pleasure cruise. I knew Abby would look in on Uncle Leo and help in any way she could.

We were just off Andros Island in the Bahamas. This one-hundred-mile-long island was surrounded by dozens of palm-fringed white beaches. Nowhere else in the world could you find waters of such luscious blue hues with beaches so white, the skies so softly azure, yet vibrant with color. It was paradise, but the beauty masked the danger.

Skirting the outer shores of many of these islands we found long necklaces of dangerous coral, which made for a hazardous approach to the shores they guarded so well. We kept a safe distance, as did the many small fishing boats that dotted the area. After piloting their boats for years these fishermen had learned about the dangers of coral slashing their hulls and the safety of the deep canyons between the islands. Many a pirate's galleon had been torn to shreds by the talons of the sea.

For two days now we had circled an area where Sheri thought the treasure was located based upon the map that we had pieced together from Rapture's and Coyote's photocopies. Sheri had prepared a grid and we worked it as best we could in a sailboat. She had adapted the techniques she used in the Coast Guard where she was trained at sea rescue. Patience, persistence and methodical searching made the difference. We tacked back and forth across the suspect area.

I had just received a phone call from Uncle Leo. The photos that Sheri had snapped showed Barnes at the wheel. Uncle Leo was digging up more information on what really was going on in Las Vegas. Barnes was after the map all along. Somehow he discovered the two parties who each had half of the map, and was there for the exchange. The puzzle was coming together.

We had ventured into port only once. Sheri picked up supplies while Rapture and I kept a low profile. I knew that Barnes would recognize us, and probably Sheri. But Sheri insisted on going ashore. She was pretty good at changing her appearance and fitting in with the locals. She would gab about who was sailing, and whether any party was looking for old ships. Anything unusual.

Nothing had turned up at first. Then Sheri heard a rumor of a guy who was keeping pretty much to himself, but was doing some searching off the Andros coast. Of course the stranger denied everything, said he was just fishing, but the locals knew better. His vessel was not rigged for fishing, and was too big for just trolling for local game fish. Nobody knew where this character was, since the natives appeared to mind their own business.

I glanced out the porthole at the ocean while I studied the charts. I thought about how it must have been hundreds of years ago. For as long as goods destined to and from the new world were transported by sea, there have also been pirates who have made it their business to capture ships and claim the holds for themselves. Pirates acted entirely on their own behalf, while privateers, sometimes issued with letters of marquee, worked for their sponsor.

Many a deckhand had their stomachs do flips when they turned aft and spotted an unknown Galleon following them. The ships used by pirates and privateers have been varied in type, but the requirements have always been speed and maneuverability. No ship was barred from attack and accidents had happened. The flagship of the notorious pirate Henry Morgan, the Oxford, blew up and sank in 1669, while Morgan was planning an attack on Cartagena, Colombia, right off St. Dominique. Nobody knows what Morgan's ship was carrying. But many armchair treasure hunters keep those facts in mind when reading history of other buried treasure on the high seas, or other conquests by Morgan.

"Boss, I got something up here."

I darted out of the galley and headed up the stairs to the top where Sheri was running operations. Rapture was already there and they were both studying a large yacht that was moored about a thousand yards off Andros.

"I got activity, Boss. This yacht just appeared here in the last fifteen minutes. It's a fifty-two-foot Atlantis Manta out of Florida. Very popular for divers as it has a great aft section close to the waterline. Very fast. Not many can beat her in a race, and it fits the description of what the locals were telling me." Sheri stopped and studied the charts in front of her. "It's in the northwest corner of our grid, and it's only a quarter of a mile off from what I targeted as our number one spot."

"Anybody on board?" I asked.

"Nobody has appeared topside," said Rapture putting down a

pair of high-powered binoculars.

"Look like they are preparing for a dive?"

"Could be...can't tell," said Sheri.

"Take a look about a half a mile to the right," I said. Both Sheri and Rapture panned over and picked up a speedboat cutting through the water. It had one man behind the wheel, and he looked comfortable in the open sea.

"Don't know him," said Rapture.

"Barnes is on deck," said Sheri excitedly.

Rapture and I refocused on the yacht, and sure enough, Barnes had just appeared on the top deck. He brought up a pair of glasses and studied the speedboat as it approached the boat.

"Okay" I said, "everybody down below. He might put some glass on us and I don't want to risk any chance of him spotting us."

Rapture hit the stairs first with Sheri following. Once we were down on the main deck, we were clear from being spotted by Barnes.

Sheri propped herself up on some pillows and studied Barnes. "What's the plan?"

"Oh, oh!" I said. I was watching Barnes and he was starting to scan the horizon, and sure enough he picked up Noble One and was studying it.

I put down my binoculars. "Okay. Real quick. I want both of you to go topside and go swimming. Give Barnes something to look at. Barnes needs to think this is a regular tourist boat. He's studying us."

Sheri was first on topside. "Race you," said Sheri showing a sense of humor while in great pain. I glanced up at them as they removed their tops and dove in.

I once again put my binoculars on Barnes. He was studying the speedboat that was racing his way, and then he panned again and studied Noble One. He dropped his binoculars just a bit, and then refocused on Noble One again. Satisfied, Barnes turned his attention to the approaching runabout, which was just pulling alongside. It tied off the port bow of the Atlantis Manta. I watched Barnes and he again raised his binoculars and scanned the horizon around him, stopping and staring directly at Noble One. I could hear Sheri and Rapture swimming in the ocean near the boat, playing the part of tourists, and that satisfied Barnes, who continued to pan the horizon.

The man who climbed on board Atlantis Manta was agile, and quick to move onto the deck. Barnes met him face to face. I could tell that it was not a friendly situation. They did not shake hands, but stood apart from each other. Barnes kept one foot in front of him ready to assume the position for firing, and this indicated to me that he was carrying a piece. On the other hand, the visitor to Barnes' yacht simply kept his feet spread apart, but wide. I thought he was ready for a physical confrontation, and I knew it would take a lot to knock him off his feet. Barnes was shaking his head to indicate an answer of no. The other man continued his tirade, letting Barnes know exactly how he felt. He moved toward his speedboat, looked at his watch, indicated with his right hand the number three, which I took to be hours, but could be days or weeks. Then he jumped onboard his runabout. Barnes kicked his tied down line off the Atlantis Manta, and the runabout sped away.

I moved out of the forward cabin after Barnes headed below deck. Just before he disappeared from site, he looked at his watch, and I knew that this mystery man had made an impression on him.

Once outside I called to Sheri and Rapture and let them know that we would be shifting our position soon. Rapture climbed up the ladder, and I turned to see her standing there very topless. Beads of water headed downward as they rounded the curves of her magnificent body.

"Looks like you need a towel?" I said.

"The sun will dry me, and give Barnes something to think about, if he should look this way."

He's not the only one, I thought to myself. Just because I'm a good guy I tossed her a towel. Just wanted to be polite.

"What a guy...," said Rapture smiling.

Just in time, Sheri pulled herself on board obviously in some pain. "Hi Boss. What's Barnes up to?"

"Seems like he didn't get along with his visitor too well," I said, tossing another towel to the topless Sheri. Boy, a detective's work is never done. Maybe I should make her my partner. "Those are some bruises."

"Thanks," Sheri said, catching the towel.

Rapture continued to dry herself. "How can you tell from this distance?"

"I think the visitor was expecting some cash, and I believe they set some kind of time frame. They are not happy with each other. When the speedboat left, it went at a high rate of speed."

"What's our next move?" asked Rapture.

"Sheri's going to move us a bit closer. With the sun setting behind us, it will be hard for Barnes to watch us if he stays the night. I've pulled some charts right where Barnes is sitting, and it is close to the Spanish ship San Cristabol, that sailed in 1563 at 120 tons."

"That's the one," said Sheri. "She's down there, well known, but

324

never fully salvaged. We've got video of it."

"I thought so. Two years ago we photographed it. I'll go online and pull the images from our database. But as I remember it was mostly covered in sand."

"Okay, but first, let's move in closer to Atlantis Manta."

"No problem," said Sheri. "Rapture will help me."

They both scampered up the ladder to the top deck with their towels wrapped around them. I took a long thoughtful look, and then headed toward the galley below and the forward cabin where I could watch Barnes. Boy, I thought to myself, what some detectives have to go through to make a case.

Chapter Forty-One

I CLICKED ON THE REMOTE CONTROL while Sheri dimmed the lights in the main cabin. Rapture snuggled on a sofa with a glass of wine. We had maneuvered Noble One to within 750 yards of Barnes' yacht right at sunset. The setting sun minimized any kind of view that Barnes would have of Noble One, and we felt that Sheri and Rapture had a good chance of not being spotted by Barnes.

"Here it comes, Boss," said Sheri.

The monitor was filled with the light colored sand characteristic of these islands. A few manta rays skirted out of the way as the camera moved slowly over the bottom of the ocean. We had shot this about two years ago to document the faint outline of the San Cristabol and her position. Suddenly the hull of the San Cristabol appeared on the monitor.

"So if it's down there, and this ship has been salvaged before," said Rapture, "how come nobody has found it?"

I leaned back against the small sofa next to Rapture. "Well, actually, we don't know that for sure. Most salvage recovery operations accurately document what they bring up. One reason is they were not looking for a cross-encrusted in precious stones. They probably found silver and gold bars and figured that was all that was of value on board."

The camera panned back and forth over the wreck. It had the characteristic of a skeleton sitting on the bottom of the ocean half buried in sand.

"So, is Barnes going to go for it?" asked Sheri.

"I think so," I said. "I can't imagine what else he would be out here for. From what you can remember of the map, Sheri, where do you think it is?"

"The notes indicated that it was under the main beam."

"From what I saw," said Rapture, "I would have to agree."

"So if somebody knew where the cross was, why would they not just take the treasure?" asked Sheri.

"Well," said Rapture, "The current thinking, according to the story my dad told me, is that the map was created by a sailor who participated in the first salvage operation at the time of the ship's sinking. Not wanting to let his superiors know, he kept the information to himself, and was able to pass it on to his family in the form of a map. The map stayed hidden for centuries, and then was divided by a family when they had a dispute over who owned the treasure. Until the dispute was settled, no member of the family would be able to find the treasure. Either half of the map did not reveal the name of San Cristabol, so the ship's secrets were safe for hundreds of years. We only know that the map was dug up by my father. We do not know where Coyote's half of the map came from."

"She never talked about it did she?" I asked.

"No, she just maintained that she had the other half," said Rapture. "And quite frankly, I was not really interested."

"What happened to Coyote?" asked Sheri.

"I spoke with her briefly when she gave us her half of the map. She's talking to the IRS about her money," I said.

"How did you find that out?" Sheri asked.

"I talked to Uncle Leo via short wave late this afternoon. She gave all the details to the police concerning what happened at the roulette table. It has been confirmed by the Treasury Department that Barnes is on the run. Coyote reviewed the videotapes with the Treasury Department, and was told that since a member of their department took the monies that were due her, they would return it to her. It was stipulated that since the money was changing hands, that she would have to pay taxes on it. She readily agreed, and they produced a check."

"So Coyote did get the money after all?" said Rapture.

"Yes, she was certainly smart in just reselling the map, instead of going for the whole treasure."

Sheri looked at me. "That's a nice thing to say, Boss."

"Well, what I mean is...."

"You don't think I should have gone for the treasure then?" asked Rapture, smiling and picking up on Sheri's comment.

"Well, I ...."

"Real nice, Boss."

"Hey, listen...."

"Let's see him get out of this one," said Sheri.

"Yeah, I'll be real interested to find out how I'm smarter then Coyote."

"Well, it's quite simple," I said, trying to get my mind to figure out how I was going to overcome three million dollars profit, instead of maybe finding the buried treasure.

"We're all ears," said Sheri.

"Well, three million dollars is one thing, and Coyote was smart in taking her money and being happy with her profit. But finding the cross on the bottom of the ocean... that's all about the lore of treasure hunting. I have spent many a week in the desert searching for possible signs of gold, not thinking about what it could do to my bank account. It's the same here, the lure of gold, silver and diamonds encrusted on a cross that has been buried at the bottom of the sea for centuries, and a map that tells you were it is. What could be more exciting?"

"That's why I'm here," said Rapture. "My dad always talked about going treasure hunting ever since they found that map on lower Sahara. When I was a kid growing up we used to study maps of possible lost gold mines. When my dad and J.T. unearthed half of that treasure map, it became his passion, his quest. I am here to complete his dream." Rapture raised her glass and toasted me. "To finding the treasure," and sipped her wine.

I raised my glass and toasted Rapture. "To treasure hunters everywhere."

Sheri raised her glass to Rapture and me. "I myself, would have put the three million right in the bank, and called it a good day."

We all laughed, and dreamed about the treasure buried for centuries under the beam of a Spanish galleon.

Chapter Forty-Two

THE OCEAN WAS ALMOST BLACK WHEN Sheri and I checked our masks, and quietly slipped off Noble One into the murky waters of the Atlantic. We had risen early in the morning, ate a light breakfast, and prepared for our first dive of the day. I wanted to be underwater staking out our Spanish galleon when the sun first appeared on the horizon. Rapture, not having any experience in diving, stayed on board to handle cell phone communications with Uncle Leo, and keep a steady eye on Barnes' yacht, which showed no signs of activity. We had scanned the horizon with infrared nighttime binoculars, and picked up only two small fishing trawlers just behind us, which was normal, being this close to the island.

We waited below Noble One, and as the sun hit the water, Sheri led the way down to the bottom, orientated herself in terms of direction, gave me the thumbs up, and we slowly began to move in on the San Cristabol. Noble One was equipped with Neptune gear for communication between divers, and direct communication with Noble One. I decided against any voice transmission, so as not to risk any possibility of Barnes monitoring our radio signals.

I did not think we were going to locate the buried cross on our first outing. The odds were against that. I was more concerned about what Barnes was up to and whether he was going to make any dives in an attempt to locate the treasure. We did not know how long he had been moored over the wreck when we arrived, and we had no idea of his diving capabilities.

We swam quietly along. Sheri swam slowly because of the bruises that still remained from Barnes' attack on her. Fortunately she had no broken ribs. I saw Sheri stop and gradually sink to the bottom, hiding behind some coral. A school of brightly color fish darted in and out of the coral. I did not recognize them, but there were hundreds of varieties to track in these waters. Thinking something was wrong, I quickly came to her aid, but she gave me the thumbs up, and indicated to look straight ahead. There it was. The San Cristabol was lying in its grave of hundreds of years, undisturbed, but not forgotten. Sheri gave me one tap, signaling me to follow her. We swam to another location further away, and slipped behind a larger piece of coral, that helped to break up our air bubbles that would give away our location. We settled in for a watch-and-wait stakeout.

We had agreed that when we came upon the shipwreck, we would first watch it for a while to make sure no other divers were approaching the wreck. We settled in for about a twenty-minute wait. Through hand signals I was able to communicate with Sheri pretty easily. I usually knew what she was thinking, and she was used to my routines and operating procedure. If one can describe it as such, we snuggled into the coral and began our wait. Looking at the San Cristabol I was awed by the beauty of the waters surrounding her, and the added thrill of studying a ship that had seen adventures far greater then one can imagine. Just thinking of its history made me shiver: being on the high seas, tracked by pirates, losing her battle and tumbling to the ocean bottom, taking secrets, dreams and passions with her as she settled into her final resting spot in the deep sea.

I nodded to Sheri, and we moved out of the coral very slowly circling around to the left. As agreed, we were going to make one pass around the San Cristabol just to see if we could spot any activity. We wanted to approach the rear end of the hull slowly as this is where the location of the treasure was marked on the map. It was lighter now. A manta ray appeared out of the sand along with a school of blue parrot fishes as daylight began to seep onto the ocean floor.

We circled all the way around, then moved in slowly on the hull of the San Cristabol. The black ancient wood was a harsh contrast against the blue waters and white sand of the ocean bottom. We were lucky, as storms during the year left the hull visible.

Sheri and I stopped and looked at the hull together. Sheri traced the main beam with her hand down to where the sand buried the beam. She moved to the right about three feet, and indicated to me that this is the location of where the treasure ought to be. I moved back a bit and studied the beam from a distance, and was able to determine that the treasure could be about ten feet down from where Sheri had indicated. Taking into consideration the slope of the beam as it entered the sand, and a guess on what the curvature of the beam was beneath the sand, I had an idea of how much digging was necessary. This certainly was not the most scientific exploration of the ocean's bottom, but neither is digging in the desert because you felt like it.

Chapter Forty-Three

CARL COLLINS, THE MAN WHO MET with Barnes on his boat, worked his way up a hill on the island of Andros carrying a long slim case. Collins, a professional hit man who worked for Barnes, was not happy. Being denied payment for services rendered was against his code of ethics. Even in the community in which he moved, there were ethics. Assignment was done; payment was due. None of that Treasury Agent crap that Barnes threw at him made a difference.

He moved quickly and expertly through the thick brush to a point overlooking the ocean. From his side belt he pulled a spotters scope. He focused on Barnes' yacht, then on Noble One, and then back to Barnes. Seeing no activity, he began to set up. From his case he pulled out a Remington 700 bolt-action sniper's rifle. It had a heavy varmint barrel, which helped to neutralize vibration when fired. He carefully placed a hand-loaded .308 Winchester cartridge in the chamber and slid home the bolt. Collins moved behind the scope, resting his elbows on the packing case he had so carefully carried up the hill. Using a Leupold 10x, he focused on Barnes' yacht, which jumped into crystal sharp focus. It was magnified ten times, and seemed brighter with the unparalleled optics of the Leupold scope. Collins tested the wind, and started to make critical adjustments in his scope to hone in on his target.

At over a thousand yards away, with a glare from the clear ocean it was hard to focus. Plus, a constantly changing wind and a slight downhill angle tested Collins' ability. But Collins had been tested before. The government had for years called him in for the impossible shot. With military action as a sniper in Vietnam, and then private wars around the world, he was always being tested. Now, as a rogue sniper, he had no spotter, no backup and no one to report to except his Remington 700. For once, he was his own man, responsible only to himself and to his ongoing fantasy that he was the best and would always be the best.

What disturbed Collins more right now, was his decision to work for Barnes. The cowboy of David Holden had been easy, but Collins' thinking process had been wrong to take an assignment under the conditions that were offered. Not paying Collins upfront was a deadly mistake for Barnes. Very deadly.

Chapter Forty-Four

SHERI AND I SWAM ALONG the bottom of the ocean and I glanced toward the surface and spotted the hull of Noble One. There were no other craft tied off on our bow or stern, and I knew it would be safe to surface. Sheri climbed up the ladder first and then I followed. Rapture was there to meet me.

"Everything is moving quickly. Brad Gibson should appear at any time," said Rapture.

"Good," I said, as I threw my fins onboard and then gave a helping hand to Sheri.

"The San Cristabol is down there," said Sheri, bursting with excitement. "She's in great shape, and the beam is exposed."

"And the treasure?" Rapture said, pulling Sheri on board.

"Don't know."

I picked up a pair of binoculars and spotted Barnes working on deck. He looked up and toward the stern of his craft, and I panned the horizon and spotted a sleek craft gliding over the water with the greatest of ease. I knew this boat had a lot of speed. It moved in a wide circle around the Atlantis Manta and Barnes never took his eyes off this craft as it circled. We had worked out all the details, and Uncle Leo communicated them to Gibson. I knew Gibson would circle and then sit one hundred yards off the bow of the Atlantis Manta. Then in exactly ten minutes, he would make his approach.

Gibson, owner of the Noble One, had agreed to make a direct confrontation with Barnes. Sheri and I were going to try and board the ship during their discussion and capture Barnes. It was that simple. Gibson was former military and knew how to handle himself around dangerous people.

"You ready Sheri?" I called. Sheri appear from below deck carrying recording equipment especially designed for underwater use.

"Just about."

"Gibson is making his final turn and is going to be sitting off the bow of Barnes' boat here real soon. We don't have much time."

"I know, Boss. I know."

Rapture worked with Sheri getting her set up and I slipped on the new tanks and then pulled on the mask. "Rapture, you watch from below deck. I want you to stay out of the way. It's my job to bring in Barnes."

"Just get rid of Barnes," said Rapture. "We can go after the treasure when he's not around."

"If Sheri and I get into trouble we're going to dive over the side and swim under Noble One and then board. If you see that happen, keep out of sight.

"Change of plans, Boss."

I looked at Sheri, and she nodded toward Gibson. He was already moving along side of the Atlantis Manta. "This is not good."

I put some glass on Gibson and watched as Gibson, under gunpoint, boarded Barnes' craft.

Sheri put down her binoculars at the same time I did. "This is not good at all," she said. "What are we going to do about Gibson?"

"We'll work it out when we get there."

"We're not going armed."

"I know," I said.

"Want to go with a spear gun?"

"No, I don't think so."

"Is Barnes armed?"

"So it appears.

"I know, but so is Gibson."

"Not any more," Sheri said. We both watched as Barnes removed a small handgun, which Barnes had tucked in the small of his back.

"Yeah, you're right about that."

I looked at Sheri. "You ready?" Sheri gave me a thumbs-up, I slipped my mask over my face, and we both jumped off the stern of Noble One into the waiting waters of the Atlantic, for a showdown, Vegas style.

Chapter Forty-Five

BRAD GIBSON STUDIED THE ATLANTIS MANTA with great curiosity. He had just made his slow turn around Barnes' craft, and was going to wait out his ten minutes giving Fargo time to make an underwater approach. Then he saw Barnes waving him over. Deciding not to wait the entire ten minutes, he started to make his approach.

Not often did he get called out of a peaceful retirement for confrontation at sea. But Gibson knew that if Barnes was a Treasury Agent, then he was trained, had the advantage, and the motive, to do battle without hesitation. Brad Gibson was also well trained. He had seen action all over the world, and was prepared for any situation dealing with the sea. Gibson checked his watch, and them slowly moved toward Barnes' boat, who was now standing topside, with a shotgun cradled in his arms.

"Ahoy," Gibson yelled, as he came along side of Barnes boat.

"Sorry, not expecting anybody today, so I thought I should find out who you are right away." Barnes said.

Gibson raised both hands over his head. "Hey, just want to talk. Got an offer you might be interested in."

"Sorry. Not interested."

"You haven't heard my offer."

"Don't want to."

"It's a good offer."

"Don't care. I don't like strangers knowing my business."

"Just want to talk. Nothing more, nothing less."

"Strip your shirt off," demanded Barnes, aiming the shotgun at Gibson.

"Not wearing any wires, if that's what you're interested in," said Gibson.

"Just the fact that you know about wires makes me nervous. Anybody onboard your craft?"

"Nobody."

"You wouldn't mind pushing it off and stepping aboard would you. I hate surprises."

"Actually, I don't like them either."

Barnes took a moment to study the horizon and scan the boats that were bobbing in the distance. "Board, and keep both hands in the air. Gibson jumped off his runabout and climbed over the railing of Atlantis Mantis. He slipped a tie-down rope over the railing as he did so. Barnes leveled the shotgun at him.

"Off with the shirt."

Gibson removed his shirt tossing it to the deck.

"Spin around, slowly."

Gibson turned around and Barnes pulled out a small handgun that had been tucked into his waistband. "Looks like you were preparing for trouble."

Gibson turned around and faced Barnes. "Pirates, you know how much of a nuisance they can be."

"Only too well. What's your offer? Make it in thirty seconds or less."

"I have the cross."

Barnes studied Gibson. "How convenient."

"I thought so."

"How do you know I'm interested in the cross?"

"You rented diving equipment and a salvage boat. You're sitting over the wreck of the San Cristabol. I want to sell you the cross for cash."

"Why sell the cross when it's worth twenty times that amount."

"I have problems...details I would not like to go into right now. I'm moving on, as they say, and want cash for my travels."

"Escape is expensive."

"I'm glad you understand."

"How much?"

"Two million."

"Payable when?"

"Now would be fine."

"And when would I get the cross?" Barnes asked.

Gibson looked at the hull of his boat, and then back to Barnes. "How long before you can raise the cash?"

"I have the cash on board."

"How convenient."

"I thought so."

"About this cash," Gibson said, "is it traceable?"

"Everything is traceable."

"How clean is the money?" asked Gibson.

"Right off the tables in Vegas."

"Big winner I take it."

"You might say that."

"Government work does have its advantages."

Chapter Forty-Six

SHERI AND I SWAM UNDER THE HULL of Gibson's boat and the Atlantis Mantis. We moved toward the rear of the boat where we figured it would be easier to board. But also the most dangerous, as this is an obvious place. I pulled myself up slowly, flipped off my mask, and listened for voices. I heard nothing. I nodded to Sheri, and quietly dropped my tanks and removed my flippers. I passed them to Sheri who was going to tie off the tanks below the hull of the boat. Just then the boat began to rock back and forth, the result of a speedboat kicking up a wake as it passed. I ducked down as Barnes appeared on board from below deck, and surveyed all the boats in the area. I watched Barnes walk to the bow of the boat and look over the side at the waters below. He then moved along the starboard side of the boat and studied the waters carefully. I had no time to escape, so I squatted down in a crouching position, and when Barnes looked over, I sprang straight up, grabbed his shirt and pulled him overboard.

Underwater Barnes was upside down, eyes wide open and completely taken off guard. Sheri let him have it. With one quick punch to his stomach, Sheri knocked all the air out of Barnes. Choking on seawater, Barnes started to desperately kick for the surface, when Sheri pulled him down further and delivered one more blow to his stomach. I grabbed his arms and pulled him to the surface. Sheri held him against the boat, and I crawled onboard and pulled him up with me, which was no easy task.

On board, I tied off his arms, and left him on the deck coughing and choking, spitting up seawater. Sheri boarded, removing her tanks, flippers and mask, and sat down, trying to catch her breath, holding her side.

"You pack a pretty mean blow underwater," I said.

Sheri gasped for some air after her struggle. "Yeah, but I've been waiting to do that."

"Watch him," I said as I moved toward the doorway leading to the ship's hull. It was easy to locate Gibson, he was tied to a chair, with his mouth taped. His eyes went wide with surprise when he saw me, and then relief hit him when he saw it was not Barnes. It looked like he had taken a bad beating from the red marks on his face. I untied him at once.

"Thanks," said Gibson. "You get him?"

"Yeah."

"Don't trust him. He's full of tricks."

"Boss," came the muffled shout of Sheri.

We both climbed up from below deck to find Barnes arms around Sheri's throat. He definitely had the negotiating advantage.

Barnes turned and leveled a gun at us. "Both of you. Hands in the air. You make a move and I'm breaking her neck, just for the fun of it. Now!"

Our hands went in the air, and I could not even guess how Barnes had made his escape so easily. I expect he was playing possum all along and waiting for his opportunity. I looked into Sheri's eyes, and I could read her thoughts. Do something quick. Just then part of Barnes head exploded, and he fell limp to the deck. Sheri scrambled away, and Gibson and I also hit the deck. Barnes did not move. It was over. But who made the shot?

Gibson and I both stood up slowly and I moved to help Sheri. She was okay, but still shaken by the surprise attacks.

"One second he was laying on his stomach, the next thing I knew he rolled over, and then sprang at me."

I held Sheri. "It's okay now."

We stood up slowly and scanned the horizon. There was no other craft bobbing in the distance, and land was at least a thousand yards away. But nobody that I knew could make a shot from land, over water, on a target standing on a bobbing boat. Nobody.

The Atlantis Manta was crawling with officials from different police departments of Andros. I had returned to Noble One and had brought it alongside. It was a complicated situation, as we had to explain to local authorities that we had not made the shot, and ballistics would prove that we had no weapon aboard that could match the fatal gunshot to the head. The bullet had been recovered by a medical examiner on a cursory examination. Everybody kept looking toward land. An impossible shot.

Local agents of the Treasury Department arrived and took possession of the monies that Barnes was carrying. Technically it belonged to them as they had already paid off Coyote. Rapture would have to wait in line for her money.

Chapter Forty-Seven

NOBLE ONE BOBBED GRACEFULLY in the warm clear transparent water. We were all here. Abby had flown out with Uncle Leo to join us for a couple days of relaxation. Another assignment had ended, and we were all safe, well and happy.

I thought back over the last two days and the excitement of pulling treasure from the San Cristabol overwhelmed me. Using the most modern electronic exploration gear, we had pinpointed the location of the cross and using Barnes boat as a platform to work from, we brought in divers to raise the beam of the San Cristabol. Word had leaked out about finding the treasure, and the news media, sightseers and anybody who had a boat surrounded us as we raised the treasure. It was early evening. The staging area was lit by the news media's portable lighting equipment.

Out of the black waters we started to bring up the treasure that was attached to a cable. Majestically the cross appeared out of the water. It was covered with a thick deposit of ocean life that had used the cross as its home. But even so, brief flashes of diamonds, emeralds, and rubies brought a cheer from the crowd. There was wave after wave of applause as the cross danced quietly in the midst of flashing strobes. As the cable twisted, the cross actually bowed as if in appreciation for being recovered. Rapture glowed, her eyes filled with tears. It was a moment in treasure hunting I will never forget. It would take many months of careful meticulous restoration work before the real beauty would be seen.

Las Vegas Metro had determined that Barnes was responsible for the death of J.T., and there was no sign that Rapture's father been involved in any foul play. This allowed Rapture to come to peace with her father's death, and seek the fortune hidden in the San Cristabol.

I sat on deck with Rapture, Abby and Sheri enjoying the view thinking about the last couple of days. Uncle Leo was on the short wave and was getting the morning line. Uncle Leo was hooked on the ponies, but I knew that a long time ago Uncle Leo had his own adventures in some far off distant lands in Southeast Asia, something he didn't talk about much, but someday his stories would be told.

"Okay, now tell me again. The locked room. How did J.T. get killed if the room was locked from the inside?" Sheri asked.

I looked over at Rapture and made sure she was okay talking about J.T. She nodded behind dark glasses.

I started slowly, working out the details as I went. "First Barnes obtained a passkey from one of the maid's laundry carts. I had noted that the maids hung their passkeys on the inside of the cart, which they use to block the doorway in the room they were cleaning. Then Barnes entered J.T.'s room and unlocked the connecting door leading to Dean Michael's room, which was just a deadbolt. He then exited J.T.'s suite and entered Michael's room using the passkey, and repeated the process. He then placed the passkey back on the maid's cart."

"Okay, that makes sense." Sheri commented. "But there's more."

"Right. The night of the murder, Barnes secured three ropes to the side of the hotel and threw them out. This was to decoy the police, which it did. Barnes then knocked on J.T.'s door, gained entry, and shot J.T. He bolted the door behind him, then entered the connecting door into Michael's room, locked the door in the connecting room as it was just a deadbolt, and exited the hotel room. He then ran down the hallway and entered his own hotel room. The police missed that J.T.'s connecting door to Michael's hotel room was unlocked, but it was locked from Michael's hotel room, and Michael's hallway door was locked."

"But, it sounds so simple. Why did it baffle everyone," Sheri asked.

"Sometimes it's the simple things that go unnoticed that turn out to be the key. It had been very well thought out, and stumped Las Vegas' Metro's finest."

"What about Barnes?" Rapture asked. "Who shot him?"

"All part of the mystery. No one knows. I think that Barnes was in deep. Really deep. And it got him into a mess of trouble."

"Who ever took the shot was good," Sheri said.

Uncle Leo turned toward us. "No, he was great. The guy was one of the best shooters around. A hit like that over a thousand yards on a rocking boat, with two heads bobbing in the scope. No, he was great."

"We'll probably never know who shot him, and it's a shame as he probably saved your lives," Abby said, as she lacquered herself up with more and more suntan lotion. She was sitting in the shade and was covered up. She couldn't afford tan lines in the wrong spot with her job at the Trop. But she was a trooper and enjoyed the islands as much as we did.

Rapture adjusted her sunglasses. "So Fargo, tell me about your first gold find."

"What!" I said somewhat surprised.

"You told me it was a long story. And we agreed that when I had the money and the map and the treasure, you would tell me the story."

"But...."

"You promised," Rapture said.

Abby at times was able to capture the moment, and provide the necessary encouragement to make me talk. "No story, no sex," she commented.

Somehow that put everything into perspective. "What?" I managed to stammer.

"You made a promise, and now I think we are all in a good frame of mind for a story."

"Okay. Here goes. I might have mentioned in the past about an old guy named Gerry Heisig. He was an old prospector that I met while waiting to testify in court."

"Yeah, you mentioned him once," Sheri said.

"Well, he and I really hit it off. He invited me to go into the hills with him, so I took him up on the offer. I had two weeks of vacation coming, so I outfitted myself and spent one day driving deep into the desert where I hooked up with him. He had horses waiting, and we loaded up and proceeded to move deep into the mountains. It took over two days to get there. Gerry was old, but he was solid muscle and had more energy than I did. Finally we came to the entrance of the mine. It was completely hidden from view and protected from overhead. No one knew this mine was there."

"He took you to his mine?" asked Uncle Leo.

"Yep. He told me he wouldn't live forever, and he wanted someone to know where it was. He told me he had even taken the steps to add my name to the claim."

Rapture was listening closely to the story. "You're kidding," she exclaimed.

"Nope.

"What happened?" Rapture asked.

"Basically he put me to work on his mine."

"It was your mine too." Abby said.

"Yep. My name was on the claim. Gerry passed away not long after that."

"Oh my goodness!" Rapture said, "You own the mine?"

"Yep. That I do. So we worked and worked. He taught me how to work the mine, how to dig, how to examine the contents. He taught me miner's geology, sort of a short cut of exactly what you need to know. On the last day before I was to leave I found a nugget. Gerry gave it to me and told me it would make me come back. All things have to come to an end, and since Gerry was staying on, he told me I was going to walk out by myself."

"You're kidding," Abby said.

"Nope. He had two reasons. One is he wanted me to learn the ways of the desert. He also said if I walked out, I would be able to find my way back when he was gone and I was ready to return."

"So what did you do," Uncle Leo said.

"I walked out."

Rapture stood up and leaned against the rail. "I have to ask, Fargo. Have you ever been back to the mine?"

"No. When I heard Gerry had died I realized that I owned it. But that's about when I launched Fargo Blue Investigations, and like anything else, I got tied up."

"You've never been back?" Rapture mused. "Can you find it again? Do you remember where it was located?"

"Like it was yesterday."

Rapture sat down next to Fargo and put her arms around him, and caught Abby's eye and winked at her. "Fargo, from one treasure hunter to another, it looks like we need to think about taking a trip. You've got some unfinished business, and I'm here to help."

"I want to go along too," joked Sheri.

We all laughed.

Epilogue

IT WAS ELEVEN. I sat at a picnic table in Paradise Park right off of Tropicana just past The Gun Store, a favorite haunt when I wanted to use a firing range. The store also had a wide assortment of firearms to test fire, and I always tested at least one every time I went there. Sheri happened to love the place.

I studied the area around me and wondered what would happen in the next few minutes. There was a swing set behind me, a public restroom off to my left, and only a few people out for a morning walk. It was still a little bit cool. There were a few families out for a picnic, two old guys playing catch, and the normal park people. Trees provided shade from the blazing sun for those who wanted to catch a quick nap in the heat of the day.

Sitting on the park bench, I turned and checked the area behind me, seeing nothing, I turned and watched a black Lexus drive by, followed by a Ryder truck, and then a delivery van. I thought about the phone call I had received earlier.

"Hello," I blurted into the phone at three in the morning trying to bring my mind into focus at such an early hour.

"Eleven this morning, Paradise Park. Be there," a woman's voice had said.

"What?"

"Eleven. Paradise Park. You do know where Paradise Park is, don't you?"

"Who is this?"

"You do know where Paradise Park is?"

"Yes..."

"Good, come alone. Paradise Park."

"What if I don't chose to come alone," I threw out trying to gain some time.

"I would not want to do that if I were you."

"Maybe..." and the phone went dead. I laid awake the rest of the night trying to figure out if I should call Sheri for some backup surveillance, or go it alone.

I decided not to call Sheri, but brought along my Glock 9-milimeter for company, which was tucked into a shoulder holster. The feel of the shoulder holster made me feel comfortable, like it was a partner.

I continued to watch the early morning traffic. I spotted the black Lexus again. It slowed, signaled to make a left-hand turn, and then swung into the parking lot. My senses were alive with anticipation. My BMW was parked on one side of the lot. The Lexus turned into the slot on the other side, away from my car.

The door opened a crack, and I waited to see who it would be. Coyote stepped out dressed sharply in a three-piece suit holding an attractive alligator slim lined brief case. Her eyes were hidden by dark sunglasses. She walked toward me, her high heels clicking on the parking lot pavement. When she reached the curb by my car, she removed her heels, and stepped onto the grass and continued to walk in my direction.

"Morning," I said as she approached the table.

"Good morning, Mr. Blue," said Coyote. She stopped directly in front of the picnic table and removed her sunglasses. Her eyes were dove

351

gray, almost fluorescent. "I have some files for you."

"Who are you, really?"

"Of no importance."

"I like to know who I'm dealing with."

Coyote studied me. "I'm an agent."

"With who?"

"The U.S. Treasury Department." Coyote pulled out a badge and flashed it.

"Been a lot of Treasury agents around here lately. Who do you work for?" I asked, admiring Coyote.

"Come now Mr. Blue. I'm doing the job that was assigned to me. You need to know nothing more."

"I'm a detective. It's my nature..."

"Here is the first file," said Coyote interrupting me. She pulled it out of her briefcase and placed it on the table, flipping it open to several stills. I glanced down at the photos. Coyote continued. "This is the subject that was targeted. Dick Barnes, U.S. Treasury Agent."

"I know who he is. Why was he a target...?"

Coyote pulled out a second file and placed it open on the table. "Here is Barnes and his hired gun, Carl Collins. Carl is out of New York and was hired by Barnes to cowboy Barnes' Treasury Agent partner, David Holden." The one I had driven by. Coyote flipped over the picture and it showed the brutal murder of Holden in his car on Las Vegas Boulevard. "This file contains additional photos of Barnes and Collins lunching in New York. They go back a long way."

"How do you know this?" I asked focusing on her eyes.

"It's my job," said Coyote. "This is Carl Collins seen entering

Florida on his way to the Bahamas. It was Carl who shot Barnes."

"From where?"

"Andros Island."

"We were over one thousand yards from the island!" I said astounded.

"He's one of the best. The very best."

"Why?"

"Business disagreement."

"We're looking for Carl Collins now. If you run into him, please let us know."

"Just one question."

Coyote cocked her head to one side.

"Where did you get your half of the treasure map?"

"It's a need to know issue," Coyote responded.

"Did you plant the map for Rapture's dad to find?"

"Need to know," said Coyote, who replaced her sunglasses. "You played a fair game, Mr. Blue." Coyote turned and walked away.

"Who are you?" I asked, knowing I would never know.

Coyote stopped, turned around, and faced me once more. "Please, Mr. Blue, you need not know," and turned and walked softly across the grass, stopping to put on her shoes when she reached the parking lot, and continue on. I listened to the click of her high heels as she walked across the pavement, entered her Lexus, exited the parking lot and then disappeared behind some trees as she drove away.

Someday we'll meet again, I thought. Somewhere. Someday. And it's true...Coyotes do run wild.

About the Authors

Don McKenzie

Don, identical twin to Ron, passed away suddenly on September 7, 2008 in Arcata, California, after The Coyote Trap manuscript had been completed and the authors were in the editing process. Don graduated from Foothill College, Los Altos, California with an Associate of Arts degree, and Humboldt State University, Arcata, California with a Bachelor of Arts in Theatre. He had written other novels, screenplays and award winning plays. He had worked for Entertainment Tonight as a Senior Video Tape Editor, had lived in Japan and later owned two book stores in Oregon.

Ron McKenzie

Ron lives in Illinois with his wife Pamela and continues to develop novels and screenplays. Ron graduated from Foothill College, Los Altos, California with an Associate of Arts degree, and California Polytechnic State University, San Luis Obispo, California with a Bachelor of Arts in Architecture. He and his brother Don had developed many other projects, which Ron plans to complete in memory of Don.